S0-CWV-118

"I didn't mean to startle you."

Oh, sure, Vana thought. Probably the same thing the coyote said as he stepped into the chicken coop.

"Is there something wrong?" he asked.

Was this guy playing some kind of game with her? She wanted to lash out at him, but her voice wasn't functioning.

He cleared his throat, and she realized he wasn't going to go away until she said something, so she summoned up enough inner strength to single-handedly tip over a John Deere tractor and used it to look up at him.

"What do you want?" she demanded hotly.

"What do *I* want?" he asked incredulously, but there was amusement in his expression. "It's you who's been watching me. I should get to ask what you want."

Dear Reader,

Spellbinders! That's what we're striving for. The editors at Silhouette are determined to capture your imagination and win your heart with every single book we publish. Each month, six Special Editions are chosen with *you* in mind.

Our authors are our inspiration. Writers such as Nora Roberts, Tracy Sinclair, Kathleen Eagle, Carole Halston and Linda Howard—to name but a few—are masters at creating endearing characters and heartrending love stories. Their characters are everyday people—just like you and me—whose lives have been touched by love, whose dreams and desires suddenly come true!

So find a cozy, quiet place to read, and create your own special moment with a Silhouette Special Edition.

Sincerely,

The Editors
SILHOUETTE BOOKS

CAITLIN CROSS
A Natural Woman

Silhouette Special Edition

Published by Silhouette Books New York

America's Publisher of Contemporary Romance

SILHOUETTE BOOKS
300 East 42nd St., New York, N.Y. 10017

Copyright © 1987 by Caitlin Cross

All rights reserved, including the right to reproduce
this book or portions thereof in any form whatsoever.
For information address Silhouette Books,
300 East 42nd St., New York, N.Y. 10017

ISBN: 0-373-09413-2

First Silhouette Books printing October 1987

All the characters in this book are fictitious. Any
resemblance to actual persons, living or dead, is
purely coincidental.

SILHOUETTE, SILHOUETTE SPECIAL EDITION and colophon
are registered trademarks of the publisher.

America's Publisher of Contemporary Romance

Printed in the U.S.A.

Books by Caitlin Cross

Silhouette Special Edition

High Risk #272
Catch the Wind #341
Shadow of Doubt #380
A Natural Woman #413

CAITLIN CROSS

has traveled throughout the United States and Canada, and she has lived on both coasts and in the heartland of America. She has been active in the diverse worlds of pro-rodeo, horse racing and high fashion. Caitlin is currently living in New York and pursuing her lifelong dream as a professional writer.

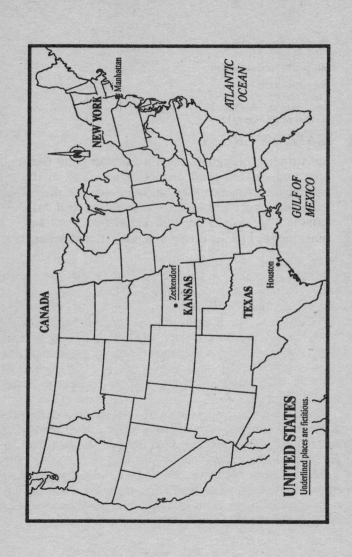

UNITED STATES
Underlined places are fictitious.

CANADA

NEW YORK

Manhattan

ATLANTIC OCEAN

GULF OF MEXICO

Zeckendorf

KANSAS

TEXAS

Houston

Prologue

*S*he stepped out of a taxi. She was alone, but she wasn't lonely or afraid.

The city beckoned her in every direction. So much to see and do. She paused a moment on the broad, bustling sidewalk, considering her options and choosing among them as if they were chocolates in a sampler box. A photography exhibit, maybe? A Broadway musical or a gallery opening? A foreign film? Maybe a museum? Yes, a museum. Something historical.

Bright, busy people in elegant clothes passed by her. Sometimes they smiled. They saw her as one of them. She was infused with their energy. She felt light and free, and she felt strong—she was somebody.

She entered the museum, and the beauty and spectacle of history enfolded her. She savored each display. There was no need to be greedy or rush—this museum was hers to visit as often as she chose.

Suddenly she was aware of a presence, of someone watching her. She turned. It was a man. A man unlike any other man.

The light in the room intensified until everything was brilliantly white. The scene around her lost color and substance.

He was the only reality.

And she knew the moment their eyes met.... "Van-ess-a! Are you deaf or something? Didn't you hear me yelling at you?"

The man and the museum and all the elegance and beauty faded. She blinked her eyes and shook her head in a moment of confusion. It had been just another dream...or another version of the same old dream.

"Jimminy Christmas, Vana! Come home from the fair, will ya?"

She looked up into her sister's frowning, exasperated face. Margaret had her hair hidden under a red bandana and dirt smudged one of her smooth round cheeks. She looked like the peasant women pictured in Vana's history book.

"The racks are all full...so you're done, aren't ya?"

Vana looked out across the lots. Indeed the hay racks were all overflowing with delicate, gray-green alfalfa. She had finished without realizing it.

"You're done, right?"

Vana sighed and tucked gloves, bale cutters and hay hook into the leg pocket of her overalls. Obviously Margaret wanted something.

"I guess I am finished," she admitted.

"Well then—" Margaret smiled "—I have just one teeny little favor to ask...."

Vana waited, knowing she would do whatever Meg asked if it sounded like her sister needed her.

"I really need you to help me fix the front pasture gate," Margaret said, her voice sliding into a cutesy babyish whine.

Vana pushed her bangs back and wiped the sweat from her forehead with her shirtsleeve.

"I don't want to fix the gate," she said. "And it's so yucky when you talk like that. I don't know why goin' to high school made you start talking like that."

"All right," Margaret said petulantly, but in her normal voice. "But I didn't ask you if you *wanted* to help fix the gate. Who'd *want* to? For somebody who's smart in school you can be really dense, Vana."

Vana snorted in the sarcastic little almost-laugh that usually drove her sister crazy. She turned to walk toward the barn.

Margaret hurried into step beside her.

"Oh, come on Vana, please! Besides—what's it to you? You don't have anything important to do."

"How come I always end up doing part of your chores, Margaret...or at least helping you? Nobody ever helps me."

"But you never *need* help, Vana. If you ever asked me I'd help you." Margaret looked hurt. "And you don't *always* help me—just sometimes."

Vana drew in a deep breath and blew it out through slack lips in silent complaint. She had been planning a walk up to the north forty to look for the foxes. She'd only spotted the mother so far, and she was anxious to catch a glimpse of the little kits she knew were hidden somewhere close by. Margaret was right, though; it wasn't anything really important.

Vana glanced over at her sister. Margaret's big blue eyes were pleading and threatening to fill with tears. Her lips were going into that you-don't-really-love-me pout that could get a yes from the devil himself, and Vana knew that she couldn't say no. She never could refuse if her sister really wanted something. But then she'd never seen anybody else say no to Margaret, either—except Papa, of course, whose standard answer to every question was no.

The thing that bothered Vana was not the saying yes. It was the fact that this was just another case of her own plans or ideas always being unimportant when compared to whatever Margaret was cooking up. The proof seemed to be everywhere—Vana was dull and insignificant in the shadow of her older sister.

It was the growing weight of this truth that burdened Vana, making her ever more tough and defensive. Even in the closeness of night, when the sisters huddled together in their narrow beds whispering secrets in the darkness, Vana could not reveal the deep, sensitive things—the wishing and hoping, the somedays...the wanting. She had to protect this side of herself, this soft, vulnerable underbelly.

She knew how easily Margaret could destroy this part of her. Her sister could belittle her with a look, completely humiliate her with a scornful laugh and devastate her with a well-flung word. And somehow, no matter what she was feeling or how justified the reaction, Meg could twist it around and make her feel guilty over it.

Other people—even Margaret—thought that Vana wasn't afraid of anything. They thought she was never anxious or worried. Mama often remarked on how Vana was such a fearless child that she'd marched right off to kindergarten alone without a backward look and how she never had nightmares like other kids.

But Vana had fears. And the worst and most chest clutching of all was the fear of losing her dreams. That fear was constant. Her dreams were the magic that kept her alive inside.

So she took no chances. She kept everything special locked safely in her head, and the only secrets she shared with Margaret were silly inconsequential ones. She never let her sister peek inside. She never gave Margaret a chance to smash her dreams and make them as dull and insignificant as the rest of her life.

Vana looked at Margaret and a feeling of resignation crept through her. Of course she would help her sister. Hadn't she always?

"Please!" Margaret pleaded. "Fixing that gate will grunge up my hands, and the coronation banquet is only one week away."

Vana studied a spot in the distance as though thinking. She never liked to say yes too quickly. She always enjoyed hearing Margaret beg a little. It was the only time she felt more important than her sister.

"Coronation?" Vana repeated the word with a wrinkled nose. "You mean like the Queen of England? Do they really coronate an FFA Sweetheart?"

"Well, maybe it's not exactly the same. But, you know...they give you flowers and stuff. And I think they give you a jacket with the official Future Farmers of America seal on it."

"Oh brother!" Vana wrinkled her nose again. "How dumb."

"What do you know? You're not even in high school yet!"

"I'm only one year behind you."

"There's a *big* difference between bein' in the eighth grade and bein' a freshman in high school," Margaret announced knowingly. "Now come on." She reached over and adjusted Vana's braids the same way that Mama always did. "I really need you behind me, Vana. FFA Sweetheart could be the start of big things in my life."

"Huh," Vana snorted sarcastically. Her sarcasm wasn't directed at the idea of this title leading to something big, but rather at Margaret's gushy delivery of the thought.

Margaret's eyes were glued to Vana's face, her expression like that of a puppy waiting to find out if he was going to be patted or kicked.

"Okay." Vana sighed. "I'll get the tools."

Margaret beamed.

Vana stopped walking and pointed toward the weanling pens. "You better skedaddle over and feed those weaners first, though, before we start on the gate," she cautioned, her tone a conscious imitation of their papa's stern, admonishing one.

Margaret stomped her foot and screwed her face into a grimace. "I hate to do that! Why do I always have to do that? I hate smelling like that junk Papa makes me put in their feed.''

"Papa gave you that job because you whined so long about doing the nurse calves,'' Vana reminded her.

"Well, I hate doing the nurse calves, too. You can't go into that pen without getting manure on your clothes.''

The girls fell into step together and crossed the hard packed earth of the empty front lot. It was midafternoon, so the milk cows weren't in from pasture yet to fill the lot with their restless mooing.

"There's only one good thing about Sunday,'' Margaret observed quietly. "It's the last day of the weekend. If only school was every day. . . .''

Vana didn't comment. It was understood that she agreed. School was their only refuge from Papa's glowering presence and endless assigning of chores.

"When I'm older,'' Margaret said confidently, "I'm going to get us away from all this.''

"You're gonna be famous and rich for sure,'' Vana agreed.

Meg nodded. "And I'll fix it where we never come back here. Ever.''

"What about Mama?'' Vana asked. "Won't we miss Mama?''

"Oh, Mama will come too,'' Margaret assured her quickly. "I'll have this big house with rooms for both you and Mama, and you guys can come shopping with me and help me decide things and I'll take you to fancy places and introduce you to all my neat friends. It'll be great!''

"That part don't sound so great.'' Vana sniffed. "Tell me again about the good part, about how you're gonna be the best and how the crowds are gonna cheer and everything.''

"Well, I'll have the most beautiful, fastest horse anyone's ever seen, and I'll have satiny shirts with fringe and sparkly stuff. . . and when I ride into the arena people will oooh and aaah.''

"And when you win?" Vana prompted so she could hear the rest of the familiar picture.

"When I win they'll all stand and cheer. And someone will take my picture and send it to the *Zeckendorf Weekly Gazette*."

"Do barrel racers get rich?" Vana asked.

"I won't just be a barrel racer," Margaret declared as if the idea were vaguely insulting. "After I'm famous I'll get smart in business and have a big ranch and oil wells and stuff—maybe even a helicopter."

Vana nodded. If Margaret had said she was going to be empress of Mars when she grew up, Vana would have encouraged her and accepted it as the gospel.

Vana was impressed as usual with talk of Meg's glittering future, but she ended up feeling squirmy with guilt. She knew her sister's offer to include her in this golden future was downright charitable, but instead of making her feel grateful, the idea of living in a room in Margaret's house, helping her pick out shoes and dresses that matched and meeting her neat friends, made Vana want to throw up.

"I don't know if I'd be very good at all that." Vana protested weakly.

"Ohhh," Margaret scoffed. "What's there to be good at? I'll take care of everything. Besides . . . what else would you ever do?"

Vana shrugged.

Margaret slowed. Raising her hand to shade her eyes, she looked across toward the house. "Do you think she's asked him yet?"

Vana kept walking, pretending not to have heard the question, and Margaret didn't repeat it when she caught up. Together they finished the gate. That is, Vana did the work while Margaret chattered and raved about how strong and capable and efficient her little sister was. It felt good to have Margaret praise her so highly, and though she wouldn't have admitted it out loud, it felt good to have her beautiful, talented, perfect big sister need her for things.

The cows were trailing in from the pasture by the time the work was finished, so Vana resigned herself to having only a short break before the start of milking chores. There would be no aimless walking or daydreaming or searching for foxes today. Reluctantly she joined her sister, who was headed for the house.

She followed Margaret through the gate in the electric fence and into their mother's yard. The farm might be Papa's, but the yard and the house were their mother's undisputed territory, and woe be to the animal that broke through that electric barrier and stole a bite of geraniums or sunflowers.

Papa's voice boomed out at them through the screen door. "Don't you understand my words anymore, woman? I told you *no*. And *no* is my answer."

Vana froze. She turned her head toward her sister and their eyes locked in the same desperate, helpless stare they'd been sharing since Heinrich had become their stepfather. They waited. They didn't dare interrupt or try to join the argument.

"But it's her graduation, her eighth-grade graduation, Heinrich. And she's been chosen as the valedictorian. She's going to give a speech. She's being honored, Heinrich. Honored for being smart and doing her homework."

"Honored! You know what that means? It means nothin'. It don't teach her nothin' but false pride. Did you or me graduate from the eighth grade in some fancy do up? Did you or me make a speech? In a pig's eye, we did! Honors'll get her about as much as that fancy name you hung on her will."

"Times are changin', Heinrich." Mama's voice was fearful and timid. "It ain't the same as it was for us when we was young."

There was a loud clattering noise as though a pan had struck the floor and Vana saw a picture in her head of her papa knocking the pan to the floor and her mama cringing and pressing her lips tightly together.

"Maybe over to Wichita or some other big city times are changin', but here in Zeckendorf ain't nothin' different then it's ever been. I'm plumb fed up with you fillin' your daughters' heads with foolishness behind my back. Why don't you teach them somethin' useful? I teach 'em about honest work, but what do you teach 'em? Can they bake or sew or help at a butcherin'? What has book learnin' and winnin' contests got to do with makin' good headcheese or puttin' up vegetables?"

"But the graduation..."

"I said no. Not on a Saturday. She works in the fields on Saturdays."

There was a silence and Margaret reached out to grip Vana's hand.

"It doesn't matter," Meg whispered in a comforting voice. "Wearing one of those getups and having to talk into a microphone is pretty dumb anyway."

"Yeah," Vana agreed quickly. "Who needs it?"

Margaret dropped Vana's hand and hugged herself as though suddenly cold. "I wonder if she's already asked him about my banquet," she whispered in a quavery voice. "I deserve to be FFA sweetheart. It's mine. I'll die if I have to turn it down."

"Mama will work yours out somehow," Vana said without malice. "It's at night, so maybe she'll lie like that other time and tell him we're goin' to a quilting or something."

She looked out across the fields. A hawk was drifting lazily over the wheat.

She felt no disappointment or anger. The school honor was something she could live without. And the knowledge of that gave her a strong, free feeling. Other people's plans and other people's dreams ruled and overshadowed her. But someday...someday...

Chapter One

The crowd pressed in on her. She had never seen so many people packed together at one time. She was intensely aware of the dull, constant roar of their shifting and talking. She could smell their cigarette smoke and spilled beer and overflowing cardboard buckets of popcorn. She could feel their eyes, feel them watching, waiting, wondering who she was and what she could do.

The strangeness of running indoors suddenly overwhelmed her. The walls and ceiling closed in on her. The stale, dust-filled air was suffocating.

She'd been flagged for a go, but she held Buck tightly a moment. He danced and fought against the bit, resenting her hesitancy. Her heart thudded in her chest and she was drenched with perspiration. How in the world had she let Meg talk her into entering such a big-time barrel racing?

She sneaked a look up. The building soared and yawned before her like a gaping dragon's mouth. The Astrodome! Oh, brother...

Sucking in air like a diver, she gave Buck his head. He flew to the first barrel and they swung around it as neatly as an oiled hinge. The precision beauty of that start awed her, then filled her with blossoming confidence. The crowd and the building, the lights and noise and confusion, all faded and lost meaning. Pure, joyful energy surged through her. She stretched with the horse, melding into his fluid movements.

The second barrel loomed. She leaned with the big gelding, expecting another smooth performance. But suddenly the horse was uncertain. He faltered, hesitating for a fraction of a second before committing to the turn, and then overshooting. He cut back sharply in a frantic effort to compensate, but he'd lost the rhythm. She shifted, using her legs and body weight to help him back into sync.

He lunged out of the turn and her heart sank at the dull thud of the stirrup wood striking metal. Would the barrel tip? She risked a fearful glance back as he thundered toward the final turn. The barrel behind them was rocking but remained upright.

He was running green and panicky now, letting the lights and confusion of the strange building wipe out the fine-tuned edge she'd worked so hard to develop. She took him in hand, directing him as though he were a colt in training, checking him into the last turn slowly and carefully and sacrificing their time for accuracy. Her firmness calmed him immediately and he settled and focused. She could feel his muscles responding beneath her, straining and bunching as he fought to regain his timing.

And it should have gone beautifully. It would have gone beautifully... if that idiot across the fence hadn't snapped a flash picture in Buck's face as they rounded the final barrel.

The buckskin jumped sideways beneath her, smashing into the brightly painted barrel. She fought to keep her seat as he lurched and then fell to one knee. The barrel clattered and rolled beside them and he jerked himself upright, leaped clumsily over it and charged into the homestretch in a careening effort to complete the pattern.

"...and Kansas rookie Vana Linnier hits a barrel and goes out of the running for the cloverleaf barrel-racing title at this year's bigger-than-ever Houston Astrodome Rodeo and Livestock Show, folks. And now let's take a look at..."

Vana blocked the announcer's voice from her mind as she slid from the saddle. Buck was breathing heavily through his great dark nostrils. Rivulets of sweat ran down his face and streaked his pale coat. Quickly she tied his reins to the side and snapped a lead to his headstall. Her knee ached as she headed out toward the cool-down area, and she noticed it in a detached way, registering the fact that she must have slammed it into the barrel when Buck cut back. But her own injuries were incidental to her.

She turned her head to study Buck's legs. His injuries were the crucial ones—the ones that could put them out of business. But, to her relief, he was traveling straight and solid and there wasn't a scratch on him.

She registered Margaret's approach out of the corner of her eye and knew from the determined swiftness of her sister's stride that she was about to give Vana an unpleasant earful. But there was no escaping it. She knew from long experience that Margaret could save her tirades for days so it was just a matter of now or later.

She gritted her teeth and continued to lead the rangy buckskin in the same wide circle. Meg's carefully tweezed brows knitted fiercely together as she approached, and her full, pouty lips were set in a frown. The expression was vintage Heinrich.

"What in the hell happened, Vana?" Margaret demanded as she fell into step beside her.

"It's our first indoor run, Meg. Give us a chance." She glanced over at Margaret's unrelenting frown. "Your sorrel didn't set any records last night, either," she pointed out defensively.

"Well, my horse didn't bulldoze a barrel." Meg rolled her perfectly contoured and shadowed eyes. She was obviously determined to grind Vana's nose in the bad run. "Everybody here is gonna think we're real amateurs now."

"We are new. There's nothin' wrong with that. Even the best of them were rookies at some point."

"It's one thing to *be* a rookie," Meg announced, "but we don't wanna *behave* like rookies."

"That would sound good in a fortune cookie."

"Oh sure! Be sarcastic. But the fact remains that you just screwed up in front of sixty thousand people. And you don't have a prayer of winning any money here. If this keeps up we'll be broke and heading back to the farm before you know it."

"All right! I'm not as good a rider as you. I'm not as tough under pressure as you are. I don't have my horse working as well as yours. So I don't have a prayer in this business—is that enough?"

Vana stopped walking so suddenly that Buck plowed right into her. Roughly she shoved him back, then hopped on one foot, grimacing as she massaged her squashed toes through the leather of her boot.

Meg's face softened instantly into a tender and satisfied expression. "My poor little sissy," she said, reaching out to pat Vana's shoulder.

Vana gritted her teeth again and resumed walking, yanking Buck into step behind her.

"Everything will be okay," Meg crooned, carefully picking her way along beside Vana. She was always careful when she had on her dress boots. "And," she announced brightly, "we're going to have a great time at the party tonight."

Vana groaned.

"You have to go," Meg reminded her quickly. "You promised the other day when we went to the sign-up together. You said you'd stick with me on it if I signed up. And you know how important this is...I mean...this could be the chance of a lifetime for me. I could be—'' she drew in a reverent breath and whispered ''—discovered.''

"Oh, brother!''

Vana's blast of exasperated sarcasm was aimed at calming her sister down more than anything. The truth was that she, too, believed this might be Meg's big chance. What had the notice said? They were looking for someone who was "more than pretty... Someone with that special, fresh, natural, all-American country beauty.''

Wouldn't Meg be perfect? Hadn't Meg been universally recognized as the prettiest girl in Zeckendorf, Kansas? Hadn't Meg been chosen again and again to the point where she'd been reigning over something or other for her entire four years of high school? Hadn't she set a record by being crowned Pork Queen and Dairy Queen in the same week?

It was a widely held belief in Zeckendorf that Meg would have been a shoo-in for the Miss Kansas title if her papa would have allowed her to enter the pageant. But Heinrich Linnier had held firm to the idea that no daughter of his was going to learn some useless activity like baton twirling or tap dancing just so some fools could call her talented. And *no daughter of his* was going to march around on television in a bathing suit.

So Margaret's natural beauty was an established fact—and how much "countrier" could anyone get? These other girls from places like Oklahoma City and Dallas and Austin were just city kids with Western accents. They weren't any more country than a street lamp. Meg had a good chance at being the sought after Bella Woman—Vana could almost feel it—and Heinrich wasn't around to tell her no anymore.

If Meg needed her to go to this party, of course she would go. She would tag along and lend whatever support she could—even if the evening did sound about as interesting as a dental checkup.

"There's a man over there staring at me," Meg whispered suddenly. "Toward the back wall. Be careful, he's still looking."

"So what? Men are always eyeing you, or at least you think they are," Vana said, without bothering to look.

"Just look at him, Vana," Meg insisted. "He's no cowboy or anything. What's he doing down here?"

"Oh, brother." Vana sighed, but she turned her head anyway.

Her eyes swept over the man in the briefest, swiftest of glances. She was looking primarily to satisfy Meg, and she didn't expect to see much. She certainly didn't expect the jolt that registered in her body with that one quick glance.

Meg had been right in saying that the man was staring—he was openly studying something in their direction. And Meg was right, too, about him being out of place down here among the boots and hats. What Meg hadn't warned her about, however, was his . . . what? What was it that was so strange or noticeable about him?

She continued forward mechanically, leading Buck and nodding to her sister without hearing the words, puzzling over "strange" and finally amending it. Strange wasn't right. There was something different about the man, but it was something striking rather than strange.

If there was any strangeness involved, it was going on inside her own head. Looking at him had definitely made her feel strange.

She wanted to look again, to study him and figure out just what was so different about him, but she was afraid to be caught staring. She didn't want simple curiosity to be mistaken for something embarrassing.

"I don't think he's anyone to worry about, Meg," she offered hesitantly.

"He's good-looking," Meg decided, looking him over openly now, "but he still could be a pervert or something. And besides, I don't care how long he makes eyes at me— he's not a cowboy. I'm only interested in real cowboys."

Vana was dying to look again, but she waited until it seemed safe, until a decent interval had elapsed and they'd made a full circuit walking and were passing his position again. Then she let her gaze slide casually back toward him over the top of the saddle.

His eyes locked onto hers, and the connection made her heart jump into her throat and her cheeks flush with heat. Flustered, she stumbled clumsily, lurching sideways against the gelding's massive body and barely keeping her footing. Embarrassment or self-consciousness sometimes made her act like a three-legged donkey at a sack race, but for once she was happy at her own awkwardness. Tripping and bumbling about had broken the eye contact and saved her—from what, she wasn't sure. How could a look be dangerous?

She stared at the ground, her knees weak as she forced her legs to keep pace with the horse's stride. She reached out, clinging to Buck's leather breast collar like a lifeline. She had the urge to laugh. It all seemed so ridiculous and adolescent. How long had it been since a male gaze had turned her to jelly? For that matter, when in her twenty-five years had a male gaze *ever* turned her to jelly?

"What's wrong now?" Meg asked as though preparing to be irritated.

"Nothing," Vana mumbled. But her breathing was still a trifle short and she felt like her face had caught fire. Was he still there? Was he still watching? Did she dare look again?

"You're probably just feeling bad over that rotten run you made. But you can't win 'em all, I guess," Meg said philosophically.

Meg looked back toward the wall. "Anyway, that weirdo is gone now. He probably just wanted to see a horsie up close or something. I swear, this Houston is full of crazies."

Vana's head snapped around, her eyes searching, but Meg was right. He'd disappeared as completely as one of her daydreams—as though he'd never been real at all.

"I'm going on over to the trailer to wash my hair and start getting ready," Margaret announced with excitement creeping into her voice and eyes. "Come on back soon, okay? I might need help with something."

Vana nodded and watched her sister go. When Meg was nervous or uncertain she always needed Vana's help. Approaching the corner that would take her out of sight, Meg turned and wiggled her fingers in a childishly hesitant goodbye.

"I'll be there in a few minutes," Vana assured her. Sometimes she felt very close to Meg, as if they were twins instead of eleven months apart. And sometimes, like now, she felt light-years older.

She reached out to pat Buck's sturdy chest. He felt dry and his breathing was even and regular now, but she continued leading him. She needed to keep herself moving for a while. Had that man's eyes really met hers? Or had she gone off the deep end and started mixing her daydreams in with reality?

She tried to picture him exactly but the image was blurry. He'd had silvery hair but he hadn't looked old. He'd been tall and dressed in some kind of dark slacks and a leather trench coat—magazine clothes, her papa would have called them.

Behind-the-chute security was tight at the Astrodome; what had an outsider like that been doing down here? And had he been looking at Meg, or maybe at Buck...or...could it be true that he'd been looking at Vana?

"You're going nutsy on me, Vana," she cautioned herself. "Really nutsy." The poor guy had probably just been looking in general and they'd happened to be the only live action in the area at the moment.

She chided herself for making too much out of nothing, but all through the long process of first putting Buck away, then helping Meg prepare for her showing at the party, she couldn't stop wondering.

When Meg was finally ready, they headed across the broad expanse of parking lot back toward the stadium and the party. Meg was geared up and chattering nonstop, but Vana couldn't keep up with her sister's train of thought. She couldn't focus on anything with all the questions bouncing around in her mind.

She might be able to deny the reality of that moment of contact, or she might be able to convince herself that he'd been staring in general and not specifically at her, but there was one thing she could not escape or argue away—her own reaction. Whether the exchange itself had been real or imagined, she couldn't deny the crazy, unsettling response it had stirred in her.

"I wonder who he was," Vana whispered. The musing slipped out before she could stop it and she immediately wanted to kick herself.

"Who?" Meg asked in irritation. She'd been in the middle of a discourse on the tacky attire of another barrel racer and she wasn't used to interruptions.

Vana shrugged noncommittally. "Oh, nobody—nothing—I—"

"Who!" Meg demanded.

"That guy. The one you noticed when I was cooling out Buck."

"The good-looking pervert?"

Vana opened her mouth to protest the description but decided to try dropping the subject instead.

Meg eyed her suspiciously. "So what about him? Do you think I ought to be nervous or something because he was staring at me like that?"

"I don't know," Vana said softly. "Maybe he wasn't looking just at you. I mean...maybe he likes buckskins, or...maybe he was looking at both of us."

"What? You mean wondering if we're related or something?"

"Yeah, something like that."

"You thought he was cute, didn't you!" Meg burst out as though just making some amazing discovery.

Vana frowned and worked at looking like the idea was preposterous, but Meg began chuckling and slapped her thigh.

"Well, Vana, if you're going to start eyeing strange men and getting wild ideas we're going to have to do some work on you. I mean, look at you! No makeup, and you've worn your hair the same way since you were five years old. And your clothes!"

Meg shook her head and clicked her tongue scoldingly.

Vana drew herself up. She was three inches taller than her sister and sometimes that felt very good.

"I'm not getting any wild ideas!" Vana bristled. "And I'm perfectly satisfied with myself, thank you. I sure don't want to be tied to all that paraphernalia you think you need just to get presentable. My life is too short to spend half of it getting ready for the other half."

"Don't get so huffy!" Meg acted as though she were the injured party. "I mean, come on. It's not that you don't look okay...it's just that men are pretty slow. If you want them to notice you, you have to catch their eye—kind of advertise a little, you know?"

"Why stop with makeup, then?" Vana demanded sarcastically. "Why not get one of those sandwich board signs to wear...or better yet something in portable neon? Something simple and to the point like *Available*—or maybe, *Pick Me.*"

Meg sighed in clear indication that her little sister's attitude was hopeless. When she began to talk again she steered the conversation in a neutral direction. Vana maintained a stubborn silence.

Arriving at the Astrodome, they stepped inside and exchanged hesitant, timid looks. Somehow the building felt even more imposing in its semi-deserted state. They walked down a wide echoing hallway, past the cleanup crews, and stepped onto an elevator marked with the sign: Penthouse Partyroom Express—Climb Aboard!

Vana knew she should be excited—or at least impressed—but she wasn't. For some reason she felt very touchy and out of sorts. She'd never admit it to Meg, but she did wish she looked better, or maybe just different.

She wished she looked more like a sophisticated woman of the world and less like a twenty-five-year-old small-town bank teller. And she wished she could charm people as easily as her sister could. And she wanted very much to believe that the mystery man had been looking at her—really at *her*—and not because he was wondering if she was related to Meg...and not because she just happened to be in his line of sight.

She followed Margaret, then stood quietly as her sister flashed the invitations at the uniformed guards who were conscientiously checking everyone for credentials. Suddenly the door was opened for them and Meg was pulling her inside.

A wall of sound and a seemingly impenetrable crush of bodies stopped her cold. Sister or no sister this insanity did not look like anything she wanted to join in on. The room seemed to extend forever, and she could swear there were enough people here for a legal township.

And everyone was so done up! Even Meg with her peacock-blue eye shadow and her ruffled pink dress looked bland by comparison.

Vana glanced down at her own simple denim skirt and good shirt and little flat shoes dejectedly. The shirt had seemed so elegant when she'd bought it. It was the first real silk she'd ever owned, and it was a shade of ivory that made her feel regal.

But now, taking in all the sequins and plunging necklines and three-inch heels, she felt like a cleaning lady who'd accidentally stumbled into the ball. She glanced over at her sister's face, expecting to see two-hundred-watt excitement, but Meg's eyes were wide and stricken and her carefully "blushed" face had gone white. She was obviously having an anxiety attack of her own upon seeing the glittery crowd.

Suddenly the whole thing struck Vana as incredibly funny. What was all this about anyway? Some company had announced that it would sort through all the real-life country women they could find to come up with the ultimate natural beauty to sell its soap and shampoo. What a bunch of baloney! And every woman in this room had decked herself out and was parading around like a show steer in hope of catching the judges' eyes.

Only it wasn't clear who the judges were or exactly what they were looking for. And there was no way to tell who in the room was competing and who was just there to have fun. Why were people so eager to join in on such lunacy? And why were they all so willing to set themselves up for rejection and disappointment?

Vana knew that the answers were unimaginably complex—and different for everyone. After all, none of this insanity was anything new to her. She'd been the witness to similar situations as long as as she could remember. "You have to help," she'd heard her mama say a thousand times. "We know your sister deserves to win this contest, so it's our job to keep her spirits up. And if she doesn't win . . . it's our job to make it all right." And so Vana had kept her real thoughts to herself and tried to be helpful through every one of Margaret's contests.

Vana reached out and gave Margaret's arm a squeeze. "I can't believe this," she whispered to Meg. "They're all done up like guests for the Johnny Carson show, not country girls. None of them stand a chance."

Meg's eyes flickered down over her pink ruffles and then back up to Vana with a brief registering of gratitude—a look that made Vana feel intensely loving and protective. In an instant Meg brightened and flashed a delighted, cat-eating-the-canary grin.

"What dopes they all are," Meg declared, and marched confidently into the fray.

Vana smiled to herself and followed her sister into the crowd; she wanted to stay close enough to make herself available in case Meg had another confidence crisis. As for her own appearance—she wished she didn't look so completely out of place, but what did it really matter? She certainly wasn't there to compete for anything or impress anyone.

With the ease of a bloodhound following a scent, Margaret zeroed in on a group of promising-looking men—three grown-up males dressed outrageously in enough fringes and gewgaws to make Wild Bill Hickok blush or a gang of five-year-olds go green with envy. They certainly weren't real rodeo people, so the odds for them being part of the New York Bella contingent seemed pretty favorable.

"You poor fellas look lonely over here," Meg crooned, her lips teasing and pouting in her customary animated display.

"We shore are!" the tallest man announced gaily in an overdone accent from a B Western. "Why don't you two lil' fillies come on over and get acquainted?"

Meg giggled and charged right in. Vana followed behind, carefully keeping her expression blank. Lil' fillies? Oh, brother! She hung back, hoping to make a quick getaway as soon as she knew Meg was settled.

"I'm Arthur," the tall man said, "and this is Stephen—" the stocky man tossed off a military salute "—and that's Jagger." The slight pale man nodded.

"We're not really here with the rodeo people," Arthur admitted. "We're not even gen-u-wine Texans. Fact is, it's our first trip west."

"I'd never have guessed!" Meg exclaimed. "You fellas wear those jeans like you were born in the saddle."

The three exchanged grins and Vana worked at keeping her face neutral and her mouth shut.

"I'm Megi... Megi Linnier—" Margaret flashed her most winning smile "—and this is my little sister, Vana."

Arthur and Stephen clumsily tipped their hats. Vana inclined her head in acknowledgement and silently prayed for a quick release.

"I'm a barrel racer." Meg twinkled. "From a little ole town on the Kansas prairie." She winked conspiratorially. "You fellas wouldn't happen to be connected to that wonderful Bella company, would you now?" She said the last as if the answer would be a naughty secret between them.

"Ah, she found us out!" Arthur laughed. "You Kansas gals are too smart for us city boys."

"Why I never said any such thing!" Meg declared cutely. "You boys could think rings around a small-town girl like me."

Vana managed to keep her groans silent and her expression wooden, but she doubted if she could listen to much more of this.

"So how do we rodeo gals compare?" Meg asked sweetly. "I mean, you fellas have been all over the country lookin' for Miss Bella, right?" Meg twinkled naughtily again. "Is she here?"

"Now there's a very good possibility of that," Stephen began earnestly.

"We don't want to be too hasty with our remarks now, do we ma'am?" Arthur cut in quickly.

"Well, I just don't know how you guys do it," Meg said. "All the traveling and looking and... well... so much responsibility and..."

"And a new boss, too," Stephen commented unhappily. "Vandy, Ltd. stepped in and bought Bella lock, stock and paper clips, right in the middle of this huge national campaign and—"

"But it doesn't change the image we're after," Arthur said reassuringly. He shot Stephen a warning look, and Stephen mumbled something about not having any more of those Texas-sized drinks.

Arthur had one of those instant-on smiles that looked as though he practiced it in front of the mirror every morning. "No sir," he said, switching the smile back on. "A change in ownership doesn't change that special look we want for the Bella Woman. In fact, the Vandy people are very enthusiastic about this program."

Vana was suddenly aware of Jagger's eyes boring into her.

"How about you?" His voice was curtly businesslike and vaguely challenging. "We haven't heard a word out of you . . . Vana, is it?"

Vana shrugged.

Arthur put his hands on his hips and did a scolding kindergarten teacher impression. "Now, now . . . Where's that famous country charm? Where's that friendly winsomeness?" he asked in a direct quote from one of the Bella circulars.

"My sister got it all," Vana said with a teasing show of regret. Margaret beamed, and Arthur and Stephen grinned like idiots. Quickly, Vana moved back a step, hoping the line would buy her an exit.

"Oh, come on," Arthur urged. "A frisky little filly like you ought to have something to say."

"Yeah," Stephen spoke up jovially. He puffed out his chest and toyed with his fuchsia suede vest and his giant concho bolo tie and silver collar tips. "Bet we had you fooled at first, too, huh? Bet you didn't guess who we were."

"Shoot, yes, you have me fooled," Vana said, finally losing control. "I was just sure you were game show hosts— or maybe some of those car dealers who always advertise on TV in California." She grinned innocently.

She knew Meg would make her feel guilty about this later, but it felt pretty good right now just the same.

The men's mouths hung open and the expression in their eyes wavered on the edge of anger. Margaret's face registered plain, undisguised fury.

"Whoops," Vana said, biting her lip to keep from laughing. "I guess I'm just a bad little filly who needs to get out of Dodge because this town's not big enough for the five of us . . . right?" She backed up as she spoke.

Turning before anyone could say anything, she plunged into the crowd. Meg would get over being mad. She always did. And if nothing else Vana could point out that she'd charitably given Margaret a chance to demonstrate one of her primary talents—soothing ruffled male feathers and re-inflating male egos.

As soon as she'd put at least half the room between herself and Meg's little tea party, Vana drew in a deep breath and relaxed. Her sister wouldn't need her for a while—probably wouldn't even want to speak to her for some time. She was officially off duty. She let her gaze wander. The people-watching looked promising, and she might even have fun if she could avoid being a part of any more nauseating conversations.

She drifted about, watching and listening, feeling deliciously invisible and unfettered. Occasionally some overheard snippet of conversation would trigger a joke or comment in her head, and she allowed her lips to turn up in private amusement, but she kept her thoughts to herself. This might be a party—and half the merrymakers might be feeling pretty good about now—but she didn't have any illusions. There wasn't a person in the place who really wanted to talk to her or hear her comments, joking or otherwise.

The knowledge didn't bother her—she'd been told to keep her mouth shut and her "smart talk" to herself as long as she could remember. And she knew it was wise counsel, especially when you were a nobody in a room full of sequins and somebodies. Besides, it was easy to see that most of the men in the room were pretty caught up in the sound of their own voices and most of the women were involved in being awed by the men.

She could never fit in as a participant here, but she was comfortable and thoroughly entertained with her role as a spectator.

But then she saw him—and everything else in the room, every other thought in her head, faded into unimportance.

Chapter Two

Was it really *him*? Vana's breath caught and her entire body tensed with the question, even as some shred of common sense responded, of course it was him, and why should she be so shocked? If he had had the pull to get down into the contestant area, why wouldn't he have the pull to get in here?

She moved sideways, using the crowd as a screen, until she reached a better vantage point. The light in the room was low, but she could see now that her blurry first impressions had been right. He did look too young for his thick silvery hair, and there was something about him...some special quality that set him apart...though she couldn't exactly pin down what it was.

This is so silly, she chided herself. Sneaking around a party to stare at some man! She hadn't truly stared at a male since Jeremiah Waldenheim had left the bathroom door open in first grade.

But then watching wasn't really staring, and why shouldn't she watch him? She'd been watching other people all evening—why was this any different?

She moved a tiny bit closer. He was dressed in a bulky pullover sweater and dark slacks—maybe corduroys, but tailored and expensive looking—and he was probably the only man in the room who hadn't tried to look Western to one degree or another.

Yet, he appeared to be completely at ease and unconcerned about his differentness as he leaned nonchalantly against a wooden railing and listened to his companion, a paunchy, round-faced fellow decked out in a Western-cut suit. Undoubtedly a local livestock show and rodeo official, the man seemed to be working very hard to be clever or likable, with fits of forced laughter and extravagant nervous gestures.

A woman approached them. She had frothy hair and a glittery dress molded to a very noticeable body. The official welcomed her expansively and made a big show of introducing her. Vana's mind filled with a hundred tacky things she could say about the woman's appearance if she was feeling jealous or mean. But then why should she be feeling jealous?

He straightened and reached forward to shake the woman's hand. She looked startled at first, then, after shaking with him, put her hands to her mouth in what must have been a giggle.

Vana was seized with curiosity. It wasn't only that it might be fun to know what they were saying—she was also dying to hear what his voice sounded like. She edged past a few more people. The official began gesturing again and the woman laughed. Still, Vana couldn't quite hear their voices. She circled a large group to try another angle, but as she moved she kept him constantly in sight.

He was bored. She was almost certain of it. He was listening to the official and the woman all right, and even nodding or briefly smiling here and there, but his responses seemed to stem from mere politeness.

Damn. If she could just get close enough to hear him! But then he wasn't saying much anyway. The other two were doing all the talking.

He turned his head slightly and she ducked sideways with her heart in her throat. Had he seen her? She would be so embarrassed if he knew she was staring. Especially after the incident that afternoon....

Come on, Vana! She stopped herself cold with a little self-disgust at the realization that she was being as silly and presumptuous as Meg at her worst.

First of all, she wasn't certain he'd even been looking at her that afternoon—or had noticed that she'd looked at him. And even if he had, there was a good possibility that he could see her tonight without remembering her. Here she was getting all flustered and nervous, and the guy probably didn't care one way or the other if she stared at him.

Once she'd taken herself down a peg she felt much calmer, and she tentatively moved back into position and sneaked a glance between some bodies. Everything still looked safe. At least, he wasn't pointing at her or screaming, "spy."

She eased into a good position between two groups where she could look over people's shoulders without fully exposing herself. The official appeared to be saying goodbye. He winked suggestively, said something, and pushed the giggling woman closer as he left. The intention was clear, and Vana gritted her teeth and growled the word disgusting to herself.

The woman leaned toward him, talking and laughing, her manner flirtatious and full of invitation. Instead of softening though, Vana watched him grow stiffer and more guarded.

She realized that even when he'd been at ease he'd exuded an air of authority and control, and now that side of him appeared to be taking over. Everything in his elegant stance—from the set of his shoulders to the angle of his chin—became suddenly stern and imposing. Intimidating.

The transformation gave her goose bumps. Before her very eyes he had turned into someone she'd never have the nerve to say so much as hello to. No wonder he'd seemed so different from the beginning. It was a lot more than just his clothing or his silvery hair—he *was* different, or at least different from the men who inhabited her world.

She backed up a few steps, letting people drift in front of her until there was a solid wall of humanity blocking her view. Girls from Zeckendorf, Kansas had no business staring at men like that. Men like that belonged in private jets and fancy offices and in pictures on the pages of newspapers and magazines.

She and Meg had been exposed to an incredible cross section of people in the short time they'd been on the rodeo circuit, but she'd never lost sight of who Vana Linnier was or where she belonged. And this guy was way out of her league. She and Meg . . .

Meg! She'd completely forgotten about her. Quickly Vana turned and scanned the room. It had been over an hour since she'd last seen her sister. What if Meg had been looking for her?

Vana moved a few feet at a time, standing on her tiptoes every few minutes to scan the tops of heads for Meg's blond hair. In looking around she noticed that the man was no longer near the railing where she'd been watching him. He and the woman were gone—undoubtedly together. And, as her mama would have pointed out, Vana was sticking her nose where it didn't belong by even taking notice.

She sighed deeply and dropped her head to stare down at the floor for a moment. The fun had gone out of the evening. If she could just find Meg, maybe it would be all right for her to leave now. Drawing in a deep breath, she turned, taking a step forward as she did—and nearly ran head-on into a male body.

"Oh, I'm—" she began, but the words of apology died on her lips. The forward momentum that would have carried her around and past him died as well. It was him.

"I didn't mean to startle you," he said.

Oh sure, she thought. Probably the same thing the coyote said as he stepped into the chicken coop.

She prayed first for invisibility, but when that didn't work she simply wished for movement. If only her feet would come unstuck and her heart would start beating and her brain would send signals to her muscles, she could turn and run away.

"Is there something wrong?" he asked.

Was this guy playing some kind of game with her? She wanted to lash out at him, but her voice wasn't functioning. She couldn't even scowl at him because she was afraid to look up at his face. She just stood there in mute, frozen silence with her eyes fastened to the intricate gray-blue weave of his sweater. If he had noticed her staring and was mad, why didn't he just say so and get it over with?

He cleared his throat and she realized that he wasn't going to go away until she said something. So she summoned enough inner strength to single-handedly tip over a John Deere tractor and used it to look up at him.

She tried to make it appear casual, as though she'd just noticed his existence: tilting her chin back, raising her eyes to his in one quick questioning motion—and intending to say something like, "Yes? Were you speaking to me?" But her mouth opened and then closed like a fish out of water and all she could do was swallow.

Yikes!

The word echoed through her brain from the dim recesses of childhood. Yikes! She remembered saying it in the face of deep unfixable trouble. And now, standing so close to this man that she could almost hear him breathing and feel the warmth radiating from his skin...so close that there was no question as to whether those wonderful intense eyes were really seeing her and only her...now "yikes" had suddenly reentered her vocabulary.

"I caught you," he said with the deadpan seriousness of a television police detective.

And she was suddenly furious. What in the hell did he mean by that, and who in the hell did he think he was?

"What do you want?" she demanded hotly.

His eyes were the color of the ocean in magazine ads for the Caribbean, and his hair was salt-and-pepper rather than the pure silver it had looked at a distance.

"What do *I* want?" he asked incredulously, but there was amusement in his expression. "It's *you* who's been watching me. I should get to ask what you want."

"I wasn't watching you!"

He had the angular facial features that made a man handsome without any prettiness and his hair fell across his forehead in a well-groomed but unstudied way. For some reason the very fact of his close-up attractiveness made her even angrier.

"Why would I want to watch you?" she demanded, intending to finish off with some homespun insult.

He held up his hands as though stopping traffic.

"But it's only fair if you were," he said, "since I was staring at you this afternoon."

"You were?" she said coolly. She could feel the beat of her own pulse quickening. He really had been looking at her! "I must not have noticed. Where could that have happened?"

He grinned, almost laughed, the corners of his eyes crinkling wonderfully and long, deep lines accenting the upward curve of his mouth. Seductively attractive. She'd read the description in a book. Now she knew what it meant.

But suddenly his amusement felt like ridicule; he was making fun of her.

"My mama told me never to talk to strangers," she announced haughtily, and wheeled to stalk off.

"Don't go...please," he said, and the sincerity of the plea completely deflated her.

Turning her head slightly, she shot him a measuring sideways glance.

"I'm Schuyler," he said quickly. The name rolled off his tongue with a faintly foreign sound. He repeated it again as though to correct himself and this time it sounded more like Skyler. "And you're Vana. See—we're not strangers."

Slowly, she turned back to face him. He was very tall and looking up at him gave her a nice feeling. With most people her five-foot-ten frame made her feel gawky and graceless, but next to him she felt almost petite.

"How did you know my name?"

"I watched you in the barrel racing this afternoon. I listened to the announcer."

"Schuyler, huh? What kind of name is that?" she asked suspiciously. She had been thinking that he had the most elegant, sophisticated way about him—as if he were from some more advanced, more refined world. She would have imagined a different name for him.

"What kind of a name do you want?" he asked.

She eyed him critically. "Ummm...a French name, maybe, or one of those long English ones."

He laughed and she suddenly felt buoyant and lightheaded. He was enjoying the exchange with her!

"My father was enamored of his Dutch heritage," he explained wryly. "I didn't have a single teacher who could spell it correctly...and my middle name's Ahrent. Not much simpler, is it?"

She studied him in silence. What did this man want, anyway?

"It could have been worse," he said, talking quickly as though he were trying to save himself in some way. "After I was born my father became obsessed with wars. First it was the War Between The States. I could have ended up as Beauregard or—"

"Or Stonewall," she said. The spirit of his conversation was catching and she couldn't resist joining in.

He pretended a frown. "You're right! Just think, I could have gone through life as Stony. Or if Dad had been up to the French wars and his Napolean Bonaparte phase I could have ended up as Nappie or Bony." He sighed in mock relief. "But I was lucky, I guess."

Vana smiled widely. She would have laughed if she hadn't been so nervous. Her anger had completely dissolved, but in its place was an escalating case of nerves that felt like borderline insanity.

"You should do that more often," he said quietly. "You have a lovely smile."

She dropped her eyes and cleared her throat self-consciously.

"Smooth talk like that makes me think I shouldn't believe anything you say." She tried to make it sound a little bit like kidding, but the thought was deadly serious.

"You could be the Houston strangler or something for all I know." She looked up at him sideways a moment. "My sister thought you looked like a pervert."

"Your sister? Now where and when would your sister have seen me?"

"This afternoon when—" Vana stopped mid sentence and all the blood in her body rushed to her cheeks.

"When you were walking your horse and not the least bit aware of my presence, maybe?" he teased gently. "So the blond woman with you when you didn't notice me was your sister?"

For the first time in history she could not think of any sort of comeback. She was totally silenced.

"Would they give a gold badge to an undesirable?" he asked, indicating the Houston Rodeo and Livestock Show pin on his sweater.

She eyed the pin closely. "So you're an official, then?"

"An honorary one," he said. "Advisory capacity only. Let's say I've been pressed into service."

She studied the pin. So that was it. He was probably here giving some kind of advertising or organizational advice to the rodeo committee. That explained his presence.

"Come on now," he said. "Why all this suspicion and hostility? Has the significant man in your life armed you against forward males?"

She smiled shyly at the intent of the question. It was so flatteringly obvious.

"There is no significant man," she said.

"Then we have a great deal in common," he said. "My life is free of significants as well."

She loved the phrases he used and the way he shaped his words.

"That doesn't sound like a great deal in common to me," she tossed back lightly.

"Oh, but there's more," he assured her. "Much more."

"And how would you know that?"

"I knew it the moment I saw your eyes," he said, giving no clue as to whether he was serious or kidding. "And now I think it's our mutual responsibility to investigate the matter and find out exactly what this involves."

Taking her arm, he began steering her through the crowd. His light touch through the silk of her sleeve seemed to burn right into her skin.

Thankfully disengaging her arm, Vana sat down across from him at one of the small tables in the quietest, darkest corner of the huge room. The rest of the party faded into background noise. She felt almost too alone with him. Dangerously alone.

"Did that sister of yours come tonight, too?" he asked.

Was it Meg he really wanted? Was he talking to her only as a way to meet Meg?

"She's here," Vana said, looking around quickly as though Meg might instantly pop up from any direction. Just minutes ago she'd been searching for her sister, but now Meg was the last person she wanted to see.

What difference would it make, though? Vana thought in sudden resignation. If it was Margaret he really wanted to meet, there was certainly nothing she could do to change his mind. Meg might just as well appear now and take over. From long experience Vana knew that she didn't begin to exist for most males until Meg had put them through their paces and broken their hearts. Then they were willing to look around for a second choice.

It wasn't Meg's fault. It was just the way things were. It was just the way men were.

"She's here somewhere...in a pink dress." Vana waved her hand vaguely at the crowd behind her. "She's campaigning. You know about the big Bella search, right?"

"Oh...of course..." he mumbled. "But I don't...I mean I'm not..." His voice trailed off, then picked up again hesitantly with, "Well, yes, I do happen to know about it...of course."

"Oh, sure, of course you'd know. I suppose it's a big publicity gimmick for the rodeo," she said quickly to put him back at ease.

His sudden discomfort was puzzling and made him seem vaguely mysterious. It also served to make her feel more at ease. Apparently she wasn't the only one who was a little bit nervous and fumbling for words.

"Anyway—" she smiled to reassure him that everything was fine, and her newfound confidence radiated inside her "—my sister is doing her best to convince some wild-looking guys that she's a good choice for the Bella Woman." Vana shook her head. "To me, this whole Bella contest looks kind of like playing Monopoly blindfolded."

"Then you aren't trying to campaign?" His eyebrows raised slightly in question.

"Oh, no." Vana scoffed at the idea. "Not me. I'm not what anyone's looking for. It's Meg—Margaret, I mean— who has all the right stuff for that sort of thing. She always has. I'm not the front pasture material in the family."

Vana grinned, lapsing into what her mother called "that fresh attitude," with the word *fresh* having distinctly negative connotations.

"My mama always said," she began as if dispensing some gem of wisdom, "that Meg got the gift of looks and pleasantry, and I got the gift of capability and loyalty. She said that put together we made a truly fine human being."

As she spoke, Vana smiled the teasing little one-sided smile that she usually didn't allow herself in public. Both Meg and her mother had always found the smile somehow threatening or irritating.

"What does that make you separately?" he asked, joining in her light sarcasm.

"Ummm...two good dogs, maybe?" She tapped her bottom lip with her index finger to signify further clarification was brewing. "Depending, of course, on whether they were huntin' dogs or cow dogs or just plain yard dogs," she added.

A sense of wonder stole over her as she finished talking. She felt so natural and easy with this man. But how could that be possible? He wasn't the sort of person she should be able to make friends with, the sort of man she should be able to feel comfortable with.

Had she fallen down the rabbit hole or stepped behind the looking glass? Was she dreaming?

What would her mama say about this if she was here to see it? Probably something about Vana getting too big for her britches or too smart for her own good. Or maybe she'd just be full of cautions: Don't let him see what a fresh mouth you have. Don't smile at him sideways like that or he won't know for sure what you're thinkin'. Don't let him know you're smart as he is. And, whatever you do, get somethin' in writin' before you let him take any of your clothes off.

Oh, Mama, Mama, Vana thought. *I believe I'm just about ready to throw everything you ever told me right out the window.*

He leaned back in his chair slightly and cocked his head to the side as though analyzing her in some way.

"Are there any other children besides you and your sister?" he asked.

"No," she answered. "How about you? Any brothers or sisters?"

He shook his head no and she could tell he wasn't interested in pursuing that line. He was obviously preoccupied with some other thought.

"Mothers are often blind to their children's true qualities," he said quietly. "And frequently misguided in their dispensing of advice."

She wondered at his train of thought and his sudden seriousness. Did his comment relate only to what Mama had said about her and Meg making one decent person or was it maybe tied to some thoughts he was having about his own mother?

His new seriousness spawned a silence between them. It grew and built, humming in Vana's body until her nerves were stretched tight with it.

"Sooo..." she said when she couldn't stand it any longer. "This Astrodome would hold a lot of hay, wouldn't it?" It had to be the stupidest thing she'd said this month, but at least it broke the silence.

He smiled as though genuinely amused. "A lot of hay," he repeated, chuckling. Was it possible he'd never heard that one?

"Is it all right if I call you Sky?" she asked timidly.

"Yes," he said. "I'd like that."

He grew thoughtful, and she loved the way he leaned his elbow on the table and cupped his chin with his hand while his blue-blue eyes drifted into a faraway look. She tried to think of words to describe his eyes: aquamarine, maybe, or—what was that other one?—azure.

Suddenly he straightened, full of purpose.

"I was born and raised in the East," he said crisply. "My father was eccentric, my mother was seldom present and my cat's name was always Butch."

"Always?" she asked.

"I had a succession of cats, but I named them all Butch." He grinned. "I was terrific in math, I loved to read and I won the gold medal for my poster on dental health in the fifth grade. I was considered a recluse until I turned fourteen, at which time I became a discipline problem instead. I've had too many embarrassing moments to pin one down as the worst and my fondest memories all involve mean practical jokes that I'm now ashamed to recount."

He paused and pinned her with a mischievous look. "Now. Tell me about you."

She opened her mouth to protest, but he cut her off firmly with, "It's only fair since you just listened to all of *my* secrets."

"My sister and I grew up on a farm in Kansas," Vana said hesitantly as if that might explain everything. His expression told her she couldn't get away with stopping there.

"There's not much to tell. Really. My papa was a farmer and my mother did the usual farm wife stuff—canning and baking and tending the chickens . . . you know."

"And . . ." he said, gesturing with his hand for her to cough up more.

"No pets—but sometimes we got to ride the horses that Papa boarded for town folks. That's about it." She shrugged.

"Come on," he insisted. "You're not playing fair. You owe me at least two fond memories and one embarrassing moment."

"Okay." She laughed. She was beginning to feel as giddy as the time she'd downed all that champagne at Margaret's best friend's wedding.

"Let's see. . . ." She tilted her head toward the ceiling in thought.

"I won a tractor-driving competition once, but they disqualified me because someone said a girl shouldn't have been allowed to enter at all. And I would have been eighth grade valedictorian if I'd gotten to go to the graduation."

She drummed her fingers on the table a moment and nibbled the inside corner of her lip.

"I guess my most terrible moment had to be when I was trying to help my sister at the Miss Heartland pageant. They had crowned her—" Vana reached up with her hands to pantomime placing a crown on her head "—and there was going to be lots of picture-taking, so I rushed over and fluffed her hair up around the crown and gave it a heavy-duty hit with the hair spray to make sure it stayed put."

She wrinkled up her nose and peered across at him sheepishly.

"The spray dissolved the glue somehow, and all the corn and soybeans started falling off the crown. They bounced and clattered all over while Meg took her victory walk down the ramp."

At his hearty laugh, a warm glow spread through Vana's body.

"Small-town farm life wasn't very exciting or exotic," she assured him.

He smiled. "How can you say that? You almost won the tractor driving, didn't you? That's not only exciting—it adds to your air of mystery."

Now it was her turn to laugh.

"Air of mystery!" she repeated as she laughed so hard she had to dab tears from the corners of her eyes. "Oh yeah, that's me!"

"You don't think you're mysterious?" he asked.

"Are you kidding? Kansas farm girl turned bank teller turned barrel racer... hardly exotic. I'm the bread with the balloons on the wrapper."

His mouth softened into the barest of smiles.

"Maybe you just don't see yourself as others see you," he said, and the look in his eyes made her breath catch in her throat. "You have an intriguing, elusive quality.... And you have very wise and generous eyes."

A shiver ran through her entire body. Cheeks burning, she stared down at the table, overwhelmed by a kaleidoscope of delight, embarrassment, disbelief, fear and excitement. Her whole sum of male-female experiences had not begun to prepare her for this moment.

But everything was shattered by the sound of a voice.

"There you are! You naughty girl. I've been looking all over for you," Meg sang. She stared unabashedly at Sky as he rose politely from his chair.

"This is my sister, Meg...Margaret..." Vana said dully. Her stomach had developed a lead bottom.

"Megi—call me Megi," Margaret insisted cutely.

Vana ignored the interruption and continued. "And Meg, this is Sky...Schuyler."

Margaret was focusing a thousand-watt look on Sky, and Vana couldn't stop herself from adding, "You remember him...the one you thought looked like a pervert."

Meg shot daggers at her but recovered quickly and turned back to Sky with a sparkling smile.

"Pleased to meet you, I'm sure," she said, stretching "sure" into two syllables. "Well," she declared, looking around, "if I could just find a chair, I'd sit myself down and join you two." She fanned herself with her hand. "The smoke and the noise in here is about to overcome me."

Sky pulled a free chair over from another table and Vana studied her sister critically. Had Meg always sounded so phonily Southern Belle? And what was this "Megi" business? She hadn't called herself Megi since babyhood.

Mama had always set such store by what she termed "Margaret's naturally feminine ways," and Vana herself had always had a great deal of tolerance for Meg's excesses in behavior. Meg couldn't help being flirtatious—it seemed a built-in part of her nature. Ordinarily, Vana dismissed it as harmless. But now, here with Sky, Vana wanted to wipe the coquettish smile and the peacock eye shadow from

"Megi's" face and order her to cut out the nonsense and act real.

Sky held the chair while Margaret seated herself, and then he returned to his own seat.

"Well now," Meg purred up at him, "I'll bet you have some stories to tell." It was the same opening line Vana had heard her use on men for years, only now it seemed downright sinister.

"He won a gold medal for his dental health poster in the fifth grade," Vana announced in a sing-song voice. She received another fleeting glare from Margaret for her efforts.

"I swear," Meg said with a delicate sigh, "all this hobnobbing with Yankees can get a bit wearing. I mean, have you *seen* that group of men who are here from the East to find the Bella girl? They all look and act like—"

"I know what you mean." Vana cut her off. She had an idea what Margaret was about to launch into, and she was embarrassed for Sky to hear any hint of her sister's narrow-minded attitudes.

"Sometimes it's hard to visit and really get acquainted with people from such different upbringings and ways of life," she said with a sympathetic tone—as if that had been the idea Meg was about to express. "But after a while the differences don't seem so important, do they? Just like Sky here . . . his being from the East and me the West isn't causing us any problems at all."

"Ohhh!" Meg squealed. "You're one of those sophisticated Yankee types, too!" She gave the word *Yankee* a whole different tone now, and suddenly it became a compliment.

"I never would have guessed by your accent. Your voice sounds so much like a movie star. . . ." Meg flashed him a smile that could have caused cavities and fluttered her eyes a little, straightening her back and thrusting her bosom slightly forward as she did. "And what part of the East do you hail from?" she asked as though fascinated with whatever he might have to say.

"Various parts," Sky said. He was leaning back in his chair now and his mouth had a tiny curve of amusement to it. "But I went to school in England. That's undoubtedly the reason my speech patterns fooled you."

"England! How very interesting! Tell me—"

Vana jumped to her feet so suddenly that she tipped her chair over. She bent to retrieve it, dodging the startled looks on both Margaret's and Sky's faces.

"I've got to turn in," she mumbled hurriedly. "It's getting late. Have to work my horse early tomorrow, get him back on track...." Her voice trailed off and she wheeled around, lunging into the crowd before she could make an even worse fool of herself.

She hoped he might follow her. She hesitated a few minutes at the door after she'd finally worked her way through the crush of bodies, then stalled another five minutes before going down in the elevator. But there was no Sky behind her. He was staying—staying with "Megi."

She stalked out of the building and across the expanse of pavement toward the trailer, her mind reeling with the idea that he was sitting with her sister at that very moment, falling for the phony act. He was probably going all soft right now over some corny stuff about lil' ole Megi findin' a gentleman like him so fascinatin' and impressive. The thought made her want to gag.

Men always got so puffed up by Meg's flattery. Men were such fools, such gullible simpletons, such...

Oh, God...she'd almost been convinced that Sky was different. And she'd thought that he liked her enough to somehow be immune to the baloney her sister dished out. A dull ache began in her midsection. She'd seen that look of amusement on his face, seen the way he was enjoying "Megi's" wide-eyed fluttering and little girl squealing. He was a lost cause the minute Meg showed her dimples and batted her peacock-shadowed eyes at him.

How could Vana ever hope to compete with Meg's act? If that behavior was what interested him, how did she stand a chance at holding his attention? And, if that was what he wanted in a woman, why would she even want to try to compete for him?

She didn't. It was that simple.

Since she wasn't willing—and, in fact, didn't even know how—to fight that kind of battle, losing his attention to her sister seemed inevitable. And now she'd foolishly and impulsively hurried the inevitable along by walking out and leaving them alone together. Meg couldn't be blamed. A good-looking man to her was like a plump mouse to a house cat. Even if she was too full to want to eat it, she couldn't resist playing with it a while. In stomping off, Vana might as well have presented the mouse to Meg on a silver platter. What a stupid move!

Hadn't she learned anything in twenty-five years? After all her mama's lectures about keeping her smart mouth and her impulsiveness under control—and after all her conscious efforts to do just that—couldn't she have managed to overcome that brash, thoughtless urge to stomp away?

Since reaching adulthood she'd made lots of progress in learning to keep quiet and think twice before she spoke or acted. Why was she slipping all of a sudden? Why now, when something was this important, couldn't she have found the strength to do the prudent, thoughtful thing? Was it being free of Zeckendorf and her old life that was unhinging her—or was it this sudden, unsettling interest in a man that was causing her to come "untrained"?

She jammed the key into the trailer's lock and threw the door open, muttering to herself and banging her elbow painfully as she stepped inside. *Serves you right,* she told herself spitefully. *You're so stupid!* she repeated over and over to herself as she kicked the door shut and jerked off her clothes. She was still saying it when she climbed between the cold sheets in the cab-over bed.

Chapter Three

Vana tiptoed quietly around the tiny living space of the trailer, hoping that Margaret would sleep late as usual. Carefully taking a small carton of juice from the miniature fridge, she tucked it into the pocket of her down jacket. She had pretended sleep when Meg had crawled into bed sometime in the middle of the night, and now she hoped she could get away this morning, too, without talking to her sister.

She didn't want to hear anything about last night. She didn't want to know what had happened between Meg and Sky after she'd left. She didn't want to think about Sky at all, and if it were possible, she would have erased him completely from her mind. Most important, she didn't want to acknowledge the jealous rage she felt toward Meg.

She was determined to concentrate on Buck today. The horse needed work. Vana was not driven by an ambition to be a top barrel-racing competitor, but she was concerned about her horse. Without her direction and guidance, Buck could be headed toward some very bad habits. He was a natural runner and had the potential to make a good barrel horse, so Vana saw it as her responsibility to nurture his talents.

The Astrodome had enough facilities to allow a roomy stall for each of the timed-event contestants' mounts. Vana wished Buck could appreciate how lucky he was as she threaded through the barns and alleyways. Later on in the year there would be rodeos where he'd spend the night tied to a tree instead of luxuriating in a cozy stall.

Activity was just starting up on the grounds as people began to stir. The 4-H and FFA kids were gearing up for the never ending washing of their show animals, and the sanitation men were tootling around in their little tractor-and-cart outfits, delivering clean sawdust for bedding and hauling off the old.

She greeted Buck cheerily, not reminding him of his errors the night before, but he was his usual grumpy early-morning self, nonetheless. He pulled back when she tried to lead him out of the stall, and he refused to step on the section of the floor where puddles stood from a dripping water spigot. Sniffing and snorting at the wet spots as though they were evil, he shied sideways, finally forcing Vana to take a circuitous route to restore harmony.

She tied him outside where they could catch the early morning sunshine and went through her routine of brushing and combing. The big horse slid into ecstasy at the first touch, his long lashed eyes sinking to half-mast and his lips turning slack and rubbery. Once in a while his hide twitched when she hit a particularly pleasurable spot. The grooming was always therapeutic for him, and, by the time she threw on the lightweight barrel-racing saddle and swung up onto his back, he was responsive and eager to begin.

She walked him aimlessly at first, enjoying the feel of his strong body beneath her and the exhilarating sense of freedom that riding gave her. Somehow the world always looked better when she was in the saddle.

It was funny that she was the one who loved riding so much when it was Meg who'd always dreamed of a life as a professional barrel racer. In fact, sometimes she thought that her sister would have liked barrel racing a hundred percent better if there wasn't a horse involved at all.

Meg had always hated dirt and outside work and the relentless caring for the animals. And after finagling her way through beauty school and becoming Zeckendorf's star blow-dry artist, Meg's aversion to dirt and animals had quadrupled. But still, the barrel-racing dream required a horse, so Meg had gritted her teeth and continued riding.

Now they were living Meg's dream. Vana had no real desire to be a world champion barrel racer. She didn't yearn for the glory like Meg did or feel that keen competitive pull that she supposed drove Meg. Tagging along with Meg had just been a means of escape from the farm and her dull job at the bank and her dead-end life—and almost any means of escape would have been acceptable.

Yet, for all this, Vana felt like she was the only one who was enjoying herself. Meg was constantly too depressed or too critical or too impatient or too frustrated or too dissatisfied to ever relax and appreciate the fact that she was getting what she'd always wanted.

Vana shifted in the saddle and took a deep breath of the tart, fresh air. God, they were in Houston, Texas! They were getting to travel and meet all sorts of people. They were free to set their own schedules and arrange their own priorities. And Meg was running barrels on *the* professional circuit— living her lifelong dream! It was beyond Vana how Meg could approach all this with such a negative attitude, with no sense of joy or wonder.

Vana was tired of hearing how rodeo wasn't as glamorous as Meg had imagined and how the other barrel racers were either idiots or scheming witches. She was tired of hearing Meg complain about how something wasn't fair or wasn't enough or was too much. And she was sick to death of Meg's flirting and fickleness and . . .

No. She couldn't let her thoughts go in that direction. Jealousy was an ugly, destructive monster and she refused to let it take root between them. Besides, wasn't that jealousy newly hatched and caused specifically by one man and one incident?

At least she could refuse to let herself be guilty of negative thoughts. She'd escaped Zeckendorf, hadn't she? And Meg's dream had gotten them out. Meg's dream had saved her. She couldn't lose sight of how grateful she was to Meg—not just for this, but for years of smaller things as well. It was Meg who'd always led the charmed life and who'd generously shared the good fortune and excitement with her less stellar sister.

She owed Meg a lot. Sometimes she felt like it was almost a tangible debt with interest building up and payments due. And right now her obligations were clear: she had to continue to humor Meg and work at keeping her spirits up, and she had to constantly remember where her loyalties lay. She owed her sister loyalty no matter what. And if Margaret charmed Sky, she would have to silently accept it and not let jealousy or resentment drive a wedge between them.

Vana patted Buck's firm neck and let him ease into a short gallop. The horse had come a long way since she'd first bought him—but then so had she. She drew in a deep breath and smiled to herself as she headed him toward the outdoor practice arena that was designated for barrel racers' use. The area was deserted except for a lone figure leaning against the fence near the gate.

She was preoccupied with her thoughts, and it wasn't until he turned that she realized just who the figure was. Heat rushed to her face and her heart thudded in her chest. She tried to appear casual as she slid out of the saddle to open the gate, but when he smiled she was suddenly all thumbs, dropping the rein and fumbling with the latch and pinching her finger.

"Good morning," he said, his warm smile echoed in his sea-blue eyes.

She was afraid to hope for anything. How could he possibly be here to see her when he'd had a full dose of Meg the night before? Was he looking for Meg?

"You're up early," she remarked a little too curtly.

"I like to get up early."

"I'd have thought you'd need to catch up on your sleep this morning after staying out so late last night," she said pointedly.

There it was—that ugly monster germinating inside her. She busied herself with leading Buck through the gate and refastening it. She avoided meeting his eyes.

"I'm not much for late nights," he said. "I left right after you did."

"You did?" she asked, a little too eagerly. She wanted it to be true, but it was so hard to believe.

"What, did Meg desert you for another run at the Bella guys?"

"No," he said.

She held her breath, waiting for him to say more, but he didn't.

"So..." She swung back into the saddle. "Why are you on the grounds so early? If you're trying to catch Meg, you're about three hours too soon."

"I was hoping to catch you," he said simply.

Her heart did a little somersault in her chest and she fought down the grin that threatened to take over her face.

"I really do have to work my horse," she said apologetically.

"I know," he said. "I thought I'd just pick a good spot on the fence here and watch. That is...if you don't mind."

"Oh, no!" she said quickly. "I don't mind at all." She allowed herself a brief smile. "And Buck loves to show off," she added, reaching down to pat the gelding's neck.

A great joyful energy coursed through her as she took Buck through his paces, working on his lead changing and his turns. This man had gotten up early and come all the way down to the practice arena just to see her! He was still interested in her, in Vana Linnier, even after a straight shot of Meg's finest efforts.

She worked Buck till he was dark with sweat and his movements were Swiss-watch perfect. Then she rode to the fence and stopped in front of Sky.

"That's it," she said. "I'm afraid it wasn't very entertaining."

"I enjoyed it. I'm a city boy and horses have always fascinated me," he admitted.

"Do you ride?"

He chuckled. "I have ridden," he said, "but I wouldn't say I ride."

"Buck's very gentle," she said. "Would you like to take him around a few laps to cool him out?"

"Really?" he said with the excitement of a child being offered some wonderful gift. He jumped down off the fence eagerly. "Are you sure?"

"Yes." She smiled and swung down from the saddle. She handed Sky the reins and quickly adjusted the stirrups for a longer-legged rider.

Holding Buck's head, she encouraged Sky as he climbed hesitantly up onto the barrel-racing saddle. She showed him how to hold the reins and explained that the exaggerated horn on the saddle was so the barrel racer could hold on for balance if necessary as the horse made his hairpin turns. If the rider got off balance at any time during a run, her weight could throw the horse off balance and the race would be lost.

He listened intently to her tips and explanations.

"Are you certain Buck approves of this?" he asked when she'd finished, but she just laughed and waved him off.

Vana perched on the top rail and watched the duo make their rounds. It was perfectly safe. They were locked inside the arena and the worst thing Buck might do at this point was put his head down and go to sleep. She smiled indulgently as they passed. Every successful round brought a delighted look to Sky's face, and she was filled with the most intense surge of liking.

A funny word—*liking*. But how else could she describe it?

She liked the way he'd openly declared that he'd come specifically to see her yet hadn't made it sound like the beginning of some smooth pitch. She liked the way he'd made himself at home while watching her and hadn't demanded any of her attention during the workout. She liked the way he'd allowed himself to revert to boyish delight at the prospect of riding a horse. And she very much liked the way he hadn't been embarrassed or threatened to admit that he wasn't an experienced rider and that climbing aboard the big animal scared him as well as thrilled him.

He insisted on helping her put Buck away, and he was full of questions, interested and amazed by every facet of caring for a horse and keeping the animal fit of competition.

"I never realized how much went into this," he said as they shut the stall door and gathered up her gear. "Do all the barrel racers here work this hard to take care of their horses?"

"Sure. I'd say being smart about your animal's health is a big part of being good at the sport."

She swung the headstall over her shoulder and started down the wide barn aisle. Horses in stalls on either side nickered softly as they passed or peered out at them as if to ask who they were.

"It's the same way in the men's timed events . . . the roping and the steer wrestling," she explained. "Only in those you get more people being 'mounted.' That means riding someone else's horse and paying them a percentage of any winnings for the use of the animal."

"And do contestants all train their own horses?" he asked. He had insisted on carrying her saddle back to the trailer for her and now walked with it clumsily tucked under his arm.

"No. Some people can ride just fine but couldn't train a duck to swim. There are always plenty of good trainers around, though, who get a horse going well and then sell it to someone who wants to compete."

"So who trained Buck?"

"Well, he'd already been started before I got him by a woman in Kansas who got pregnant and decided to quit. So all I really had to do was put a finish on him."

"And is he a quarter horse?"

"Yes. He's registered. His paper name is Dekes Bumble Bars. I just call him Buck because he's a buckskin."

"Buckskin?"

"His coloring. He has this certain pattern where his hide is pale yellowish-tan and his mane and tail and lower legs are kind of blackish . . . you know?"

Sky laughed and she felt a rush of self-consciousness.

"I don't see anything funny about that," she challenged.

"I'm sorry. . . . I'm sorry. Really." He grinned widely. "I can't help it. I just love the way you talk and the way you describe things. It's so different from what I'm used to."

She frowned at him. Was he serious or kidding? Had he been poking fun at her? Did he see her as some ridiculous country hick?

"Come on," he coaxed. "Please. Can't I enjoy the differences between us?"

She drew in a deep breath and a smile crept to her lips. Yes. It was all right. And the differences between them were wonderful. Very, very wonderful.

"So," he said. "I think it's time for brunch, don't you?"

Brunch! She'd never had brunch before.

"Do I need to wear a dress?" she asked in panic. The only skirt she had with her was the one he'd seen her in the night before.

"No," he said gently. "If they don't like us in jeans, we'll just take our business elsewhere."

He smiled down at her and she had to turn and rush into the trailer to escape. She wanted to spin in circles and dance wildly and shout to the sky, but Margaret was still sleeping so she held it all inside.

"Going out for brunch with Sky," she scrawled on the refrigerator noteboard. She paused and studied the words a moment then erased "with Sky." She would keep that part to herself for now. The sisters weren't in the habit of keeping each other posted as to whereabouts or plans and had learned that getting along in their cramped quarters depended pretty much on going their own separate ways, but "Going out for brunch" was just too delicious to keep to herself.

Quickly she washed off with the little hand-held shower in the toilet cubicle and pulled on clean jeans and her best sweater. She stopped in front of the mirror to smooth back the strands of hair that had escaped from her tightly braided ponytail.

"Tidiness," her mama had always insisted. "There's no use in your being vain, daughter—you can't invent what's not there. But tidiness is a pleasing feature in itself. You can be appreciated for your neat appearance."

Meg was wrong, she thought. She hadn't worn her hair exactly the same way all her life. She had eliminated the thick awninglike bangs of her childhood. The memory of Margaret's critical comment the night before stirred up a hornet's nest of insecurity inside her.

She had never liked her own reflection, but today the feeling verged on despair. She frowned at herself and a heaviness settled over her. How could that man possibly be attracted to her? What was he seeing?

She squinted at the woman in the glass. She hadn't changed since leaving the employment of the Zeckendorf Security National Home Bank and Trust. She was still the same boring, bony person with too many angles in her face and not any of what her mama called "feminine softness."

The plain brown woman, was how she had always thought of herself. All-over brown, like grocery sacks or mutt dogs or field stubble—not even a rich, dark brown that might be a little exotic, but this weird light brown, varying only slightly in shade between her eyes and hair.

And her eyes weren't wide and round like her sister's, and her lips wouldn't pout—even after she'd held the bottom one out with her finger for two weeks in high school—and her skin wasn't perfect and creamy like her sister's or dramatically tan like the women in the movies. It was some strange shade in between. Another weird variation of the same brown that colored her eyes and hair.

She turned away from the mirror and peeked out around the edge of the curtain to see if he was still there. She didn't want to go anymore. He couldn't possibly be interested in her. Not really. She was just a funny hick to him—a walking aggie joke. She wished he'd just go away and leave her alone.

What more could he want, anyway? She'd already introduced him to her sister and let him ride her horse. She had no more to offer.

She stepped out the door, ready to tell him she'd changed her mind; but before she could speak he reached out and took her hand.

"You look terrific," he said with a warm genuine smile.

And all of the doubts and negative feelings dissolved into crazy, magical swirls of something heady and intoxicating that must have been the fairy dust she'd searched for as a child.

Climbing into the front seat of his car and making comfortable small talk with him as he sped along the Houston freeways in search of brunch was hazy and unreal. Sliding into the plush-leather rounded booth beside him and looking at him over the top of a huge menu was positively unbelievable.

As in a dream, the fabric of time stretched and warped, first seeming to speed and then to slow. Her awareness of everything was heightened—the languid heaviness of the plants that filled the restaurant, the stiff white cloth of the napkin as she unfolded it, the heat from his body whenever they casually brushed against one another.

The food arrived and she had to force herself to eat. She had no appetite at all. She only wanted to look at him and to bathe in the glow of his eyes on her. She wanted to luxuriate in the wonder of their being together.

And she wanted to listen to him. She loved his voice. She drew in his words like a starving person devouring food. She listened to amusing stories about New York and London. She listened to his fondness for Houston and his interest in the rodeo. And she found herself smiling more than usual and laughing more than usual, and responding easily to questions and telling long stories of her own and joining in jokes unself-consciously.

And when he mentioned something about his trip being too short and his flight leaving that night she was as stunned and breathless with pain as if someone had delivered a surprise punch to her solar plexus.

"Tonight! But—"

Sky stopped her with a firm shake of his head. "No. You didn't let me finish. I *had* a reservation to return to New York tonight, but I've changed it. I'm staying over."

"I don't understand," Vana said weakly.

After all their conversation, she still had no sense of what he was doing in Houston.

"You're leaving, then you're not leaving. You say you're not really here on business. Why did you come in the first place and how did you get hooked into helping with the rodeo? What's the big mystery? Why are you being so secretive?"

He toyed with the spoon resting in his coffee saucer and kept silent as the waitress cleared away the dishes. Something was making him uncomfortable again. She had the crazy thought that he might be with the FBI or the CIA or some kind of Mafia gang. Why was he so damned hesitant to discuss his business and his trip to Texas?

He cleared his throat. "I've been working too hard, I'm told—developing tunnel vision—and I was ordered to get away." He inhaled deeply, set the spoon down and smiled ruefully.

"I'm just a boring guy, I guess. I couldn't think of anyplace I wanted to go for a short break—not by myself, anyway—and I was having trouble coming up with a plan." He paused as though taking great care with his words. "I have business connections to the Bella team, and I heard about the trip they'd planned to Houston." Another pause. "I'd never been to Texas before, so I thought, why not?"

"Then the Bella guys are friends of yours?" Vana pressed. Something bothered her—both about his having a connection to Bella and about his not having mentioned it until now. She tried to recall exactly what she'd said about Meg's campaigning to be the Bella choice. Had she said anything she shouldn't have or compromised Meg in any way?

"No. Not friends," he said firmly. "Business acquaintances." He began fiddling with his spoon again. "It was just something to do to get away, and I knew if I came with them I'd get an insider's view of the rodeo and the city."

"I guess I shouldn't have talked to you about Meg's wanting to be—"

"No, no, no," he insisted, shaking his head. "I've got nothing to do with that. In fact the reason I was trying to keep such a low profile—" he looked across at her and gave a charmingly boyish shrug "—is primarily because I was afraid my connection to the Bella team might give rise to all sorts of assumptions about me having some part in the selection. I didn't want people—"

"By people you mean women," Vana cut in dryly.

His manner was definitely sheepish now. "Yes, I suppose that's what I mean," he admitted.

"All right, I can understand that," she conceded. But she didn't want to let him off the hook. This seemed like a good time to have some other questions settled.

"So exactly what *do* you do?" Vana quizzed insistently. "I mean, you keep saying you're a businessman. Shoot, that could mean anything where I come from."

He smiled, but his eyes were vaguely troubled. "I work for my family's company," he said. "Just like my father worked for it and my grandfather before him. Old Kiliean Van Dusen, my great-grandfather, set us all up for life when he started his little import-export business all those years ago."

"That's nothing to be ashamed of," Vana insisted in mild reprove.

Suddenly everything was falling into place, and she felt a sense of relief. There was nothing ominous about his hesitancies. There was no life-of-crime or wife and kids hidden in the woodwork.

"Do I sound ashamed?" he asked.

"Yes. But there's no call for it. Just because you didn't have to go out on your own to make your way doesn't mean you shouldn't be proud of what you're doing. If you're working hard and doing a good job and satisfied with yourself... that's all that's important. Most farm boys just step into the family farm operation—rural folks look on that as the natural order of things."

"I don't know... I guess I was always afraid of being lumped with all those snotty blue-blooded old family business types in my neck of the woods. I hate the thought that people assume I'm like that."

"How could anyone ever think you were like that!" Vana declared.

He smiled at her gently, tenderly, and leaned forward slightly. He rested his hand so close to hers on the table that she could feel the nearness of it without having to look down to see it. His smile faded and he held her with a look that grew in intensity until she could barely breathe.

She pulled her eyes away, fixing them on the safe haven of her coffee cup. Her heart hammered wildly in the charged silence.

"Do all New Yorkers put that much milk in their coffee?" she said. Her voice sounded shaky and desperate to her ears.

"Generalities are never true," he said lightly. "But in general I'd have to say we Yankees have a tendency to like our coffee on the tan side."

"Whenever anyone offered my uncle milk for his coffee he'd always act offended and say, 'I was raised on a steer outfit!'"

Sky's unbearably sea-blue eyes filled with puzzled delight. "What in the hell does that mean?" he laughed.

His laughter saved her and returned her equilibrium.

"It means," she explained with a grin, "that Uncle Jim thought it was sissyish to put milk in coffee. And he figured that since they don't run cows on a steer outfit then there was never any milk for coffee there—and sayin' he was from a steer outfit was all that needed to be said to prove that he'd never consider puttin' milk in coffee and darn sure wasn't a sissy."

Sky shook his head as though completely lost. "I detect a thread of logic there somewhere," he said.

"Cowboy logic." She grinned. "Boy, he could really get me mad, too, when I was little by tellin' me I'd never make it on a steer outfit. That meant I was a sissy for sure."

"Wow." Sky laughed, shaking his head. "Sounds like this Yankee boy has a lot to learn."

"Jim was my mother's brother. The kinda crazy Irish-Spanish side of the family." Vana studied her empty cup for several beats. "You'll just have to come back west soon...to learn some more," she said. The words didn't come out as light and bantering as she'd wanted them to.

Had he heard the yearning in her voice? Could he tell how disappointed she was at the thought of never seeing him again? Disappointed. That didn't even begin to describe what she felt.

"And I can't believe you ever considered leaving tonight!" She worked at putting the fun back into her tone.

"I mean, how could you leave before you found out who won the barrel racing? More important, how could you leave before you saw Buck make his second run?"

He held up his hands in a show of helplessness.

"I don't know what I could have been thinking," he admitted in mock seriousness.

"And of course you have to find out if they pick a Bella girl here. You did come out with that bunch. Don't you have an obligation to stay through to the finish?"

His eyes changed as she spoke and she sensed that she'd said something he didn't like. Oh, hell, couldn't she do anything right with this man?

"I told you," he said sharply, "I have nothing to do with that."

Vana swallowed hard against the burning in her throat and pushed a few strands of hair back off her forehead in the frustrated gesture her mother had always said was unladylike. She so badly wanted Sky to like her. She wanted everything she said to be right.

She didn't know how to cope with this whole situation, and she had so little time to figure it all out if he was flying back to New York in a matter of days. New York! It might as well be the moon.

Why was this happening? Why couldn't she have felt this way with Bubba or Olaf or Wiggy? Why couldn't she have lost her sanity over some dull, familiar guy back home— somebody she had a chance with?

Then it struck her—there was another way to look at this. What did she have to lose here? She could go with her crazy feelings, full speed ahead. She could do or say whatever she damn well pleased. She could even make a total fool out of herself.... And what would it matter?

When these few days were over she would probably never see this man again. She wouldn't have to face him like she would a neighbor, and she wouldn't have to worry about him telling stories about her to the gang back at the Zeckendorf domino parlor. What more could she ask? What better situation could she find to try out her wings and experience her first case of complete madness?

She looked up at him and smiled.

"How about dinner tonight?" she said impulsively.

He looked surprised.

"My treat," she added quickly. "Maybe Mexican?" Surely she would be able to afford a Mexican place.

She held her breath for his answer. She wished he'd smile, but he didn't. He just studied her and she could tell from his eyes that he had some kind of conflict going on in his mind.

"It's not really important or anything..." she added quickly. "I just thought...if you weren't doing anything...I mean Texas is famous for it's Mexican food...and even if you don't go tonight, with me, you should—"

"I'd love to have dinner with you," he said quietly.

She closed her mouth in the middle of a word and slumped back in the booth with a quiet sigh of relief.

"Oh...okay," she said lamely. "Since my truck is connected to the trailer—"

"We can use my rental car," he said. "What time is good for you?"

What time is good for you—just as though she was somebody important with valuable time! She'd always had dates where the guy said, "I'll come git ya at seven" or "Meet me at the gas station at eight," just assuming that whatever was good for him was automatically okay with her. Of course, she'd never had a date where she was the one who did the inviting. Maybe this sort of thing had a whole different set of rules.

"Do you compete every night?" he asked as though just realizing that was a possibility.

"No, but I'd like to catch tonight's barrel racing," she offered hesitantly.

"Fine," he said. "Just say when and where and I'll meet you."

"Are you going to the performance?"

"I'll be around," he said noncommittally.

"How about if we meet at my trailer about nine-thirty? Is that too late for you?"

He laughed. "No. We Yankees are fond of late dining."

There was a long silence while more coffee was poured and more attention than necessary was given to adding milk and stirring.

"I have to go back," she said finally. She'd ignored the fact of the fading afternoon as long as she could. "I have to take care of my horse and..."

"Of course," he said as if apologizing for thoughtlessness. "I shouldn't have kept you."

He paid the check and they started out for the car. When he took her arm for a moment as they stepped out the door, his touch sent a jolt of sensual electricity zinging through her body. A strong current of awareness sizzled in the silence between them.

On the drive back she seized every opportunity to look in his direction. Whenever they stopped or turned she would let her gaze slide sideways toward his face. And she caught him looking at her, too: furtive looks, guarded, questioning looks, looks that told her this was not simple for him, either.

She said a shy goodbye to him at the gate and started across the grounds to the parking area. The air was crisp and tangy with the mingled smells of sweet horse feed and baled hay. She felt like breaking into some crazy song and dance routine but settled for humming and adding a little bounce to her walk.

As she rounded a stock barn, the sight of the long, blue-and-white metal trailer—its back half for horses and its front half for people—stopped her. The unlikely beat-up contraption had been their ticket out of Zeckendorf, their magic carpet ride, and it stood before her now in mute accusation.

Even though she would never have admitted it to anyone, Vana had been as active as Meg at harboring big dreams. While Meg's had all been centered on being a barrel-racing champion and being rich, Vana's had been less concrete and not so easily expressed. But they'd been inside her just the same. She'd always been full of wanting.

She'd dreamed of a different kind of life than what Zeckendorf had to offer—a life with more potential and more surprises. A life that included travel and art and ancient castles and towering mountains and endless oceans. A life where it was possible to try snow skiing and scuba diving and flying in an airplane. A life that included the taste of unfamiliar foods and the sound of all kinds of music. A life that pulsed with the energy of a city.

A different life. Such a vague thing to want.

She had spent her childhood feeling secretly ashamed because she knew deep down that no amount of Zeckendorf's offerings would ever be enough. She knew that others would see her as greedy and ungrateful if they knew. She wanted too much.

Just three months ago she would have sworn that having this trailer and seeing Zeckendorf fading in the rearview mirror was all she would ever ask for again. Escape had been a rebirth for her, and she felt as though her previous twenty-five years had been lived in some suspended fetal state.

Did she dare want more now? Did she dare want...? She couldn't bring herself to even think his name. She took a deep breath and blocked the question from her mind as she stepped into the trailer.

"Long brunch, huh?" Margaret commented sarcastically as Vana entered. Meg stood studying herself in the mirror on the closet door, pushing her hair this way and that.

Vana didn't respond. She pulled off her coat and slid into the little bench that nestled between the built-in table and the wall.

"That was really rude the way you cut out last night," Meg accused. "It was really inconsiderate. You could have destroyed my whole evening."

"I'm sorry," Vana said woodenly. She couldn't possibly discuss the reason she'd left.

Meg sighed in exasperation. "God, you're so weird around men sometimes! What'd the guy do that made you run off like a scared rabbit?"

Vana shrugged. "I was just tired of the party. Are you changing your hair or something?" she asked, hoping for a change of subject.

Meg frowned. "I don't know.... I was just trying to decide which way to wear it tomorrow. What do you think?"

Vana knew her sister didn't really expect any suggestions, so she just watched silently as Margaret tugged on her shoulder-length, blond hair. Meg had been born sort of blond—or dishwater blond, as Mama called it—but in her second week of beauty school she'd gone *blond*! The shade, called Champagne Sonata, was a silvery-beige that always reminded Vana of the old dun mare that had been struck by lightning behind the barn one spring.

"I wish I knew exactly what they wanted," Meg declared petulantly as she studied her reflection. "I mean, when they say natural, exactly what are they talking about? And when they say fresh and country, do they want freckles and pigtails or what?"

She turned toward Vana with a deep frown creasing her forehead.

"I could be anything they wanted," she said with almost religious fervor, "if I just knew *what* they wanted!"

"Just calm down and be yourself," Vana advised halfheartedly.

"Oh sure! That's easy for you to say." Margaret paced a few steps in either direction in the tiny enclosure. "You just don't understand, Vana. You don't know what it's like to really want something."

Vana observed Meg's overly dramatic movements and facial expressions without comment. Bubbly and animated—that's what men always called her.

"Now tomorrow afternoon they want us to show up in jeans and looking..." Meg paused and picked up a printed sheet from the counter. She held it up and read, "'...looking fresh and simple.' God, can you believe this!"

She dropped the piece of paper to the table and rolled her eyes. "I guess they want to march us around, eyeballing our behinds in tight jeans and checking us out in the daylight to see who has pimples or false eyelashes."

Vana smiled and shook her head. "Will you settle down? Getting yourself all lathered up over this is not going to help you look better to those guys."

"I know." Margaret wrinkled her nose and pooched her lips out. *"I. Want. To. Be. Miss Bella!"* she announced dramatically. Then she sighed and smiled dreamily. "I might even forget about being barrel-racing champion if I could be on the cover of *Vogue*."

Vana laughed. "How about *Playboy*?"

"Mama would die!" Meg squealed. She drew in a deep breath and looked thoughtful a moment. "Just think, Vana, if I could pull this off we'd be set. We could live anywhere we wanted and we'd never, never have to go back to Zeckendorf."

"Except to ride in the parade," Vana said.

"Oh yeah, yeah!" Margaret chuckled gleefully. "We could be the visiting celebrities in the parade, couldn't we?"

"You mean *you* could," Vana corrected her gently.

"Have I ever left you out of anything?" Meg demanded in a tone that implied a wrong answer might easily hurt her feelings. "Haven't I always included you? Always made sure you and Mama got to come onstage and help and everything?"

"Yes. Always," Vana said, feeling a sudden wave of tenderness as though she were talking to a misguided but adored child.

"Well, then—" Meg beamed "—this will be no different! We're in this together, like always. What does it matter who wins or who gets the fuss made over them? The main thing to remember is that this deal could set us up for life."

Meg reached for her jacket. "I haven't even worked my horse yet!" she exclaimed as she started for the door. "Now keep in mind for tomorrow," she cautioned, "we have to *be there* at noon."

"I'm still stuck with coming, huh?" Vana asked, but she already knew the answer.

"Of course you have to come! I'd never go without you! Besides, I heard a rumor that they might actually announce a choice tomorrow. If that's true I'll really need you there— whatever happens."

Meg finished zipping her jacket and reached for the doorknob.

"Oh, say..." Vana said casually. "Do you mind if I borrow one of your dresses tonight and maybe a purse?"

Meg stopped and turned back toward her in surprise.

"It's not a big deal," Vana said quickly. "Everybody just seems to dress up more around here, and I thought..."

"Too bad you don't have one of those sexy bank uniforms with you," Meg teased.

"Sure," Vana said, and threw a crumpled paper napkin at her.

Margaret laughed and ducked out through the door. "Borrow anything," she called. "See ya later."

Vana took a deep breath and let her head fall back against the plastic, wood-grained paneling behind her. Meg hadn't asked her anything about her brunch date.

It used to make her mad the way Meg always just assumed that Vana's dates were boring and not worth discussing, but today she was grateful. She could never explain to her sister the way she felt about this man. And she wouldn't want to if she could. She didn't want to share him with Margaret in any way. She didn't want her sister to know anything about him.

Meg had had frequent mystery dates through the years, but most of the boys Vana had dated had been Meg's castoffs—boys they'd both known for a hundred years. Now Vana had a mystery man, and she wanted to keep him all to herself. And, there was still the raw fear that Meg would captivate him if given half a chance.

Dinner tonight. Vana grinned and hugged herself. She was having dinner with *him* tonight. The delicious excitement of that fact traveled through her body in a heated, tingling rush.

Chapter Four

Yes." "No." "Sometimes." "A little." Those were the only responses Vana had managed in the past hour and, in fact, the only words she'd spoken at all.

She felt stiff and unnatural in the borrowed dress, and the purse she hugged so closely to her side throbbed with an incriminating life of its own. What if she dropped the purse and it fell open? What if a robber appeared and made her dump the contents in front of everyone?

The purse contained the proof, the evidence of her questionable intentions.

She'd walked beside Sky into the rambling, red-tiled restaurant with her eyes downcast. The dinner itself no longer seemed important to her, and she felt detached and distanced from the whole scene. The only important thing now was her decision and how she would carry it out.

No one who knew her would believe it if they could see into her thoughts right now—or her purse. Meg would go into shock, and the boys she'd dated around Zeckendorf would double over with laughter. Vana, the town prude, had gone off the deep end.

And it couldn't be blamed on impulsiveness. Not this decision. She had been slow coming to it that afternoon, but once the idea took hold she'd tiptoed around it and worried it for hours. She could never use a lack of thought as an excuse.

She intended to make love with Schuyler Van Dusen tonight, and she simply was not going to allow herself to weaken or change her mind.

The decision was set in concrete. But now she was worried because she didn't know the first thing about flirting or seduction or how to give a man whatever signal it was that women were supposed to give. And she was worried about the contraceptive paraphernalia she'd scooped off the drugstore shelf so hurriedly—it lurked in her purse, ready to scream her intentions to any who looked. And she was worried about making a fool of herself. And most of all she was desperately worried about her lack of sexual expertise. She'd had a boyfriend she'd said yes to, but the furtive fumblings with him in his parked pickup had not taught her much about lovemaking.

But she was not going to weaken. She was determined. She was a grown woman, yet she had never felt these deep stirrings or beckoning passions before. In all those years of holding sweaty farm boys' hands or kissing behind the hedgerows or giggling with Meg about how cute a guy from the next county was, she had never once felt true sexual attraction. She hadn't ever burned at a touch or melted at a glance or ached or yearned.

When she had finally given herself it had only been to prove that she wasn't abnormal. She had felt neither desire nor pleasure, though, and the incidents had left a residue of sadness and frustration in her, and she'd feared that maybe what the other kids said was true: She was a prude, and she was missing some basic womanly need.

But now, for the first time in her life, a man had awakened something powerful and urgent within her. This was genuine, not something conjured up to satisfy her sister or prove something to her peers. These feelings were real and intoxicating and rare, and she might never experience them again in her entire life. She might never again have the chance to make love with a man who made her feel this way.

The years of waiting, of watching her life tick away in time to the bank's old clock, had made her painfully aware of how few chances a person is given. Of course there were lucky people who seemed to be showered with opportunity, but people like her—nobodies—were allotted precious few shots at the brass rings in life.

This was her chance to experience passion and fulfillment, and she was not about to let it slip away. And she refused to ruin it by thinking about the future or about what her mama would think. Or about how she'd hurt when he left. Or about whether he cared as deeply as she did. Those were worries she was saving for later.

"You're very quiet tonight," he commented after the waiter had taken their orders.

She couldn't think of anything to say to that, so she nodded.

He laughed.

"Are you making fun of me?" Vana asked.

"No. Why do you always think that?" He frowned slightly. "I was laughing because . . . oh, never mind."

"What?" she said. "Are you angry at me?" Oh, God, this was a lousy way to begin a seduction.

He shook his head in a show of bewilderment. "Why should I be angry at you? I'm just afraid you might take offense at whatever I say. You seem very . . . touchy, tonight."

"Touchy! I am not touchy!" She glared at him across the table until the absurdity of it all began to seep through to her. She grinned ever so slightly, then drew in a deep breath and laughed.

He laughed with her and raised his margarita glass. "To a lovely dinner with an enchanting, but not touchy, woman."

She touched her glass to his and willed herself not to sink from her chair into a puddle of jelly. An enchanting woman—did he really mean that?

The tension finally broken, Sky began asking nonstop questions about barrel racing and farm life. He asked her why she and Meg had suddenly decided to quit their jobs and try the barrel-racing circuit, and she tried to explain about the lives they'd led when Heinrich was alive. About how Heinrich had charged them rent as soon as they'd taken jobs and ceased doing all the chores. And about how they'd never had enough money to break free completely.

Then she explained how everything had changed with Heinrich's death. How their mama had helped them get horses and then surprised them by cleverly trading Heinrich's fancy coyote-hunting rig and automatic dogbox for the truck and trailer that had finally enabled them to make the rodeo circuit a reality.

They talked without pausing until their food arrived. She welcomed the intrusion of the fragrant and steaming plates as a chance to withdraw from the conversation and plan. Cutting into her chicken, sour cream and green chili enchilada, she puzzled over the problem of how to go about being seductive. Maybe if she said a few suggestive things he'd get the message.

"My mama didn't even use salt and pepper in her cooking when I was growin' up, but I've learned to crave all this spicy stuff," she said between bites. She gathered her courage and fumbled for an opening phrase. "But you know what they say about spicy food," she offered hesitantly. "It makes people . . . you know . . ."

"Sleepy?" he filled in. "Or unable to sleep—I've heard both."

"Well, yeah," she said helplessly. "But also . . . isn't it supposed to—" She gestured with her fork.

"Help prevent clogged arteries? You're right. I did read that in the *Times* not too long ago."

Vana smiled stiffly and turned her attention back to her food. This was going to be harder than she'd imagined.

"Would you like a bite?" she asked, holding out her fork, a ripe green chunk of avocado speared on the end. She'd seen people feed each other in the movies and it always looked very sexy and seductive.

"No, thanks," he said. "I've got the same thing here on my plate."

"Well how about a drink?" she asked, offering her glass. She remembered reading a story where the man's lips touched the same spot on the glass rim the woman's lips had just touched; the sexual significance had filled pages.

"My drink's the same as yours," he said with a perplexed smile. "But thank you for the offer."

When they were nearly finished eating, she reached out, intending to stroke his hand with her fingertips in what she hoped would be an obviously suggestive move, but the wide sleeve of her borrowed dress snared her spoon as she lifted her arm. The spoon hung on the sleeve a fraction of a moment, then dropped with a resounding clatter that brought startled glances from the tables around them.

She quickly cut her reach short and gave it purpose by plucking a tortilla chip from the basket, then returned to her eating in embarrassed silence.

Nothing was working. Their intimate dinner was almost over and she was running out of ideas. She tried to imagine herself as Meg. Meg would know just how to handle this. But she wasn't Meg and she never had been, and the truth was she didn't really want to become Meg anymore.

The waiter appeared and cleared the table and Sky nodded when the man asked if they were ready for the check. Sky was apparently in a hurry to leave. So what was she going to do? If she couldn't be manipulative and flattering like Meg, then how was she going to handle this?

The check appeared. She reminded Sky that it had been her invitation and she overruled his objections and paid it. Before she knew it they were back in their coats and headed across the parking lot toward his car. She had to think of something witty or charming or clever very, very quickly.

"How about going someplace fun for dessert?" he said as he unlocked the door on her side. "Or—"

"Or going to your room to make love," she said quickly. The words tumbled out without any planning.

He stared at her a moment, then grinned quizzically as if to ask if she were kidding. "How many margaritas did you have?" he teased.

"I'm serious."

His expression changed and sobered.

"Vana," he said earnestly. "You don't know what—"

"I do. I know exactly what I'm saying. I..." She fumbled for words. She couldn't tell him how much he meant to her. She couldn't say those things to him yet.

"I want to be with you," she said. "I need to be with you...to be close to you."

"I don't want to hurt you, Vana. I won't make love to you. Now let's just forget all this and—"

"You what?" she stammered in wounded amazement. "You won't? But I thought—I mean, don't all guys want to all the time? Am I that terrible?"

Sky studied her a moment as if to gauge her sincerity. He began to laugh gently as he reached out and gathered her into his arms. "Oh, Vana, Vana, Vana. There's not one terrible thing about you. You're too wonderful to be true. But don't you see what a big mistake—"

"Why?" she asked. Her face was pressed against his coat and the word was muffled. She was glad that she didn't have to look at him now as she spoke.

"This feels—" he chose his words like a man picking his way across a rocky precipice "—like a dangerous situation. I'll be leaving soon, and I don't want either of us to have regrets or resentments or—"

"My only regret will be if this doesn't happen. What do you care? What can it possibly matter to you? Men don't—"

"What do you know about men? Do you think a man can't have feelings or fears? Do you think a man can't be hurt?"

"No, it's not that." She tilted her head back to look into his face. "It's just, well, men are raised to enjoy casual sex, aren't they?"

He released her and let his arms drop limply to his sides. The action was disappointing. She wanted him to hold her tightly again. She studied his face but his eyes were turned toward the night sky.

Suddenly he riveted her with a hard look. The lines of his face were stern and his eyes were narrowed. "So you want us to have casual sex."

"No." She sighed. She was so very bad at putting things into words. "That's just it. It wouldn't be casual for me." She sighed again and turned her gaze sideways, out across the dark horizon with its thousands of twinkling lights. "This is the first time I've ever felt that it would be something special, something other than casual. That's why it's important to me."

"But, Vana—" his voice was full of emotion "—that's exactly why I think it's a mistake for us. Because it's not casual for me, either. Neither one of us can shake hands and smile and go our separate ways when it's over. We could hurt each other terribly with this."

She turned to look him straight in the eye. "So what you're saying is that people who have feelings for one another should never make love. That it's too dangerous. The only time people should let it happen is when it's meaningless, when they don't give a damn." She shook her head fiercely. "Well, I don't buy that. And I refuse to live my life like that."

Sky turned away from her and then turned back. He raised his hands in a gesture of hopeless confusion. "But we have to face realities here."

"What realities?" she demanded. "That we don't live in the same town? That we'll be going our separate ways shortly? That we may never see each other again? Yes, those things are true. But don't you see? That's why we have to make use of the time we have together. That's why we can't afford to wait and test the ice and make sure it's safe to go any farther."

He stared at her for what seemed a very long time. The silence settled in around them. She could hear the faint whine of the cars on the distant interstate. She could hear him breathing. She almost imagined she could hear him thinking.

Suddenly it all seemed bitterly funny to her and she started to laugh. "All those years of batting off groping hands and fighting my way out of parked pickups. And now here I am trying to talk a man into bed with me. What a joke!" She laughed till there were tears in her eyes and she had to lean against the car for support.

He reached out and pulled her roughly against him as though his own feelings were as raw as hers. "Baby, baby," he breathed into her hair. "Shhh, it's all right."

She realized that the sound she was hearing was her own sobbing. He held her, stroking her hair and murmuring softly, until she was calm. Then he helped her into the car.

They drove in silence. Vana had no idea where they were headed, and she didn't care. She felt drained and totally humiliated. What a stupid fool she'd made of herself!

Without warning he pulled the car to the side of the road and stopped. He turned to face her and the hand he left on the steering wheel looked white with the effort of his grip.

"What a fool I am." His words were forced and startling because they echoed her own. She kept silent.

"I want you," he admitted. "I've wanted you almost since the first moment I saw you. That's what scared me, I suppose—there was too much importance attached to it.'' He gave a short rueful laugh. "It's been years since I've slept with a woman I wanted or cared about. Not that I've met many women I cared about—but even if I had, I probably would have denied myself intimacy with them.''

He ran his fingers through his hair in frustration. "It's nothing you've done wrong. The fault isn't yours—it's mine.'' The look he gave her was full of pain and apology and self-defeat.

"Stop,'' she said, reaching out to touch his arm. "You've said enough. Don't punish yourself.'' She blinked at the mysterious burning in her eyes and tried to smile. "I'm glad to know you wanted me. I'll always remember that.''

He leaned towards her and cupped her chin with his hand. His eyes were nearly black in the darkened car and she wasn't sure what they held as he studied her face so intently. She was afraid to breathe.

He bent his head and brushed his lips across hers. It was a tender kiss, more like a friend's than a lover's, but it made her feel hot and liquid inside. She didn't respond. She was afraid to move.

"Are you angry at me?'' he asked.

"No.''

His lips touched hers again and he pulled her close, locking her in the strong circle of his arms. Her heart pounded wildly and a rush of need pulsed through her entire body.

"Would you still come to my room?'' he asked in a small voice.

"Yes,'' she said without hesitation or pretense.

They drove toward his hotel without speaking. The tension sparked around them in the confines of the car. She didn't dare look at him. She didn't trust her voice to speak. And her thoughts careened so crazily that she had nothing coherent to say anyway.

She had never been so nervous in her life. She felt like she could easily die of nerves or explode into a million fragments. She felt sick and weak. Her cheeks burned and her hands were icy. Why had she ever wanted to do this?

From the corner of her eye she saw him move slightly. Without a word he extended his hand to her. Silently she took it, holding on for dear life as they sped through the Texas night.

She was still holding tightly to that strong hand as he swung open the door to his room. He stood patiently and she knew that he was waiting for her to decide. Did she still want to go in? She didn't honestly know now, but she had complete faith in him. She knew that she could walk into that room and still change her mind later. He would release her at any time without ugliness or anger.

That knowledge about him touched her, reaching down inside her to bring up a well of emotion. She had never known a man like him before—a perfect man...a dream man.

She dropped his hand and stepped through the door. It was a beautiful room, spacious and furnished with real antiques. The bed was a massive four-poster of polished cherry. The top of the bed was a soft tumble of pillows and someone had folded the spread to the foot and turned down the blankets, exposing perfectly smooth, white linens. The sight of it sent her nerves into orbit again and she quickly moved to the huge window and opened the heavy draperies.

The city lights winked in the velvety darkness below her, spreading out in patterns as far as she could see.

"This is a long way from Zeckendorf," she said under her breath, but he heard her and laughed.

"Every place is a long way from Zeckendorf," he said.

There had been a bright overhead light on in the room. He crossed to the dresser and switched on a small lamp with a stained-glass shade, then crossed back and turned off the overhead. The room was bathed in a jewel-like glow.

"You can spend the rest of your life a long way from Zeckendorf if that's what you want. Because you have what it takes Vanessa. You can conquer the world and put it in your pocket if you want to.''

Vana stared at him in brief confusion. Then she understood. He had it all mixed up. He was talking about Meg, not her. He had to be thinking about Meg. But she didn't want to correct him now—she didn't want to spoil the moment.

"Well," he said. "There's a soft-drink machine down the hall or there's room service. Would you like something?''

She was amazed to see that he was edgy too.

"No," she said, and reached for something calming to say. "I didn't know hotel rooms like this existed."

He looked around as though seeing the room for the first time. "I'm glad you like it."

The space between them seemed like miles. She wanted to go to him but her knees felt too shaky to make the crossing. She took several uncertain steps.

He rushed forward as though he'd been waiting and wrapped his arms around her, crushing her to him. "Oh Vana, Vana," he whispered.

Their coats were like a thick shield between them and she was suddenly hungry for the feel of his body against hers. She pulled back from his arms and tugged her coat off, letting it fall to the floor beside her. He followed suit and then stood just inches away from her, looking down into her eyes, holding her with the intensity of his gaze.

She moved forward, reaching up to circle his neck with her arms. Slowly she drew him closer, pressing her body against his. She was acutely aware of his skin just beneath the fine cotton of his shirt. Her breasts and thighs heated with the contact, and her body felt incredibly soft and yielding against the muscled length of him. A sweet, aching need blossomed inside her and she felt something within her unfolding and bursting to life like a flower eager to receive the sun.

There were no more doubts in her mind. She excused herself and carried her purse to the bathroom. She had to work to steady her hands and she had trouble reading the directions. This was it. With this act of preparation she was totally committing herself.

When she returned to the room he kissed her and she twined her fingers in his hair, pulling him closer, wanting to devour his mouth with her own. He drew back, leaving her dizzy and momentarily disoriented. Gently he guided her to the bed and sat her down on the edge. First he pulled off her shoes, then he lifted his hands toward her hair. "May I?" he asked and she nodded without knowing what he intended. She trusted him completely.

Carefully he pulled her hair free from its thick plait. He combed through it with his fingers, then lifted it and shook it so the waves fell softly around her face. He pulled her back to her feet and looked at her with what appeared to be wonder.

"My God, you're beautiful."

No, it's Meg who's the pretty one, she wanted to say, but when she looked into his eyes she actually felt beautiful. Somehow, this man was magically transforming her into a beautiful and desirable woman.

With trembling hands she unbuttoned his shirt and pulled it free of his slacks. She touched his bare chest with her fingertips, amazed at how wonderful his warm skin felt.

He pulled the shirt off in one quick motion and reached to unzip her dress. She felt suddenly shy. What would he think of her body? She wished she had a nicer slip or maybe a lacy bra.

"Could we turn off the light?" she asked timidly.

He smiled gently and stroked her cheek with his fingers. He lifted her hand to his mouth and kissed her palm. The soft brush of his lips sizzled through her veins.

"Please," he said. "You're so beautiful. I need to see you. It's *you* I'm making love with—not some faceless body in the dark."

The beauty of his words broke through her hesitancy. She closed her eyes and pulled the dress from her shoulders, letting it slide unhindered to the floor. She was afraid to open her eyes. She felt completely vulnerable.

His strong hands gripped her bare arms, and she felt his lips brush her closed eyes and trace the line of her neck. His mouth at her throat made her gasp with pleasure, and she found herself hoping for more, wanting that mouth on every inch of her body. But he stopped.

She opened her eyes and saw that he was looking at her again, and she wished she could capture that look and keep it with her the rest of her life.

She shivered and he gathered her up, swinging her easily into his arms. He carried her to the bed and lay her down, tossing ruffled pillows this way and that. Then he tucked the covers tenderly around her body. She watched as he stepped out of his clothes. She'd never seen a man completely naked before. Her previous experience had included fumbling through layers of clothing.

"I might not be any good at this," she said shakily.

"You aren't a—" he began with alarm.

"No," she assured him quickly, knowing immediately what he'd been about to ask. "It's just...well...for instance, I've never been in a bed. And I've never had my clothes off, and—"

He stilled her rush of words by placing his fingers to her lips. Then he slid into bed beside her, propping himself on one elbow so he could look at her as he spoke.

"I'm sorry," he said. "It sounds like it's never been beautiful for you."

She swallowed hard against the threatening tears and reached for him in the drifting, snowy linen.

"I want to make it beautiful for you..." he whispered, but his words were cut short as she covered his mouth with her own and gave in to the heated longing bursting within her....

"Now...have to...come on!"

The words filtered into Vana's consciousness, mixing into her sleep as part of a dream at first, then finally drawing her into groggy awareness.

"Ummm," she said without opening her eyes.

"I can't believe this! Is this happening? My little sister coming in at dawn? My sister sleeping till noon? We oughta mark this on the calendar."

It was Meg's voice.

Vana opened her eyes reluctantly and groaned at the flood of light that assaulted them.

Meg laughed. "You are something, Vana. When I found out ... well, let me tell ya, I was just so amazed!"

Vana glowered at her and wondered whether Meg was amazed at the fact that she had stayed out all night for once or the fact that she'd finally found a man she wanted to stay out all night with.

Meg grinned. "Go ahead," she said affectionately, "be secretive if you want, but I know what's going on now. I know everything. And I just wanna say that, well, I think you're pretty terrific."

Vana shook her head to clear it as she sat up in the bed. Had she missed something? What was Meg up to?

"You mean about Sky?" Vana asked groggily. "You found out I'm seeing Sky?" She reached up to scrub at her face with her hands. "You're glad?"

"Of course I'm glad, silly!" Meg chuckled. "Just take your time," she said generously as she gathered up her jacket and purse. "I want to be there early, but you've still got an hour or so before I really need you to be there." She chuckled again and winked. "You can tell me everything when you get there."

Vana stared at her and blinked a few times. Meg couldn't be serious about expecting Vana to tell her everything, could she? Her vision had cleared to the point where she could focus on Meg now. But taking in the outfit that was apparently designed to bowl over the judges started her blinking again. A study in ruffles and ponytails and bows, Meg looked like a character from a Saturday morning cartoon. Somehow the total effect made her appear shorter and rounder than usual.

"You're awake now, aren't you? You won't fall back asleep as soon as I leave?"

Vana shook her head, holding up her palm and crossing her heart with her index finger. "An hour, I promise," she grumbled. She was getting off easy and she knew it. She'd expected Meg to roust her out without mercy and demand that she be ready to leave for the Bella barbecue early.

Meg opened the door and stopped to throw Vana a conspiratorial look. She giggled. "You are so sly," she said. As she left, Vana noticed an embroidered heart on the back pocket of her jeans.

Vana stepped down out of the cab-over bed and stretched. Her sister had apparently learned about her and Sky some way or another. But her reaction had certainly been easy to take. In fact, she was being kind of sweet about the whole thing. Vana felt a little guilty now about not sharing her feelings with Meg in the first place.

She stretched again. Her body felt deliciously sexy. She touched her mouth. Did her lips look as bruised as they felt? She closed her eyes and let her hands slide slowly down her body, remembering where his mouth and hands had been. Her breasts felt pleasantly swollen and her nipples were tender and responsive.

She threw off the oversized T-shirt she used as a nightshirt and stepped into the tiny bathroom cubicle. Adjusting the hand-held shower to pulse, she let the hot water play against her skin.

Sky. Sky. Sky. Her mind was filled with the sound of his name. She leaned her head back, exposing the line of her throat to the water, and the throbbing heat in her veins seemed connected to the pulsing spray. She drew in a deep breath and tried to concentrate on soaping herself. But her skin tingled with the memory of his fingers, and a sweet ache built deep and low inside her.

Finally the hot water ran out, and she stepped from the cramped, steamy bathroom to dry herself. The chilly air made her shiver and hurry into her clothes. She pulled on a comfortably warm pair of jeans and her favorite sweater, a loose-fitting, intricate pattern she'd worked on one whole winter with her mother's guidance. She'd made it all in ivory, intertwining silk and angora with the plain wool yarn. She loved it partly for the way it looked and felt and partly because it had seemed so extravagant and luxurious when she'd made it.

As she moved across the small space of the trailer, she was acutely aware of the worn denim whispering against her legs and the softness of the sweater brushing against her breasts, arms and the sensitive skin of her midriff. She had never been so aware of her own body. She had never felt so—her mind searched for the right word—consumed? Obsessed? What was she? What was this powerful tangle of thoughts and feelings that had taken over her life?

She brushed out her still-damp hair and gathered it high on her head. Standing in front of the mirror with a mouth full of hairpins, she wrapped it around and around into a thick glossy knot, fastening it as she went. The face in the mirror looked different. She reached up to touch her cheeks, and her forehead creased with the questions tumbling through her mind.

Was she still the same person? Or had she become so bewitched that the old Vanessa Linnier no longer existed?

She closed her eyes and images of his face, the width of his shoulders, the supple strength of his hands came rushing into her mind. Her breath sharpened and threads of need tugged at her belly.

She opened her eyes to escape and was surprised to see that the pink of her cheeks had heightened and her pupils had widened, giving her eyes an almost feral look. She was changing even now! She was still changing, hours after being with him.

What more would happen? What had she gotten herself into? Would she ever be the same again?

There were no answers. And the questions were quickly pushed from her mind by more thoughts of him. She would be with him shortly. She would hear his voice and see the smile touch his mouth and eyes—a special smile just for her.

She glanced quickly at her watch. He'd said he'd be there around noon. It was three minutes till then. She pulled on her sneakers and scooped up her keys from the counter. In just minutes she would be with him. What did it matter that they would be surrounded by all the rest of the people at the barbecue? The others barely existed for her. The reason for the gathering, the excitement being generated by it and the nervous hopefulness her sister and so many others were feeling were totally unimportant. Sky was the only reality. Sky was all that mattered.

Chapter Five

The day was bright and full of promise as she walked across the parking area and cut through the poultry show barn. She smiled at the young competitors so seriously hovering over their chickens and turkeys and silently wished them all luck. She was full of good spirits and brimming over with joy and she felt a great generosity toward every creature on earth.

She emerged from the long low barns into the clear afternoon light. It was a beautiful day. The sun was gently warm with the promise of spring just around the corner. She was glad the barbecue was outdoors.

Circling the huge coliseum, she saw the hubbub in the front parking area immediately. The festivities were well under way. Catering vans and enormous portable barbecues were set up near clustered tables and crowds milled everywhere. At one end a band played on a recently erected stage. Strains of western music drifted to her ears with the buzz of the crowd. In just moments she would see Sky. She smiled to herself and quickened her pace.

A figure broke from the crowd and came racing toward her. It was Meg, wide-eyed and breathless. "There you are! I was afraid I wouldn't catch you."

Vana tried not to conceal her impatience. Meg would only be anxious to see her if she needed something or if there was a problem she thought Vana could fix. And right now Vana just didn't have the reserves to deal with one of Meg's disasters. She scanned the edge of the gathering hopefully. He had promised he would meet her.

"I had no idea this shindig was going to be so big," Vana said. "There must be five hundred people here—how'd you even see me coming?" She started forward, pretending that her sister had raced out to meet her for no special reason.

"No. Wait," Meg pleaded breathlessly. She reached out to take hold of Vana's arm as if to physically restrain her. "I goofed. I think I *really* goofed."

Vana sighed. There was no way out. "What's wrong now?" she asked.

"C'mon. Come over here." Meg glanced around nervously and pulled Vana toward the back of a catering truck.

"Oh Meg, what is this?" Vana demanded, but allowed herself to be led until they were behind the truck.

"Well..." Meg swallowed, forced a grin and winced. "Promise you won't hate me?"

Vana rolled her eyes skyward and threw up her hands. "Just tell me, Meg. Okay?"

"I was trying to talk to some of the other girls, and they were being so stuck up and acting like I was some kind of idiot or something—and they were getting me so upset—and well, it just slipped out."

"What!" Vana demanded impatiently.

Meg winced again and ducked her head as though expecting a blow. "About you...and you-know-who."

"Who?"

"Mr. Big. Sky."

"Why should that interest anyone?" Vana asked quietly. "And why would you be talking about my private affairs behind my back like that with complete strangers?"

"Oh come on, Vana," Meg said miserably. "You don't have to pretend anything. The whole damn litter of kittens is out of the bag!" She screwed her face up guiltily. "I mean I told them everything. Who he is and how you're in so solid with him and—"

"That was none of their business! And for that matter it isn't any of your business, either!" Vana said hotly. How dare Meg spread her personal life around like a television soap opera plotline.

"None of my business?" Meg almost shrieked. "Of course it's my business. It's my life, too!"

Vana frowned down at the paved surface beneath her feet for several beats. What was her sister trying to tell her? That she wasn't allowed to have a private life separate from Meg? And aside from the fact that she was making Vana very angry, why was Meg behaving as though the Titanic had just gone under?

"All right, Meg," she insisted coldly. "Aside from the fact that you've apparently embarrassed me and made my private life into a public joke, just what is the bottom line here?"

"You aren't listening to me, Vana," Meg wailed accusingly. "I spilled it *all*. I overheard the Bella guys talking yesterday—that's how I found out—and I know everything about Vandy and everything. With you stayin' out half the night last night I never got a chance to tell you that I found out. And now they know exactly who he is and exactly what you've been doing!"

Vana shook her head as though the muddle might be some problem in her own head.

"You mean you found out about me and Sky when you heard the Bella guys talking? How would they—"

"*No!* They were talking about company stuff and then about Sky. I'd already figured out he was who you were sneaking off with—so then I put it all together. But they didn't find out about you seeing Sky till one of the big-mouthed girls I was talking to ran over and ratted.''

Vana leaned back against the truck for support. ''You mean...'' She couldn't quite put all the pieces together and she wasn't sure she even wanted to.

''Those stuck-up girls made me crazy and when I opened my mouth it just slipped out. I just wanted to make them sorry they'd treated me like that.''

But that wasn't what Vana wanted to know about. She wanted to know about Sky. She wanted to understand why—aside from the invasion of privacy it represented—it was so terrible for the Bella guys to have been told she was seeing Sky.

''Here you put yourself through all that and I—'' Meg sobbed and quickly dabbed at her eyes with a tissue to keep her mascara from smearing ''—I ruined it all.''

Vana stared at Meg blankly. Put herself through what? Nothing made sense. She didn't begin to understand Meg's supposed problem and she couldn't focus on anything except the growing certainty that something was very wrong.

Meg sniffed, signaling recovery. She had cried without any effect on her eye makeup. ''After all you went through, I can't believe I—''

Vana felt a sudden frantic need to talk to Sky. Whatever was wrong he would be able to sort it out and solve everything. She started around the truck back toward the party. ''I have to talk to Sky,'' she said.

Meg reached out and grabbed her wrist. ''Everyone knows,'' she said weakly. ''Those three girls I told had such big mouths!''

Vana pulled free and rushed away. She didn't want to hear any more. She didn't want to think about what it all meant. She just wanted to find Sky and talk to him and make sure everything was still the same between them. Nothing else mattered.

Frantically she threaded through the crowd of people, murmuring apologies for plates of barbecue nearly lost and elbows bumped. She turned and twisted and rose up on her toes every few feet. Where was he? Where could he be?

She was aware of her sister following along behind her and she had the urge to whirl and scream at her. She wanted to tell Meg to go away and leave her alone. She wanted to tell her that Sky was important, really important, and she wasn't going to allow Meg to ruin it.

And that's exactly what Meg was doing—she had no doubt of it. She didn't exactly know how and she was afraid to try to figure it out, but she knew Meg was bent on destruction just as surely as if she'd seen her sister wielding a sledgehammer.

The music stopped and there was a shuffling on the stage. Vana glanced up, then froze. Sky was up there. He was standing off to the side with Jagger and Stephen, and watching Arthur fiddle with the microphone.

Meg caught up and settled in close behind her to stare up at the stage. "Oh Lord," she breathed. "What are we gonna do, Vana?"

Vana ignored her. Her entire body was stiff with apprehension. Sky was on the stage with the Bella team. What did that mean? She was afraid of the implications but she couldn't shut them out. Schuyler Van Dusen was more connected to this Bella contest than he'd admitted.

Was that what Meg had been blabbing to everyone? Was that what she had been so worried about and so frightened over?

Vana glanced over at her sister and realized that she didn't really care what Meg's problem was right now. Right now the only important thing was the fear building inside her and the anxiety spinning and growing, spreading through her like a maddening poison. What was going on and what did it mean to her and Sky?

Arthur did a self-conscious testing routine at the microphone and then introduced himself and launched into a welcoming speech.

" . . . but I'm only one third of the Bella team, ladies and gentlemen, and now I'd like to introduce Stephen Shanda, the internationally acclaimed photographer. . . ."

Just get it over with, Vana thought as Stephen stepped forward and made a few comments into the microphone. If they would just get this nonsense out of the way Sky would come down off the stage and she could talk to him.

"And the third member of our team, a man who's a star in his own right, the award-winning beauty consultant—Jagger LeBlanc."

Now it was Jagger's turn to step forward and drone on and on about what he'd been looking for in the Bella Woman.

"Oh brother," Vana muttered under her breath. She began to edge sideways and forward toward the place where the steps came down off the stage. She wanted to be in position to catch Sky's attention as soon as he started down. Meg followed her and she had to grit her teeth to keep from shouting something nasty at her to make her go away.

Arthur had the mike again and was obviously warming up to being the center of attention. He began a long-winded spiel on the history of Bella and the idea behind the Bella Woman. He detailed the forming of the three-man team and the hunt for the woman with the right look.

Vana paid little attention. She was in a good position to see Sky now and she studied him intently. He was dressed in a finely cut suit and a white shirt and tie. There was no hint of personal thoughts in his expression. He was every inch the cool and controlled New York businessman.

She wanted to wave or call out to him. Nothing else mattered to her—not the gathering or its purpose, not the people who might stare or talk, not her sister with all her anxieties—nothing but Sky and whether he still looked at her the same way or smiled or reached out or. . .

He shifted suddenly, smiled politely and started across the stage toward the microphone.

"...the man behind Vandy, and Bella's new guiding light—Mr. Schuyler Van Dusen."

Vana reeled with the words. The head of the company? Sky was the head of the company? If people hadn't been pressing close to her on all sides she would have stumbled backward under the dizzying weight of that news.

"Thank you," Sky said as he adjusted the height of the standing mike upward. His voice was commanding and quietly self-assured.

"The Bella Company was formed over a hundred years ago by a brilliant woman with a vision. Gabriela DeVerona came to this country from Italy and she made her dreams come true here. Throughout the years her family continued the tradition of excellence and quality that made Bella a success."

Sky paused a moment and scanned the crowd. Was he looking for her? Was he thinking about her? Why had he misled her so flagrantly? Now she saw the reasons for his evasiveness and his discomfort at the mention of certain topics. Now she saw that he'd been actively misleading her from the beginning. But why? Had he been playing some kind of game with her?

"When the DeVerona family made the difficult decision to sell Bella," Sky continued, "we at Vandy were immediately interested. Vandy had never acquired an outside company before, but Bella's history was familiar because it was so similar to our own. Vandy, too, was started by an immigrant with a dream and was founded on the principles of uncompromising excellence and unwavering quality."

The shock began to fade and Vana was filled with an immense sadness. What if there'd been no reality at all to what she and Sky had shared? He had misled her greatly on this—what if he'd been misleading her on other things as well? What if nothing had been true?

"We are proud to include Bella in the Vandy family, and we intend to maintain the company without change, just as the DeVeronas would have. In that interest we have not publicized our acquisition or attempted to change the Bella image by linking it to Vandy in any public fashion."

Vana's mind raced back suddenly to Meg's disjointed ramblings. They didn't seem so disjointed now in the light of this discovery. In fact, they were starting to make a horrible sort of sense. Meg had guessed that she was seeing Sky. Meg had overheard the Bella guys and learned that Sky was the big man behind the whole operation.

She stopped herself for a moment and ran back over it. Meg had made it sound as though no one else knew who Sky was, either. Could it be possible that he'd been keeping his identity a secret from everyone and not just Vana, that he hadn't set out to mislead her specifically?

"The search for the Bella Woman was started by the DeVeronas and we have given their own hand-picked team—" Sky held out his hand to indicate the three men who stood with him on the stage "—absolute authority over the completion of that search. Vandy has faith in both the integrity of the Bella Woman campaign and the judgment of the search team the DeVeronas so carefully put together."

The puzzle pieces continued to dance around maddeningly in her mind. Just when one locked into place another popped up to taunt her. Meg must have thought that Vana knew what Sky's position was all along. What had Meg said? Something about Vana having worked so hard and now Meg had ruined it?

Oh, God! Could it be possible that Meg believed Vana had been seeing Sky *because* of who he was? Could it be possible that Meg thought Vana had been trying to influence Sky so that Meg would win? Was that what she'd been so happy and grateful about that morning and was that what she thought she'd ruined by letting "the whole damn litter of kittens" out of the bag? And was that the horrible information that Meg's "big-mouthed" companions had sup-posedly run to the Bella team with?

The possibilities flooded Vana with despair. Was that what everyone was thinking right now? Was that what Meg was so sick about? The belief that Vana had manipulated herself into a position where she had an in with Sky and could influence him on Meg's behalf? And what about Sky? Had he heard the awful story too? But then surely, if he had, he would wait to hear her side, wouldn't he? If he really cared about her as he'd said he did, he couldn't possibly condemn her and believe the worst without giving her at least the benefit of the doubt.

She glanced over at her sister's distraught face. Meg, on the other hand, was a different case. Meg might have no trouble believing that about anyone—even her own sister—because it had probably sounded to her like a perfectly ac-ceptable and normal pattern of behavior. She could see how Meg would automatically believe Vana was stringing Sky along and trying to use his power in some way as soon as she'd heard who Van Dusen was.

And Meg probably would be unable to accept that Vana hadn't known Sky's identity. Meg would certainly never have been satisfied with Sky's vague references to his life and background if she'd been the one seeing him. She would have pried and spied and investigated until she had all the answers. And she would never believe that Vana hadn't wanted to invade his privacy, hadn't wanted to know any-thing that he didn't freely tell her himself. And she espe-cially wouldn't believe that Vana hadn't cared about not knowing everything—that Vana had known all she needed to know to love him.

"And now, you've been kept in suspense long enough so I'll turn the mike back over to Arthur with a thank-you for all his dedication and hard work in making the search for the Bella Woman as comprehensive and exacting as was humanly possible."

The crowd clapped and a smiling Arthur took control again.

"This is it," he said with almost childish excitement.

"And if anybody deserves thanks for making this a reality it's Vandy and Mr. Van Dusen. They let us go with everything a hundred percent...*without interference*." Vana wondered if his stressing of this point had anything to do with the ugly story about her. "Mr. Van Dusen himself didn't even hear the final choices until just before today's program."

Was there some kind of message in that? Vana wondered. Was he reassuring all those Dallas girls and anyone else who'd heard Meg's irresponsible talk? Or was it just Vana's own anxieties making it seem so?

She felt a tugging on her sleeve. Meg wanted her attention or her reassurance or God knew what. But she had nothing to give. All she could do was try to reassure herself. Everything was going to be okay. If this thing would just be over with, she could talk to Sky....

"...so the first and second alternates hold the title if anything happens," Arthur was explaining. The huge crowd was hushed and expectant.

"It's not going to be me," Meg said in a tiny, pathetic voice. "I can feel it."

Vana concentrated on Sky. He looked so tall and untouchable up on the stage and he was so fashionable and sophisticated in the suit—almost frighteningly so. If she didn't already know him, if she didn't know what was beneath that impressive facade, she would never have had the nerve to say hello to him. She would never have believed a man like that could ever be interested in a nobody like her.

"And from Texas, the second alternate is Dena Kay Hawthorne."

Squeals and a flurry of activity erupted. Vana kept her eyes on Sky. He stood on the stage with so much casual poise, so much presence. He was every inch a somebody. He'd been born a somebody.

A grinning Dena Kay climbed onto the stage and was hugged by the three-man Bella team.

"The first alternate is Sherilyn Petigrew from New Mexico!"

There were screams this time and then laughter as Sherilyn raced for the stage.

A somebody. Hadn't her mama always said the world was divided between the men and the women and the somebodies and the nobodies? She watched Sky on the stage. He reached out to shake hands with Sherilyn and she saw the gold flash of a cuff link. She'd never known a man who wore cuff links. She'd never known a man who could look so elegant and imposing.

And suddenly she knew that there was nothing to worry about. It didn't make any difference what Sky had heard or what he thought. She hadn't stood a chance with him anyway. A man like that . . . What could he ever see in someone like her? She had just been a diversion, an amusing little experience to round out his Texas vacation.

Maybe he didn't even know that himself. But she knew it.

She knew that the moment he got back to New York and remembered how important he was, the moment he was surrounded by the glamorous women he was used to, the moment he was through relaxing—Vana Linnier, the foolish little hick, would just be an amusing sidelight to remember from his time in the West. The knowledge filled her with a vast emptiness.

Meg's fingers clutched her arm. "Here it goes," she wailed softly. "And it's not me."

The emptiness inside Vana grew until it wasn't inside her anymore but all around her, surrounding her and separating her from everything else. Meg was a million miles away and so was the crowd and Sky and Arthur with his grinning and posturing and too-loud voice in the microphone.

"...the moment you've all been waiting for. The woman who will *be* the Bella beauty in magazines and newspapers around the world . . . the woman who will *be* Bella in the minds and hearts of America. The woman whose entire life will change starting today...."

Meg clawed at her arm, but it registered only as some vague, faraway nuisance to Vana.

"Ladies and gentleman, the Bella Woman—Vanessa Linnier from Kansas!"

There was a scream from beside her. It was Meg. She felt herself being pushed and shoved. Stephen ran down the stairs and began pulling her forward and up onto the stage. Sky's set, emotionless face was very close to her now. She opened her mouth to speak to him, but she was turned toward the audience by tugging hands and suddenly her mouth was just inches from the microphone.

The mass of humanity staring up at her sent a shock through her system. There were smiles and there was some clapping, but the majority of feeling was hostile, and it hit her with the force of a tidal wave.

"There's been some mistake..." she mumbled apologetically into the stillness. The words echoed out over the PA system, but before she had a chance to finish Arthur pushed in beside her and cut her off.

"I'd say this is one excited little lady, folks! Now let's just get on with our party here and do some more dancing and eating and we'll just give her a chance to calm down." He signaled the band and they rushed into position, launching immediately into a western swing number.

Arthur took hold of her from one side and Stephen from the other. She jerked her head around to look for Sky, but he wasn't there anymore.

"I don't..." she began. The men ignored her and hustled her bodily down the stairs.

"Where..."

"Just calm down," Stephen soothed.

She tried to pull her arms free of them.

"We'll get you away from all this commotion so you can collect yourself," Arthur assured her.

She gave up and let them hustle her forward, into the back of one of the catering trucks. It was quiet and dim inside. Floor-to-ceiling wire racks were bolted to the sides and she absently noted how the tubs of cutlery and dishes fit snugly into the racks for transport. There was a semicircle or over-turned plastic crates and three people were sitting down with plates of food in their laps.

"Hey, guys," Arthur said jovially. "Would you mind taking your break elsewhere? We're badly in need of a little privacy here."

The three workers vanished without a word and Vana felt herself pushed down into a sitting position on one of the crates.

"Just relax now," Stephen told her.

"There's been a mistake here, guys," she began in as calm and rational a manner as she could muster. "I'm not the one, I couldn't possibly be. I wasn't even, you know, after it."

"We were furnished with pictures of you," Stephen said.

"But they took pictures of all the girls."

"And you came to the initial meeting and signed in," Arthur said.

"But I was just along to keep my sister company."

"And you came to the big party and met us," Arthur said.

"A lot of people did," she said weakly.

"And you're here today," Stephen finished meaning-fully.

"No." Vana shook her head. "You've got it mixed up. I can't be the Bella Woman. You must mean my sister. It's Margaret Linnier, not Vanessa."

"My dear," Jagger said, entering the van in time to hear her last sentence. "We are not idiots. We don't go just by names. We could see with our own eyes if the wrong woman was in front of us."

"But . . ." Vana felt dangerously close to tears.

Stephen sat down next to her and reached over to pat her hand. "You've just had a surprise. People react differently to big surprises. You're going through some sort of denial syndrome—"

"Please! Spare us the psycho-babble." Jagger moved over to face her. "Now. Why don't you cut all this out and let's talk about the practical side."

She looked from Jagger to Stephen to Arthur. Panic rose inside her. "Where's Sky? I want to talk to Sky!"

"Mr. Van Dusen has nothing to do with any of this," Arthur said firmly.

Jagger smirked. "You could have saved the effort. It was wasted. In fact it almost lost the plum for you. When we found out about how you'd been—"

"I don't think we need to go into that here," Arthur said uncomfortably. He smiled woodenly at Vana. "You were our choice before we ever learned about your, ah, friendship with Mr. Van Dusen. That's the main thing, and I think we need to keep that foremost in our thoughts and dispense with everything else."

Vana's shoulders sagged under an invisible weight and she sighed in resignation. She was trapped in the most impossible mess and she couldn't see any good way out.

"What about my sister?" she asked. "Can't she be the Bella Woman? She'd be very good. She'd try hard and—"

"Your sister was never under consideration," Jagger said shortly. "We want classic, not cute. And we want natural. Your sister is contrived and unconvincing, not to mention—"

"Some people just don't photograph well," Stephen cut in diplomatically. "Perfectly attractive people can look all wrong on film."

Vana stood and paced along one side of the truck. Her footsteps echoed hollowly against the wooden flooring.

"You don't want me," she said, turning to face them. "I know you're good at your jobs, but what in the world could you possibly be thinking? Is this some kind of joke? Are you wanting a plain person so other women won't be threatened or what?"

Jagger moved to stand directly in front of her. His expression was hard. "You can cut the humble little-Miss-Innocent act," he said. "This isn't a personality contest and we don't care how ruthless and conniving and conceited you are underneath. You're the *look* we want. All we care about is how you come across on film—how well you sell. We're pros. So stop pretending. It's a waste of time for all of us."

"All right, let's stop wasting time then," Vana said hotly. He was the same height as her and she stared directly into his eyes. "I don't want to be the Bella Woman."

"Oh, now—" Arthur said, rushing toward her.

"Now, now..." Stephen said, jumping up from his crate.

"Jagger can be a bit abrasive at times," Arthur said, nudging Jagger out of the way and moving in close to her. "Let's not be too hasty about all this."

"Why don't we just leave you alone to think for a little while?" Stephen suggested. "Or maybe you'd like to speak to my therapist if I can get her on the phone."

"I want to talk to Sky," Vana said. "I don't want to hear anything else until I've talked to Sky."

Jagger smirked and the other two nodded, assuring her that they would find Mr. Van Dusen and send him right over. She should just sit down and relax, they said. She should just try to stop worrying.

She watched them go and then sank back down onto a crate. The enormity of what had just occurred flooded over her in a sudden, sweeping tide. How could it be possible that they had chosen her? The world felt like it had suddenly been turned upside down.

She heard footsteps and she stood and rushed forward. But it wasn't Sky who stepped into the truck. It was Meg. Her face was pale and drawn; her eyes blazed.

"My sister!" She almost spat the words. "My wonderful sister."

"It's not what you think, Meg."

"It's not what you think," Meg mimicked in a spiteful, singsong voice. "I know that. I thought you were trying to help me—" a tear ran down one cheek "—but instead you stole it from me. You slept with him to steal it from me!"

Vana shook her head fiercely. "No Meg. That's not true! I don't even want it! I wish I could give it to you."

"Okay, then," Meg challenged. "Do it! Tell them to give it to me!"

"I tried." Vana drew in a deep breath. "I tried."

"Sure." Meg laughed hollowly. "Not very hard, though, huh? You as the Bella Woman. What a joke. You can hardly get a date!"

"Meg—"

"What are they selling? Cosmetics for wallflowers? Soap for the woman who doesn't want to appeal to men?" Tears ran freely down Meg's face and her voice was full of anger and spite.

"I know you're hurt, but please try to understand," Vana pleaded.

"Understand what? That you tricked me—robbed me?"

Vana turned away to escape the horrible verbal blows. She had failed her sister. She had ruined everything. But she stopped herself short, righteous anger beginning to brew deep inside her. What in the hell was this, anyway? She had nothing to be sorry for.

She turned back to face Meg. "Stop it! Will you stop thinking about yourself for just five minutes and try to see what's happening to me? All of a sudden everything's crazy, really crazy." Vana sank back down onto a crate.

"Yeah," Meg snorted. "It's crazy all right."

"I suppose if I tell you I was completely innocent—that I didn't even know who Sky was until the program today—I suppose you'd never believe it," Vana said flatly.

"Don't insult me by even telling me something like that," Meg spat out.

The full impact of Meg's upset settled heavily on her, adding to her already overwhelming emotional burden. Meg wasn't just upset over losing and over suspecting Vana of betrayal. Those were reactions that stirred pity and remorse in Vana, but there were other things going on here that caused her to feel a steely coldness toward her sister. There were powerful undercurrents of jealousy and hypocrisy and Vana felt suddenly compelled to flush them out in the open and force Meg to deal with them.

Vana tried to gather herself. "Okay. Let's look at this from another direction then. You thought it was great that I was using Sky and being dishonest as long as you assumed I was doing it for you, right? And you'd have tried to influence him yourself if you'd learned who he was in time."

"But I wouldn't have kept it a secret from you!" Meg protested. "And I would never have led you to think I was doing it for you, and then sneakily turned around and promoted myself with it."

"Led you to believe! I never—" Vana stopped, knowing any protest would be useless at this point. She began pressuring Meg to see realities again. "And if you'd thought the contest was between the two of us, you'd have done anything to make certain it was you who won and not me, wouldn't you? I mean, don't you always say that all's fair in love and beauty contests?"

"Well, there are limits," Meg insisted. "I mean I wouldn't ever hurt anybody or—"

"I have a few more points to make here," Vana said. "You thought the all-for-one and one-for-all spirit was just right when you were planning on winning, didn't you?"

Meg stared at her quizzically.

"Come on, Margaret, you remember," Vana prodded her mercilessly. "You said we were in this together, like always. You said it didn't matter who got the fuss made over them— that what was important was that this might be a permanent way out of Zeck. What happened to all that reasoning? What happened to it not mattering who gets the fuss made over them?"

Meg frowned. "This is different."

"Why? Because you're faced with me being the one who's successful? How is that different? I wouldn't desert you. I'll take care of you and keep us both happy and off the farm the same as you were going to do if you won. Why don't you like that? Why are you really so furious and disgusted with me?"

"I'll tell you why. Because you can't stand to see me get this. You can't stand for me to have something that you couldn't have. You can't stand to think I was picked first for something ahead of you...even once...even one damn time in our whole lives!"

Meg glared at her. "You'll fall flat on your face. They'll eat you alive in New York City. And when they realize what a loser they've got on their hands they'll throw you out like last year's catalogs."

"Maybe," Vana said. "But that doesn't mean I won't give it a try."

Meg whirled and stomped out and Vana leaned forward and buried her face in her hands. Did she really intend to try it or had she just said that for Meg's benefit?

"Not falling apart already, I hope."

She jerked her head up to see Sky silhouetted in the square opening.

"Sky!" She jumped up and ran toward him. "I'm so glad to—" But she stopped. The look in his eyes was cold, his posture stiff and unyielding.

She drew herself up. "So, I suppose you believe it all then, too?"

He raised an eyebrow. "What's there to believe or not believe? I know the facts. I know how you thought you were using me. I witnessed your sister's spilling of the beans in front of everyone here this afternoon. You know, your cleverness almost backfired on you."

Vana sighed. "All of that came out of Meg's imagination. My sister just didn't know any better. Maybe this will teach her a lesson when she cools down long enough to see the truth.''

If she could only get Sky to see how ridiculous all this was. She attempted a smile, but only one side of her mouth responded. ''You've got to understand that in Meg's book if you aren't cheating, you aren't trying.'' The smile died completely. ''You see, Meg just imagined what she'd do if she were in my place and . . .'' Her voice trailed off weakly.

His lips turned up cruelly as if to show her he had no problem putting on a smile if he chose. ''She looked pretty mad when she passed me just now. I don't think she's being quite as philosophical about all this as you are.''

''She's got nothing to be mad about. I didn't do anything wrong!'' Vana looked into the heartbreaking coldness of his eyes. ''You've already tried and convicted me, haven't you?'' she asked sadly. ''You won't allow yourself to listen to a word I say, much less believe it.''

''I believe that you and your sister probably have very different definitions of right and wrong than I do,'' he said simply.

She turned away from him, fighting down an urge to slap his face. He was stubbornly refusing to listen to her or to have any faith at all in her. He was behaving like a mule-headed idiot—not at all like the wonderful dream man she'd believed he was. She had seen the unwillingness in him as soon as he'd fixed her with that hard, uncompromising look.

This was his way of getting off the hook, she realized. Now that there was the possibility of her coming to New York he had to end his involvement with her swiftly and finally. The relationship would have been embarrassing to him in front of his big-city friends. He was clinging to his righteous anger as a way out.

''You must have been horrified when you found out it was me,'' she said, smiling ruefully.

''Yes. I was. I had heard them mention you originally— that's why I was staring at you that day you were walking your horse. But they'd mentioned a number of other names as well, and I never imagined—''

"What a surprise," she interrupted, chuckling bitterly. "What a shock to learn that your little hick friend was going to be your neighbor in New York. I'll bet that made you do some quick thinking. Lucky for you this convenient excuse popped up, isn't it? You have a way out that won't leave you feeling guilty at all."

His eyes narrowed as though she'd hit a nerve. "You're going to have to learn to curb your mouth some, Ms. Linnier. Country naiveté will buy you a lot of tolerance in the city, but it does not excuse viciousness."

"I'm supposed to stand here and take your abuse and not fight back in any way?" she challenged. "I'm not your employee yet! I can still say anything I damn well please to you, and I think your unreasoning anger is a cover-up for something else. I think you're running away from something. I think—''

"Think whatever you want!" he shouted. "But don't expect me to listen to it." He stared at her, his expression changing slowly from fury to icy coolness.

"I'm certainly not concerned about New York City being big enough for the two of us," he said sarcastically. "I doubt we'll end up neighbors, and except for occasional Bella functions, I don't expect we'll see much of one another at all. I am concerned, however, about your attitude and frame of mind—since you're to be the Bella representative."

"I'll bet you are." She laughed, but there was a great pain welling in her chest. "Only I'm not so sure I want to be the 'Bella representative.' "

"Don't be foolish, Vana." His words sounded like an order from a superior. "Don't throw this chance away just to prove some childish point. A car, a big-money modeling contract, an opening into a whole new world of opportunities—this could buy your freedom for a long, long time.

This could mean never having to go back to the farm unless you want to."

And, Vana added to herself silently, it could mean becoming the kind of woman a man like Schuyler Van Dusen would respect. The thought made her angry at herself and her own weaknesses, but in the end it was this thought that finally swayed her.

Chapter Six

Vana stepped out of the building onto the crowded sidewalk. Scowling people bumped and jostled her, and she had to fight her way across the fifteen feet of concrete to the curb. Traffic whizzed by on the street. She tried to remember what she'd been told about cabs—if the light on top was on they were off duty, or was it on for on duty? Or maybe that was the full or empty signal. She decided just to step into the street and wave and see who stopped.

The sky was battleship gray and the fine mist that had greeted her that morning was now a chilly drizzle. She pulled her coat closer around her neck and waved timidly at the passing traffic. Every second vehicle was a cab, it seemed, but none of them stopped for her.

A bus screeched to a halt in front of her, and she had to jump back to avoid being hit. Murky gutter water splattered across her legs. People pushed and shoved past her to get to the open bus doors.

"Excuse me," she said, "do you know if this bus…" But the woman she'd been addressing disappeared up into the bus before she could finish the question. She walked to the corner and tried waving again. Her arm grew numb with the effort, but finally a battered yellow taxi swung to a stop.

She felt a small measure of satisfaction as she stepped forward, reaching out for the doorhandle. From out of nowhere a woman streaked up, knocked her aside with a large briefcase and yanked open the door. "My cab," she muttered fiercely as she jumped inside.

"But…" Vana protested weakly. The cab sped away and she turned, looking for someone who had been a witness. No one was paying any attention. People hurried by, unseeing and uncaring, huddled into their coats against the rain and the world.

This wasn't the magical New York she'd always imagined. She stepped into the fast-moving stream on the sidewalk, dodging to avoid being poked by umbrellas or sideswiped by briefcases. How far could it be? There was certainly nothing wrong with a good walk.

An hour later she stumbled into Jagger's office suite, dripping wet, numb with cold and on the verge of tears.

"Yes?" said the stylish receptionist, her eyebrows raised in inquiry.

"Mr. LeBlanc, please," Vana said through chattering teeth.

"I'm sorry, Mr. LeBlanc is unavailable…" the woman began.

"Send her back, Nafa," Jagger's voice ordered from some inner sanctum. "That's Miss Kansas."

Nafa looked unconvinced but ushered Vana to a white door anyway.

"You're late." Jagger perched casually on the edge of a marble counter. The entire room was a maze of pale rose counters and mirrors and different kinds and intensities of light. The walls, ceiling and floor were starkly white.

Jagger stood and produced a folded towel from a cupboard. "Here. Dry yourself." He walked to the door and called out, "Nafa, bring hot tea."

Vana shrugged out of her coat and dried herself as best she could. She slipped out of her sodden sneakers and socks and padded barefoot to the chair Jagger was impatiently indicating.

"Stephen tells me you were a bit self-conscious and unresponsive in your modeling class this morning. I expect you to do better than that with me."

She nodded and turned to stare at herself in the silvery mirror. Her wet hair was plastered to her head. Her nose was red and her eyes were swollen and pink rimmed. Agreeing to all this had been a gigantic mistake. Nothing was going right. And Sky had never even tried to call her.

"This is never going to work," she said evenly. "Making me into a model, I mean. You've known that from the start, haven't you? That's why you don't like me."

Jagger didn't flinch. He frowned, but it was her reflection he was frowning at, not her words.

"This is a professional relationship," he said, without lessening his concentration on her reflection. "Like or dislike has no bearing on it." He squinted and leaned forward to stare at some part of her face in the mirror. His scrutiny made her extremely uncomfortable.

The tea arrived and Vana cupped her hands around its warmth and breathed in the steamy fragrance. She tried to ignore Jagger's silent scrutiny.

"Now," he said, reaching into drawers and cupboards and heaping the countertop with brushes, pencils and all manner of paraphernalia, "we have a lot of work to do." He pulled over a chair and swiveled hers around so they were facing one another with their knees almost touching.

"Stephen said you're bright, but you're so uptight you're not trying. So the first thing you have to work on with me is your attitude. I don't intend to baby you. Your self-concept stinks. I don't know how or why you ended up with such a low opinion of yourself—and I don't care. I'm not interested in your mental health and I don't do psychobabble like my esteemed photographer associate. But how you feel about yourself is going to come across on film.''

He dropped a stack of eight-by-ten photographs into her lap. ''Flip through those while I'm talking,'' he ordered. ''Those women's faces are sending out messages.''

Vana sipped at her tea and flipped slowly through the pictures. The women were stunning or exotic or mysterious or bursting with health and energy or sensual or warm and innocent.

''I could never look like any of—'' she began, but Jagger quickly dumped another stack of photos in her lap.

''Those are the same women without any makeup and shot candidly without photography skills or regard for angles or lighting.''

Vana was amazed at how plain they all looked in the second stack.

''The camera is stupid,'' Jagger began, and Vana had a brief moment of goose bumps.

Was this really happening to her? She certainly didn't deserve it. Sky had seen that she didn't measure up. He'd seen she wasn't good enough no matter how much potential she might have shown in their test pictures. Sky had had a taste of the real Vanessa Linnier and he'd dropped her like a hot rock.

''The camera has no mind or heart or imagination,'' Jagger continued. ''It can be tricked. It can be manipulated. It can be made to believe anything. A single person—either the photographer or the subject—can fool or use the camera to make a big difference. A team of people—the photographer and the subject, with peripheral support from makeup and hair and wardrobe technicians—can combine their skills to make the camera see magic.

''I could take a strikingly ugly person, dress her becomingly, find just the right hairstyle and employ every makeup art. Then I could have Stephen use the best lighting and the most flattering angles and the perfect filters—and together we could turn out a very attractive picture of that subject.''

"It still wouldn't be magic, though." He pulled several of the most beautiful pictures from the stack in her lap and held them up. "Not like these. Because to make magic that the camera will believe and record, you have to have something more. You have to have something that comes from deep inside the subject—something of the subject's essence . . . of the subject's soul, if you will."

He dropped the eight-by-tens onto the counter and nailed her with an intense stare. "It can be real or a talented act, but it has to feel genuine to the camera in order to work. And even when it's acting—" he reached out and thumped her chest so hard that she reeled backward in the chair "—it has to come from deep inside. It has to be made of your essence."

Vana hung onto the arms of the chair tightly. Her eyes felt too wide and she was afraid to blink. Jagger rose from his seat and began pacing. As soon as his back was turned Vana swallowed and blinked and rubbed the spot on her chest that he'd thumped.

"You have a natural presence that translates easily onto film. It's the primary reason you were picked. That essence came through in the most poorly constructed candid shots we took of you when you didn't even realize you were being photographed."

He stopped abruptly and turned to face her. "But your self-esteem is so dismal, your self-image is so low that the moment you feel any focus on you, on Vanessa Linnier, you submerge all that wonderful natural presence under a trash heap of self-consciousness and self-denigration. You do it with people face-to-face, and you do it with the camera. You actually tell the camera you are awful."

He strode up to tower over her and she cringed in her chair. "Do you understand?" he demanded.

She nodded. She didn't know what denigration meant but she definitely got his meaning. What Jagger didn't know yet was that when the camera looked deep inside her and saw her lacking, it was seeing the truth.

He rubbed his hands together and sank back down into the chair opposite her. "So what you have to realize first of all," he said in a gentler tone, "is that few of the great camera models are what you might consider physically perfect. They are simply very skilled at projecting an image, whether it be a natural one or a contrived one.

"This is a business. This is a skill that can be studied and learned. And you are starting with a lot of raw material that you need to recognize and appreciate and learn to make the most of.

"So." He stood and swiveled her chair around so she again faced the mirror. "Look with me," he instructed, bending close to study her reflection. "I am the expert. Forget your preconceived notions and trust me. Forget your insecurities and think of your visual self simply as a complex tool to be mastered and used."

Vana stared into the mirror at her face. Exhaustion and resignation and dejection were plainly etched on her features. She was curious now to see what Jagger would say. What did he see when he looked at her? What did any of them see? Would she ever understand why she'd been chosen?

"First," he said, reaching forward to trace the outline of her face's reflection with his index finger, "we have the shape of your face as a plus. It is a perfect oval, giving us a wide latitude with hair, earrings and necklines."

Vana stared hard at herself to see the oval shape.

As if in answer to her question he flipped open a book on the counter. Pictures of faces were superimposed with shapes and Vana saw the differences clearly.

"Next, we have your overall coloring. It's your most unusual feature and therefore one we want to pay special attention to."

"You mean all this brown?" she asked incredulously.

Jagger glared at her and she snapped her mouth closed meekly.

"Brown?" he asked, his tone disgusted. "Are you blind? Don't you realize..." He shook his head. "The thing that has continued to astonish me after twenty years in this business is how ignorant women can be about their own assets. Even successful actresses! You wouldn't believe—" He stopped himself and settled back into his calm professional manner.

Carefully he reached around and unfastened her hair. He produced a blow-dryer from a shelf and dried and fluffed the hair around her face.

"There," he said. "When it was wet it was nothing more than nice, healthy brown hair. Now that it's dry and has movement and depth—" he fluffed it again with his fingertips "—we see the fine shadings, the unique highlights."

Vana leaned forward to peer into the glass. What did he see in there that she'd never seen herself?

"Your hair is a palette of autumn colors," he said with excitement mounting in his voice. "Look, here's cinnamon, here's a touch of coppery chestnut, here's nutmeg and maple and a few strands of pumpkin and—"

"Where's the turkey?" she quipped self-consciously and Jagger glared at her again.

"I work only with people who can approach themselves in a mature and serious fashion." It was a threat.

Vana swallowed hard. "I'm sorry," she mumbled.

He began rumpling her hair again. "Brown! Ha! I know women who would spend a fortune if they thought they could buy this 'brown' hair of yours. But what do you do with it? You keep it pulled back and tied up where it can't move or collect light. You keep it hidden beneath hats and scarves. You've imagined it plain brown and then refused to let it be anything else."

He pulled a gooseneck expandable light over so it shone directly on her hair. "Look at this!" He ruffled her hair so the dry parts fluffed out in all directions. "What is all this mixed in with the colors I've already named? Look, here's honey and ripe wheat and look at all this . . . it's gold! Pure, dark, tawny gold. See how it catches the light when you uncover it and let it move? Can you even imagine how spectacular that color will be in the right hairstyle?"

Vana stared into the mirror in amazement. Could he possibly be right? Could that be true?

"Next we have your eyes. We couldn't have ordered a better eye color to go with that hair."

Sure, Vana thought. Light brown eyes. What could he possibly make of her eyes? But she knew better than to open her mouth and say anything.

"Your irises are absolutely clear. No rays or flecks or lines or outlines—just pure color."

Yeah, Vana told herself . . . paper bag brown.

"That purity makes the color even more elegant, more unique." He adjusted the light again. "Turn this way . . . now tilt your head. See how the color collects the light and stays pure and clear? It's like fine amber or expensive Scotch whiskey.

"And the slightly almond shape is very versatile. We can go either exotic or innocent with that. And your brows— thank Methuselah you've never plucked your own brows. So many women ruin their browline."

He tilted her chin up and placed a small mirror in her hand. "Now your skin. Look at it."

"It's not perfect," she said without thinking.

"No, it's not," he said impatiently. "Especially close up in a hand mirror like that. But it has no major flaws, no acne scars, no large pores. You'd be surprised how many beautiful women have skin defects they need to keep hidden under heavy makeup. You're very lucky."

She frowned at herself in the mirror. She had freckles across the bridge of her nose. Was he overlooking those?

"Your complexion shade is a tiny bit tricky."

Aha, she thought, now we get to the real stuff.

"It's such a delicate color...almost an apricot, and that dusting of freckles is charming. We can use those or cover them up depending on the look we're shooting for at the time. But we'll have to be careful about shades of blush on you and about background and clothing colors. I'm afraid you skin might translate into yellow for the camera if we get the wrong colors next to it."

He took the mirror from her hand, pulled in a softer light and had her sit back. "Gold," he said triumphantly. "Dark gold hair, amber-gold eyes, apricot-gold skin...we can make you into the most stunning golden girl the camera's seen in years."

Vana saw her own mouth drop open and her brow crease in perplexity. She had learned of Jagger's reputation and she knew how good he was supposed to be, but how could his vision of her be possible? How could she reconcile this with what she'd always believed about herself, with what her sister had always said, with what her mother had preached?

If she was so great, why had she spent her life almost dateless and invitationless and noticeless? If she was so attractive, why hadn't people looked at her instead of Meg once in a while? And if she was so uniquely terrific, why had Sky thrown her away so quickly?

Jagger rattled on and on about cheekbones and high foreheads and neck lengths and ears, but she barely heard any of it. She simply couldn't absorb any more.

In the last two weeks she'd sold Buck and spent a teary day on the farm listening to Mama wail about the mistake she was making. She'd unsuccessfully tried to patch things with Meg. She'd flown to New York with Arthur and spent days in legal sessions with contract lawyers. She'd done all the paperwork to take possession of her winnings, and she'd been moved from a large intimidating hotel to a more intimidating furnished penthouse sublet.

She'd spent almost every waking hour till today listening to Arthur and his anonymous gang plan campaigns and strategies, talking about her and her life as if she wasn't there and tossing around possibilities like she was a trained seal or a tube of toothpaste.

She'd been shepherded around in Arthur's company limousine—shuffled from place to place with just glimpses of bridges and buildings through the darkly tinted glass. She was desperate for fresh air and exercise and a little freedom. She was worried that the New York of her dreams might be nonexistent. And she hadn't seen Sky. Not at all. He had managed to shut her out of his life completely.

"That will be all for today," Jagger said suddenly. "I'll have my favorite hair man here tomorrow and maybe we'll get in a little makeup work, too. You don't have a session with Stephen scheduled, do you?"

She shook her head. "He said he couldn't go any further with me till you'd worked on me some."

Jagger chuckled. "Well, don't be discouraged. You'll be surprised at how quickly this all falls into place. And you're lucky—you don't have to get into shape in addition to everything else. So many women do."

"I won't stay in shape long with all this sitting around indoors," she said bleakly.

He looked concerned and insisted on hearing exactly what all she'd done since her arrival. Other than that morning's work on camera technique with Stephen her entire stay in New York had been sedentary.

"That Arthur—" Jagger shook his head. "He's simply unconscious. I'll speak to him."

Vana brightened. "Do you think you could talk him into a few days off? I mean, I'd love to see a museum or maybe the Empire State Building or..."

Jagger held up his hand. "You'll have some days off and I'll arrange for a membership in a gym for you. Someplace with a pool. Do you like to swim?"

Vana nodded enthusiastically.

"And I'll have Nafa give you Manhattan lessons." He smirked. "Judging from your arrival today you need city survival training."

"Oh, no...I wouldn't want to put your secretary out—" Vana protested. She wasn't too keen on spending any time in the disdainful Nafa's company.

"She's my assistant, not my secretary. And it's part of her job. Besides," he snorted in amusement, "she'll adore having an opportunity to show you how incompetent you are and how smart New Yorkers are."

He paused in thought a moment, cupping his chin in his hand. "I might have Nafa do the initial shopping with you, too. I trust her judgment, and we're getting very rushed for time here. Your first round of public appearances is only three weeks away."

"You're kidding! Arthur never said—"

"Just calm down. It's not television or anything, just a couple of parties. Society bashes...you know. Arthur scheduled them as sort of practice sessions for you so you could get comfortable with yourself as a personage before you had any real media exposure."

"Oh, Jimminy..." Vana muttered.

"Nafa! Nafa, come in here!" Jagger called.

The woman eased herself elegantly into the room and stood with perfect poise as Jagger explained her mission. She looked Vana up and down pointedly. "Looks like I'll need to get out my combat boots and start taking vitamins," she said dryly.

"All right," Jagger said, "why don't you get her into a cab and off for some rest, Nafa? Then come back up and we'll discuss our plan."

Vana stood and the woman eyed her critically. "You look terrible," she said, and Vana thought it was the first sane thing she'd heard in days. "You just settle in and take a hot bath and get into your robe for the night. I'll order some food to be sent up so you won't have to go back out for dinner."

Vana started to mumble a thank-you, but Nafa was already marching for the door. "Follow me, girl," she called. "Nafa is going to teach you special forces cab-snaring."

Vana leaned back against the seat and giggled inside the cab Nafa had snared for her. Everything seemed hysterically funny. Jagger with his rock and roll clothes and his promises to make her golden, Arthur with his wild advertising plans, Stephen with his lens-eye view of the world and now Nafa with her tough, aggressive attitude—they were all like characters in a crazy book. Was all this really happening?

She was still pinching herself the next morning when Jagger called with the news that she was enrolled as a member of a posh health club complete with pool, rooftop running track and celebrity fitness experts. He told her she had the morning to work out and then Nafa would pick her up.

Eagerly Vana headed for the club. A charge account opened in her name in the club's shop allowed her to buy a bathing suit and workout clothes. For the first time since she'd arrived in New York she felt good about something. To her surprise Nafa was waiting in the lobby after she'd finished and showered and dressed.

"Is that all you own, girl?" Nafa asked without greeting.

Vana looked down at her regulation jeans and sneakers and man-cut shirt and looked back up at Nafa in question. "Well, it's what I usually wear.... I mean I have different-color shirts and some newer jeans but—"

"Never mind," Nafa said with a toss of her perfectly manicured fingers. "Today we do the fairy godmother bit." She started for the door. "Get yourself going now. Soon as we grab some lunch, I am introducing you to your first course in guerrilla shopping."

Vana raced to catch up with her. In no time Nafa had hailed a cab.

"What about my hair and . . . ?" Vana asked as she slid into the cab behind her.

"Jagger's rescheduled it. He had to fly out to the coast for a few days . . . some movie emergency."

"But he said my hair was today." Her disappointment was mostly due to fear. She'd hoped to get that part over with.

"You think you're the only worry he's got?" Nafa asked. "He's one of the best, sweetheart. He's got people begging for him all over the world. Just like Stephen Shanda is one of *the* best photographers and that Arthur fella is one of the top ad-men in the business. That's why that whole Bella search took so long. All three guys were having to juggle the rest of their work while they did it." She signaled for the cab to stop. "And you ought to be damn grateful to him for taking the time with you at all.

"Now get moving," Nafa ordered. "I'm still trying to make a name in this business—" she shot Vana an appraising look "—and if I can get you together it's going to earn me a medal. We'll start here," she announced, pointing at the entrance to Bloomingdale's. "We'll grab lunch and check out the designer floors, then we can boutique hop in two directions."

Nafa stepped neatly into the hundred-mile-an-hour revolving door that was swallowing people in one direction and spitting them out in another. Vana rolled her eyes skyward and steeled herself to jump in and follow. She watched the door make several dizzying revolutions before she drew in a deep breath and made the leap of faith.

Nafa was standing just inside with an exasperated look on her face. "This is guerrilla shopping, Ms. Kansas—hit and run. You are going to have to shift yourself into high gear and keep up with me. Understand?"

Vana nodded contritely and followed Nafa through an incredible maze of hats and scarves and belts and jewelry and up a short flight of stairs. "The escalator," Nafa said over her shoulder, and Vana assumed that was their objective. She dodged and sidestepped through the crowds in a frantic bid to keep up with Nafa's seemingly effortless forward motions. Shoppers jostled her and she was attacked without warning by people determined to spray her with cologne. They seemed to leap from hiding as she passed, and soon she was enveloped in a cloud of mixed fragrances.

Lunch was a rushed fruit-and-cheese plate with some special kind of bottled water all the way from Italy. It didn't taste any different than the tap water she'd been drinking, but Vana knew better by now than to say anything to that effect.

She followed her leader through the displays of designer clothing like a child following a teacher. She had always disliked shopping—she'd never felt any confidence in her own judgment and she'd always been convinced that she would be laughed at or scorned if she made any attempt at all to wear something stylish. She knew that having Nafa to choose for her should have made her feel secure, but instead it only added to her general depression.

All these beautiful clothes... But *she* hadn't changed. She was still Vana Linnier from Zeckendorf, and wouldn't people know that the minute they saw her? Wouldn't she look foolish and ridiculous in all these fashionable things?

"What do you think?" Nafa asked, pushing her over to a mirror and forcing her to confront herself. She had been dressed and undressed repeatedly and she could tell that her leader—and all the assembled salesladies—thought that the current outfit was *it*.

She stared at herself in the wide, three-way glass. The suit was made of a very fine wool and the blouse was a silk that felt almost liquid next to her skin. She could close her eyes and feel terrific, luxuriating in the wonderful textures of the fabrics. But when she opened her eyes and saw herself her heart plummeted.

The cut of the suit made it magazine-cover stylish. That was bad enough...but then there was the color! The draped silk spilling out at her neckline was a luscious peachy gold. And the entire suit, every inch of that fine, soft wool, was the most seriously elegant oyster white.

"You have the height for it," a voice said. "And the coloring!" someone else added. "Good gloves maybe?" "And just the right shoes..." There was a pause as they all patted one another on the back. "Let's try the cape now."

She watched in the mirror as several pairs of anonymous hands put a matching cape on her. It wasn't exactly a cape, she thought. It did have arms, though they were big and blended with the flow. There was a wide swath of fabric trimmed in pale fur that draped around her neck and dangled in front like two long tails.

"Here, let me fix it," a saleswoman said. She stepped in front of Vana, blocking her view of the mirror, and with quick expert movements pulled the draping fabric up on the back of her head and wrapped a long piece around Vana's neck. When the woman finally moved out of the way, Vana gasped at herself.

The fabric had been pulled up into a hood. It draped softly around her head, crossed at her neck in an undefined flow and then one long piece trailed elegantly in the front and one in back. Her face was framed in pearl-beige fur and soft white, and her body was cloaked royally in the same. She looked like a snow queen.

"I can't wear this," she protested in a comically squeaky voice, and everyone laughed. "It isn't funny. I could never go out in front of folks in this."

"Take it off," ordered Nafa suddenly.

Vana hurried to the dressing room gratefully. Nafa obviously understood. Nafa saw the truth of it.

She had nearly finished and was just stepping out of the skirt when Nafa entered the room. She stood just inside the door and stared at Vana in a disquieting manner.

"You still don't get it, do you?" the woman asked with marked hostility. "You aren't just country, baby—you're dumb. A stupid twit who's gonna—"

"Nafa! What did I do? I—"

"Oh, hell, don't play Sleeping Beauty with me. I've heard all the stories about how you steamrolled your own sister and played cozy with some boss to get this."

"No! No. It's not—"

"Who the hell cares! The main thing is, you aren't any newborn baby. You know what's going on here, what's at stake. Now are you going to get tough and fight or are you going to whine your way through and lose everything?"

"I don't understand," Vana said helplessly.

Nafa puffed her cheeks out and expelled an angry breath of air. She turned away from Vana as though planning to stalk out. Then she turned back.

"Look at me," she said fiercely. "You think I bounced out of Freeburg, Mississippi looking and talking like this? This woman you're gaping at right now, this woman who wears hot clothes and talks pretty and makes more money in a year than her mama ever saw in a lifetime... You know how hard I had to work and scrabble and fight to make this woman come true?

"When I heard about you and about how they picked some nowhere farm girl who hadn't ever had much of anything—I thought: Yeah, good for her. She'll make something of this chance. She'll appreciate it and be strong enough to use it."

Nafa shook her head and looked suddenly sad. "But look at you! All you can do is whine and moan about how you aren't good enough and about how your looks aren't just right and about how you'll never fit in. Well, you're right. You aren't ever going to fit in. You aren't going to make it in this business. You aren't going to be anything more than a sideshow novelty in this town. They'll see you for the nothing hick twit you are and they won't even take the time to wipe their shoes on you. And Bella? They'll keep you till your year's up, but they won't sign you again, and you can go right back to your little farm town and tell stories for the rest of your life about how you were almost something, almost somebody. About how you almost made it."

Vana hung her head. She swallowed against the burning lump in her throat. "I wish—"

"Wish! Hah. This ain't no fairy tale, girl. This is the real world. And the real world gobbles up little wishing princesses and spits them out for road gravel.'' She stared at Vana intently for several long moments.

"Dreaming is what keeps people like us alive, Vanessa. We gotta have dreams. But then we have to get out there and work to make those dreams come true. There aren't any ivory towers or Prince Charmings. You dream and you try and you fight—and you make things real for yourself.''

Nafa shook her head in amazement. ''This Bella thing you won...I'll be damned if it isn't the closest thing I've ever seen to a fairy godmother with a wand. You are one lucky farm girl.'' She chuckled softly. ''You got a toehold on a dream without much work. But don't kid yourself—it wasn't the wishing that did it. It was pure luck. Could have happened to anybody. It doesn't make you suddenly special. You still gotta work or it's all gonna fall apart.''

"I know I'm lucky,'' Vana said, swallowing again against the lump. ''Why me? I don't understand why it was me.''

"That's it? That's why you're gonna let this all trickle out of your fingers without catching hold? 'Cause you feel guilty or unworthy or something? 'Cause it shoulda happened to someone else? 'Cause you didn't deserve it?''

"My sister should have won this. She worked her whole life for it in a way. And not only did I get it when she should have been the one, but then I abandoned her to come to New York and take it.''

"That's garbage!'' Nafa clenched her fists and shook them at Vana. ''Pure garbage! Nobody *deserves* something like this. Not you, not your sister, not anybody. Just like nobody deserves tragedy. This is something that just happened. Like a bolt of lightning or a flood or a winning number in a lottery. Things like that aren't deserved or undeserved—they just are. And you take them as they come and use the good things and ride out the bad.''

She softened slightly. ''I didn't really pay any attention to those stories about how you won. I know how envious and jealous people get when they think somebody else is getting ahead of them in some way. Most people would like to see you fall on your face. Makes them feel better about their own lives. None of that's important. Don't you see? And your sister... well, it's sad that she can't be happy for you over this, but that's not your fault. And as to abandoning her...she's a grown woman, isn't she? And besides, I thought you said she wasn't even speaking to you—sounds to me like she wanted you to leave."

Nafa fixed her with a pleading, intense look. "Don't you see, Vana? All that matters now is whether you grab hold and make something come true."

Vana knit her brows and cocked her head to stare absently off at the ceiling corner. Thoughts tumbled wildly in her mind, but somehow Nafa's words were clicking into place. This chance was hers and she'd been sabotaging it with her guilt and insecurities. She'd set herself on the road to failure in order to prove her own unworthiness.

"Guess I'm wasting my breath," Nafa muttered, and turned to go.

"No, wait. I—I'm not very good at putting things into words but...you're right. I've been mixed up about a lot of things." Vana smiled ruefully and shrugged. "I still am, I guess. But I can see that a lot of what you're saying is true."

"If you can see it, you can fix it," Nafa said.

"I want to. But I'm not sure I know how."

"Well you can start by cutting out all this 'I can't' stuff. 'I can't wear this; I can't act like that; I can't see myself as anybody special.' Of course you can! You haven't even tried. And as for this 'I'm not good enough' nonsense— most of the glamorous and sophisticated somebodies in this town started out in places like Freeburg and Zeckendorf... and don't you forget it. Old Mr. Jagger LeBlanc himself is really Sol Horowitz from New Jersey."

Nafa squared her shoulders and cleared her throat. "Now," she said firmly, "You're gonna listen to Jagger and the hair and makeup people without whining, right? And you can and you will wear that white suit, right? And you'll

PLAY
SILHOUETTE'S

LUCKY HEARTS
GAME

AND YOU COULD GET

* ★ FREE BOOKS
* ★ A FREE UMBRELLA
* ★ A FREE SURPRISE GIFT
* ★ AND MUCH MORE

TURN THE PAGE AND
DEAL YOURSELF IN

PLAY "LUCKY HEARTS" AND YOU COULD GET...

★ Exciting Silhouette Special Edition® novels—FREE
★ A folding umbrella—FREE
★ A surprise mystery gift that will delight you—FREE

THEN CONTINUE YOUR LUCKY STREAK WITH A SWEETHEART OF A DEAL

When you return the postcard on the opposite page, we'll send you the books and gifts you qualify for, absolutely free! Then, you'll get 6 new Silhouette Special Edition novels every month, delivered right to your door months before they're available in stores. If you decide to keep them, you'll pay only $2.49 per book—26¢ less per book than the retail price—and there is no charge for postage and handling. You may return a shipment and cancel at any time.

★ Free Newsletter!

You'll get our free newsletter—an insider's look at our most popular writers and their upcoming novels.

★ Special Extras—Free!

You'll also get additional free gifts from time to time as a token of our appreciation for being a home subscriber.

Chapter Seven

My, my, my. Who is this gorgeous chick?" Arthur walked around Vana slowly, looking her up and down. "What a difference three weeks makes!" He whistled and backed away to cross his arms and shake his head. "You are going to knock 'em dead tonight."

"Yeah, and you better beat off all the deadheads and take care of this girl," Nafa ordered.

Jagger and the hair stylist and the makeup assistant all laughed at Arthur's look of fear.

"Actually, that's why I stopped by. I'm not going to make it tonight. I'm on my way to the airport right now. Big emergency in Japan with one of our top accounts—Tokyo Action Toys...you know, they make all those little death-ray alien dinosaurs and vampire ninjas."

"You can't—" "What does that mean?" "What about..." Everyone leaped in to question him at once.

"Don't worry," he assured them quickly. "All systems are still go. We just don't know who Vana's escort will be yet."

wear it and everything else we pick out, including evening gowns and furs, without one complaint, right?''

Vana nodded. ''I don't know if I can act natural in those kinds of things, though.''

''We'll work on that, girl.'' Nafa grinned. ''Boy, are we gonna work on that.''

He looked at Jagger sheepishly. "I don't suppose your evening's free?"

"No. It is not," Jagger retorted haughtily. "For such an important event in the campaign—Vana's first personal appearance of all things—this doesn't sound like it's being handled very competently."

"It's not a question of competence." Arthur bristled. "I do have other commitments—just like you. This is simply a matter of unfortunate timing. But we have all afternoon to iron out the problem. The important thing is to find Vana an escort who will be able to introduce her to the right people and maximize her exposure. So I don't want to ask just anybody."

Jagger nodded and went back to staring at Vana from various angles. She stood quietly in the center of the room, staring at some distant point and barely noticing Jagger's acrobatics and consultations with the hair man. Nafa had taught her a trick—one answer to looking poised was to ignore everything happening around her with a sort of casual elegance, concentrating instead on some wild flight of fancy in her imagination. It worked for a lot of situations and kept her from having crippling bouts of self-consciousness. Unfortunately it also left her with a vaguely sad expression because whenever she let her thoughts ramble for any length of time, they always managed to come around to Sky.

"And what's going on here, anyway?" Arthur asked smugly. "Still work to do before Vana's ready to go to the party?"

Jagger shook his head impatiently and turned to say something to the hair stylist.

"They're trying to decide whether Vana's hair should be up or down tonight," Nafa explained dryly. "Shouldn't take more than another hour to decide. Then a couple of hours to fix it. Then we start putting her into makeup and then the gown. Then we do her jewelry." Nafa glanced down at her watch. "So we're right on schedule here."

Arthur stretched his mouth down into a mock frown. "Wooo... sure am glad my end of the business isn't that complicated. Guess I'd look sad, too, Vana, if I had to stand around like that for hours and let people fidget with me." He scooped up the raincoat he'd tossed over a chair. "Gotta run now. My driver's waiting downstairs. Don't worry. We'll get an escort and it'll be the same plan—he'll come here with a limo to pick her up."

Vana lifted her hand and smiled a goodbye as Arthur left. She was trying to control the nervousness and uncertainty his news had stirred up in her. The party tonight had her in knots and the thought of having to go with someone she didn't even know made it a hundred times worse.

"We've decided on putting it up, Vana," Jagger said, motioning for her to take a seat at one of the rose marble counters. "It was hard... your new cut is so perfect on you—"

"And so sexy..." the hair stylist cut in with a chuckle and a wiggling of eyebrows.

Jagger ignored him. "But this is a charity ball, very up-scale, so we've decided to go for the ultimate elegant look for your unveiling. They're expecting a perky little farm girl with hay in her hair, so we'll give them a shock...shake them up a little. That ought to get them talking."

Vana's stomach was suddenly filled with a careening flock of butterflies. Shake them up... get them talking... shock them. Jagger was expecting *her* to do all that?

"I ..." she began frantically. "I don't ..." But Nafa sent her a warning look that stopped her dead.

"This is your first real job tonight," Nafa said evenly. "A certain amount of excitement is natural."

Vana nodded. Her hair moved around her face when she did. She liked the motion. She tried to calm herself by looking at her hair in the mirror and reminding herself of how pleased she was with it and how Jagger had been right—there were a zillion colors in it and it did swing nicely and pick up the light now that it was free to move. She wished Sky could see it.

The cut was very soft with strands of hair falling across her forehead and dipping slightly over one eye. She hadn't known her hair was naturally wavy. She'd always kept it so long that the weight had pulled it down straight. Now it framed her face naturally, moving gently with the slightest breeze or toss of her head. It looked like a very complicated cut to her with the tapering around her face and the way it went from one length to another, ending up long enough to fasten into a ponytail in back. She wondered how Meg would like it.

"I love my hair," she said. It was more to reassure herself than anything else. "And the dress for tonight is beautiful." She cleared her throat. "I feel pretty good about everything...a little nervous, but pretty good." She looked at Nafa, in a plea for understanding. "I'm just a little worried about who I might end up going with."

"Don't you worry, girl. Arthur wants this thing to go well tonight. It's as important to him as it is to you. He'll find a good escort for you."

Vana nodded and submitted to the hairdresser. Now that the decisions had been made the stylists and makeup artists were eager to get on with things. She drew in a deep breath and leaned her head back slightly. This was all so crazy. She'd never spent over twenty minutes getting ready for anything in her life—except that night with Sky maybe. She'd put a lot of time and thought into herself that night. A lot of—

Stop it! she ordered herself. Tonight was business. Tonight she had obligations. She could not and would not let herself slip down into a state of melancholy or depression. She forced herself to think about movies instead. She loved movies and since she'd been installed in the furnished sublet she'd put herself to sleep each night watching film after film on the video cassette machine.

She stayed immersed in characters and plots the entire day, and when a late lunch break was called she felt so distant that she retreated to a quiet corner to be away from the joking and chatter of the assembled crew. Her fantasy world was safe and secure and she didn't want to come out of it. She didn't want her fears to have a chance to surface again.

"You tryin' to hide from the world?" Nafa plunked a plate down and sat down purposefully beside her.

Vana kept her eyes on her food and hoped the woman would go away.

"It doesn't work with me, girl. Remember? I'm the one who taught you about ignoring people and acting cool and all that stuff. I know there's really a scared little rabbit underneath all that smoothness."

"How do you know?" Vana challenged her. "Don't you think I'm smart enough to know there's nothing to be scared about? Look at me!" Vana glanced at herself in one of the room's ever-present mirrors. "Why would a woman who looks this terrific be scared about a party?"

Nafa gave her a one-sided, sarcastic smirk. "Because deep down inside, you still don't believe you do look terrific. But I want to tell you something, Vanessa, and I want you to listen good. Sometime or another you're going to lose it tonight. You're going to find yourself eaten up by those insecurities and feeling so small and awful...but you just remember this: Nobody else knows. Nobody but Nafa knows you've still got that scared rabbit inside. When you feel the rabbit taking over just stay cool, stay distant and aloof and it will be your secret. No one else will ever guess. And as long as they don't guess they can't humiliate you or hurt you. In fact they'll be damn intimidated by you."

Vana leaned over to give her a timid hug. "I'd never have made it through any of this without you," she said gratefully.

"Humph," Nafa snorted. "Let's see how you do tonight before either of us starts getting too puffed up over it."

Vana replayed Nafa's words over and over through the remainder of the afternoon as she was made up and dressed. And they gave her strength and security. She knew it was true. Whenever she withdrew, people seemed to become even more impressed with her, more willing to accept her as somebody important. She was even able to fool Jagger now with her outward coolness. And she realized that the reason she'd taken so naturally to this course of action was that it was the same thing she'd always done to a lesser degree throughout her life. She'd grown up withdrawing as an escape and concealing her true thoughts as a means of defense.

"A masterpiece!" Jagger announced finally, and everyone in the crew stepped back to examine her.

The announcement startled Vana. She hadn't really been paying attention to the time or the signs that she might be almost finished. She looked at the happy faces around her, sought Nafa's nod of approval and then followed her order to turn and "look for yourself."

Slowly, Vana turned to face the floor-to-ceiling three-way mirror. She tilted her head and stared curiously at the figure reflected there. The woman looked very tall with her gleaming hair piled on top of her head in a froth, her long emerald-and-pearl earrings dangling from her ears, her long bare neck, her long bare arms and her long ivory silk dress. Was she really that tall?

The woman in the mirror blinked at her and she peered at the stunningly natural but dramatically flattering makeup job that had been applied to her face. It seemed almost like a mask to her, hiding the real Vana underneath, safe from prying eyes, safe from detection.

"It's like going to one of those masquerade parties," she said in wonder, then laughed. "It's the best disguise I've ever had." Everyone in the room laughed with her but Nafa. Nafa's expression remained carefully neutral.

"Look at the back," someone suggested.

She turned sideways, studying herself from all angles in the reflections upon reflections that the three-way glass held. The gold beads and seed pearls scattered across the softly draped bodice of the dress shimmered and sparkled as she turned. The carefully worked thread of emerald-green beads flashed, calling attention to the subtle design they traced through the beaded bodice and repeated in the wide beaded waistband. The skirt was softly gathered from the waist, appearing almost straight—until she moved, sending the luxurious fabric flowing outward like a ballerina's gown, then returning to softly caress her legs.

She turned and posed again and again, intrigued by the perfection of her disguise. She looked so elegant. Elegant enough to fool anyone. Elegant enough to please Sky? she wondered. She imagined him looking at her, judging her. She could see him reflected in the mirror, tall and distinguished, his blue eyes fixed on her with an eerie intensity, and a chill swept over her. The image was so real! So real that . . .

She whirled to face the doorway. It hadn't been an image. Or if it was just in her mind, then it was so strong she couldn't make it fade. He took a step forward and she began to tremble. "Sky?" she whispered.

"Mr. Van Dusen!" she heard someone else say.

Jagger stepped forward quickly to take charge. "Mr. Van Dusen . . . so glad you could stop by and take a look at our progress. I'm sure you'll be happy with everything." He turned and made a grand sweeping gesture with his arms as though to present Vana to royalty. "I give you the consummate natural beauty—the Bella Woman!"

"Yes. I see," Schuyler Van Dusen said in that quiet, but intimidating, strong and assured voice of his. "Very well done, Jagger."

The world-renowned beauty consultant beamed like a child. "Ms. Linnier is a quick learner," Jagger said benevolently as though to share the praise. "She was a natural at all this."

"I'm sure she was," Sky said coolly, and Vana knew that somehow the words contained disapproval.

There was an awkward, momentary silence and Vana could feel the uncertainty and discomfort building. Everyone in the room was anxious and fearful of the all-powerful, icy Schuyler Van Dusen. She wanted to tell them all to stop worrying—it was only her he disliked.

"I'm Nafa Monroe." Nafa stepped forward courageously with her hand extended to break the uneasy silence. "And this is our beauty blitz squad...." Nafa went through everyone's names as though nothing was wrong.

"Very good work," Sky said, shaking each person's hand, "and now I think it's time for us to be off."

The words hung in the air like a trapper's net waiting to fall, and Vana's heart pounded. The frightened rabbit inside her darted frantically about in search of a way out, but there was none.

"I've been elected to be Ms. Linnier's escort tonight," Sky said evenly, and she felt the net fall around her, pinning her to the ground, making her nearly faint with fear.

Sky was taking her to the party tonight. Her deepest longings, her most heartfelt desires were being fulfilled—she would be with Sky. Only it was all wrong. He was here because he had to be, because it was a business obligation. And he was here with coldness and disapproval and resentment. He would take her to the party as an enemy, not as a friend.

She shot Nafa a look and instead of seeing strength and reassurance and guidance in her friend's eyes she saw a hint of anxious concern.

"I don't . . ." she began weakly.

"Get the lady's coat," Sky ordered.

Vana stood woodenly as the golden sable was draped around her shoulders and a beaded evening bag was thrust into her hand. Nafa leaned forward to give her a kiss on the cheek. "You can do it," she whispered.

Sky reached out to grip her elbow and the hostility in his touch was like a jolt through her body. As he walked her through the door she turned her head for one more glimpse of Nafa, but he jerked her forward and wouldn't allow her to slow her pace until they were on the sidewalk and a silver limousine was gliding toward them.

"Oh, Sky..." she began shakily as soon as they were inside.

"I'd prefer you call me Schuyler when we're in public," he said. "Now, may I pour you something to drink?"

His words hit her like a blow to the midsection. She swallowed hard against the lump in her throat, shook her head no and concentrated desperately on her surroundings. The roomy back seat was completely enclosed, shut off from the driver by a divider and shut off from the world by thick, dark glass. There were no sounds except the rustling of their clothing. The upholstery was butter-soft, silver-gray leather, and a small television screen with video cassette hookup was sandwiched between a compact refreshment bar and a complex stereo with radio and cassette player.

"Is this where you live?" she asked, her words heavy with sarcasm and disapproval. She was seized by a need to strike out at him, to break through his cold composure and wound him somehow. She wished she had the power to hurt him.

"It's one of the company's cars," he said. "Available to any executive who has a trying company mission to fulfill."

"Is this a trial for you?" The question came out as a challenge.

"Yes," he said.

"You don't like big parties or you didn't want to see me?" she pressed.

He turned his head and pinned her with a look that was absolutely controlled and absolutely decided. "I didn't want to see you."

She sagged back against the seat and concentrated on not crying. If she ruined this makeup she would fail everyone who had worked so hard on her all afternoon. But her heart was breaking into little pieces and nothing seemed to matter anymore—not the party or the Bella Company or what people thought of her—nothing mattered except this great pain welling inside her. She couldn't wound him. She couldn't even touch him. But he was destroying her with barely any effort at all.

She retreated inward, sealing herself off from him and mentally curling herself into a tight fetal ball. It took every endurance skill she had ever learned to get through the long ride with him to the party.

When they arrived at the posh nightspot and she was swept into the glamorous swirl on his arm, she didn't feel one tremor, one butterfly, one urge to run. His pointed rejection had hurt her so deeply that she arrived numb and distant, with all shields in place. The armor that had enabled her to survive her childhood was now resurrected and put to another use.

People clustered around them, with eagerly curious faces and eyes searching for one flaw, one mistake, one sign of unworthiness. She smiled upon introduction, but otherwise remained detached. Nothing could touch her. She was separate from everyone and everything.

She lost her sense of time. There was no natural light and not a clock to be seen, and she had no idea whether she'd survived hours or only long minutes. She excused herself and went to the ladies' lounge for a break.

The first room in the lounge was an old-fashioned powder room like she'd seen in old movies. There were couches and an overstuffed chaise, and the walls were lined with old-fashioned built-in dressing tables and lighted mirrors. She stopped in front of one and ran her fingers lightly over the jars and pots and bottles. Everything a woman might want was available on these little tables. Everything? Well, not quite.... She smiled to herself grimly. Not even close to what she wanted.

She studied herself in the mirror. Her life seemed so full of mirrors now. Just a short time ago she'd spent days without ever consulting a mirror. She'd felt real then. She hadn't needed to check and see whether she was still there or what others might be seeing. There had been no questions in her mind about who or what she was. Now she needed to be reassured or convinced continually. She felt like one of those dolls designed to be drastically changed. Press a button in her back and her hair goes from long to short. Press a button in her front and her eyes go from brown to blue. Change her clothes, change her nose, change her bustline. Take her from pitiful to beautiful in the twinkling of an eye.

And who are you now, Vana? she was always asking her reflection. But tonight her reflection had no answers for her. She was enclosed in a glittering shell that allowed no feelings to escape. Her image was blank.

She sank down on a couch and closed her eyes to rest. If she hid in here and drifted the rest of the night, would anyone notice?

"I thought that was you! I'm Danielle Whittenboro...of the Connecticut Whittenboros."

Vana opened her eyes to see an attractive woman with dark hair and light eyes staring down at her.

"Mind if I join you?" the woman asked as she sat down on the couch with a rustle of dark blue taffeta and a blaze of diamonds.

"Parties are so boring. Don't you agree?" she asked haughtily and Vana wanted to ask her why she had come.

"So tell me," the woman said conspiratorially. "Where did they get you? You may have started out on a Kansas farm, but you've been to a European finishing school haven't you?"

Vana shook her head no and hoped the woman would go away.

"Come on now," the woman prodded, "I can tell you're one of us. It will be just between the two of us."

"I've been to a very private guerilla finishing school," Vana whispered as though sharing a closely guarded secret.

The woman appeared momentarily startled. She blinked several times and her mouth opened into a perfect O. "I'm afraid I'm not familiar with that one," Danielle said, recovering her composure.

"It's very exclusive," Vana assured her, smiling inwardly at her own joke. Nafa would love this.

The woman studied her a moment, then took an engraved gold case from her purse. A line of diamonds formed a *D* on the lid. "I have these made for me in London," she said, flipping the case open and offering it to Vana.

"I don't smoke," Vana said without a thank-you. She had noticed earlier that rudeness seemed to go hand in hand with wealth and station among some of these people.

Danielle pulled out a jewel-encrusted lighter and eyed Vana closely as she went through all the motions of lighting up.

"How well do you know Schuyler?" she asked casually.

"Sky?" Vana asked with a little start of discomfort.

"Oh." One of Danielle's eyebrows shot up. "He allows you to call him Sky, does he?"

Vana collected herself and ignored the second question. "I met him through the Bella promotion," she said evasively.

"He's a hard man to pin down, if you know what I mean," Danielle chuckled ruefully. "All of us have certainly tried."

Vana remained silent and watched the smoke curl from Danielle's nose.

"We all thought it would be easy after his wife left—"

"His wife?" Vana blurted out in shock.

"Yes. Oh, but that's ancient history." Danielle took another long draw on her cigarette. "It didn't last long. She was a Gidell. You know...the California Gidells? New money." She smashed the cigarette into the ashtray on the end table. "No breeding.

"So tell me...." Her eyes reminded Vana of a cat measuring its prey. "I can keep a secret. This farm drivel is all just for publicity, isn't it? Is Linnier your real name? What family are you from?"

Vana rose from the couch and smiled. "I'm out of Kansas by horse trailer," she quipped in a parody of the old joke about equine bloodlines. "You know, like out of Dancer's Lass by Secretariat?"

Danielle wavered and then suddenly a glimmer shone in her eyes. "Horse talk!" she exclaimed. "That's a clue, isn't it? You're from an old horse-breeding family! Polo or racing? Give me another hint."

"The kind with the most manure," Vana whispered. She tossed Danielle a little wave and escaped back to the party.

She was surrounded instantly by a group of people. It was all so strange. She had never been popular before. She had never been sought after. She could remember wishing for just this when she was in high school and playing wallflower to Meg's bright light. But now, now that she seemed to be attracting people the way porch lights attract moths, it all felt empty and meaningless.

She caught sight of Sky from the corner of her eye and she was about to ask him how long they were staying when her hand was suddenly seized and kissed.

"My dear Vana, I've been waiting for you. Why don't we just sneak off for a bite to eat? We have so much to talk about."

Vana stared at the man in confusion. He was spectacularly handsome in a too-perfect way, with perfect teeth, perfect black hair, a perfectly practiced smile and a seductive gleam in his gray eyes. He was treating her with such intimacy—had she met him earlier and forgotten?

"I'm sorry," she said casually. "I seem to have forgotten your name."

The people surrounding them stared at one another in silence and then one by one broke into laughter. The man dropped her hand like it had turned into a poisonous snake.

He swallowed hard enough to make his Adam's apple bob and his face went from red to nearly purple. Finally, he spun on his heel and stalked away.

Vana watched him go and listened to the laughter in silent perplexity. She had no idea what had just happened. Suddenly she felt a hand on her elbow and she knew without looking that it was Sky's. She turned toward him in confusion. "What—" she began, but he cut her off with a wink and a tiny shake of his head.

"I'm afraid it's time for Vana to say good-night," he announced to the group, and she detected a curious note of smug satisfaction in his voice.

She was amazed at the groans of disappointment and the hugs and cheek kisses that followed. Were all these people really sorry to see her go? She followed Sky's example and worked her way through the crowd, passing out goodbyes but remaining steadily on course for the coatroom in the process. She had been kissed and fawned over by a hundred people by the time she finally had her fur on and was sliding back into the long silver car with Sky.

She sighed and leaned her head back against the soft leather upholstery.

"Tired?" he asked. His voice was neutral.

"No. Just glad it's over," she answered truthfully. "I'm anxious to go home and wash all this stuff off my face and order something to eat. You know, that's one of my favorite things about New York—the way you can order food to be delivered at all hours of the day and night. It's amazing."

He shrugged. "I guess I've always taken it for granted."

She felt strangely at peace with both herself and him. The worst was over. She knew for a fact now that he was not in love with her, not even in like with her. She knew that her dreams were futile. She suspected that she never had really meant anything to him. She'd been just a vacation diversion, nothing more. She couldn't fault him for that, though. He certainly hadn't taken advantage of her sexually! In fact the opposite could be seen as true. He hadn't been malicious or callous or deceitful about any of it, and he had given her a glimpse of a dream, regardless of how brief.

"You were spectacular in there tonight," he said. "Those three guys really are geniuses. I wasn't sure they knew what they were doing when they picked you.... Not that I didn't think you were beautiful," he added quickly. "I just didn't believe you'd be able to handle this high-pressure glamour life."

He chuckled and shook his head. "You had them all going. Even that Whittenboro witch. And I loved that comedown you gave Roderick Denova. That was the highlight of the whole party!"

"You mean," she asked hesitantly, "the hand-kissing guy? Who was that creep anyway?"

Sky laughed with almost childish delight. "You mean you really don't know? That's even better! That would shrivel his ego."

"I thought he was slick to the point of slimy," Vana said. "Made me want to go wash my hand where he'd kissed it, you know?"

Sky grinned as though enjoying some private joke. "He's slick all right. So slick he's seduced ninety-seven point nine percent of the able-bodied females on both coasts. He's a big television star. Has been for years. Plays a hip detective with an eye for women and a nose for crime...or so the ads for the show say."

He paused a moment and when he continued there was a brittle bitterness to his voice. "Anyway, most women seem to buy his act—both on screen and off. My—" His voice choked off abruptly as though he had come to a word he simply couldn't say. "A woman I used to know...was so captivated with him she left everything and followed him to Europe for a filming session after only knowing him a week."

Vana stared down at her hands. "I don't watch television," she said quietly. "I didn't know who he was."

He'd been about to say "my wife." She was certain of it. The ex-wife Danielle Whittenboro had mentioned was a reality. He had committed himself to a relationship with a woman, and that relationship had failed. And now he could not bring himself to even say the word. He had a past bottled up inside of him. He'd felt pain and known unhappiness.

A sense of astonishment swept over her. Schuyler Van Dusen vulnerable or hurting? Was that possible? She had thought of him as rock solid and perfect—someone who never made mistakes or had regrets or let his emotions get the upper hand. She'd thought of him as someone whose intellect ruled his life and whose every decision was based on cold, careful logic.

She had built him up in her mind as some kind of god. Some infallible, unquestionable presence—someone who could decide that a person or a relationship was not suitable and who could then simply erase all feelings for that person from his heart and mind as easily as he dismissed bad business proposals. It was a shock to realize he had weaknesses, too. He wasn't always right. He didn't know all the answers.

Sky broke the pregnant silence by chuckling again, softly this time, maybe even affectionately? The bitterness seemed to have disappeared as quickly as it had surfaced.

"In just one exposure you are the talk of Manhattan society." He shook his head in amazement. "It's the most remarkable thing I've ever seen."

She smiled stiffly at what she supposed was a compliment. "I had a very special teacher," she told him. "Nafa Monroe, you remember, the woman you met at Jagger's. I couldn't have done it without her. She's the real genius."

"Hmm, maybe I should offer her a position with Bella." He drew in a long breath. "I can't believe how effortlessly you fit in with all that tonight."

His eyes met hers and she was surprised at the sudden sadness she saw. She wanted to reach out to him and gather him into her arms. Quickly she dropped her gaze and ordered herself to be careful. Her emotions were in turmoil. She needed to sort things out.

"Does the driver know my address?" she asked without looking at him.

"Yes, but...you said you were planning on ordering food in. How about stopping for Chinese with me on the way home, instead?"

"Fine," she said casually, but her heart picked up speed in her chest.

They sat across from one another at a small table in a dimly lit corner. The restaurant was quiet and nearly empty. Glowing red paper lanterns hung all around them. She pretended an interest in her food but her appetite had vanished.

He began talking about the Bella promotion. "Are you happy with all the arrangements?" he asked. "Has everything been satisfactory?"

"Sure," she said. "It's fine. I'll be glad for more free days, though. I'd like to be a tourist for a while."

He smiled mechanically. "Yes. I suppose there hasn't been much time for any of that. And your car and wardrobe...has that been taken care of?"

"I told them to deliver the car to my mama. What would I do with a car here in Manhattan anyway? And the wardrobe...well Nafa's found me enough clothes to last me the rest of my life and she still says we're not done. I didn't know winning a wardrobe was so much work."

He smiled again but it was a little more genuine this time. "And your living arrangements? How is everything there?"

"They've found me a very elegant place. Just like a magazine cover. And it's got everything...you know, modern furniture and good silverware and real paintings and even these big glass decorations on all the tables. At least I think they're decorations. They told me it was a sublet. Everything in it belongs to other people who—"

"Yes. I know what a sublet is. But are you happy with it? Do you want to live there for an entire year?"

"No, but I don't want to complain. I've heard how hard it is to find apartments in Manhattan."

"Don't be silly. You're entitled to an apartment you feel comfortable in, within reason of course."

"Maybe I wouldn't be comfortable anywhere," she admitted. "It feels so strange to live all alone."

"A lot of very successful people live by themselves in this city," he said as though explaining something to a child. "It may be difficult for you, but being a responsible adult in the modern world often means learning to live alone."

"I always thought growing up meant learning how to live *with* folks," she said. "I've been working on that a long time. I don't want to forget how to put up with other people sharing my life. It feels more natural than bein' alone. I don't think I want to learn to like it."

He studied her thoughtfully a moment. "Well, maybe Meg could come visit you periodically."

"Maybe," she agreed. "Eventually anyway. When she gets over being mad at me and blaming me for everything. Right now she's got some girl traveling with her to rodeos in our trailer and she told Mama it's workin' out way better than travelin' with me ever did."

"She'll come around eventually," he said. "Just give her some time."

He spoke of trivial things then, unrelated things. His manner was as carefully polite as if they'd just met at a church supper. Vana couldn't concentrate on his words—his knees were too close to hers beneath the table and his eyes were too searching, too lingering, too full of unspoken emotion. Tiny arrows of hope and despair and uncertainty darted around in her stomach and pierced her chest.

He leaned forward suddenly, his eyes dark and intense, his whole body gripped by some deep disturbance. Vana pulled back instinctively. What now?

"I was wrong," he said, and the words forced their way out in an anguished rush as though they'd been festering inside him.

She wanted to reach for his hand and cry and laugh and tell him of course he'd been wrong! He should never have doubted her or treated her so harshly or driven this wedge of cold silence between them. But she kept silent, waiting for the words of love and apology that would release her and allow her to pour out her heart.

He cleared his throat. "I just assumed I'd have to spend the whole evening following after you and patching up. I assumed you would embarrass both me and yourself." His words trailed off and he looked at her helplessly a moment.

"Seeing you there tonight—" he spoke carefully now as though afraid of choosing the improper words "—I realized how right you were for all this...how seriously you've applied yourself and worked, and there is no question in my mind that you deserve to be there. I was wrong to ever think you didn't. I seriously misjudged you and I thought..."

She waited with her breath held and her heart ready to leap into her eyes and her voice. All she needed to hear was one word of apology, one tiny mention of how much she meant to him.

"I think I was convinced you'd fail," he admitted reluctantly. "I didn't believe you could pull this off. Or maybe I just hoped you couldn't. I don't know." He drew in a ragged breath. "I was so angry about them choosing you. I was so angry about feeling used. I see now I simply lost my objectivity for a while...lost my ability to see things rationally."

A heavy weight settled in Vana's chest. This was no apology and attempt at reconciliation. This was not Sky reaching out as lover or friend. This was Mr. Van Dusen admitting a business error!

"So now everything's dandy and you think I'll make a great Bella Woman," she said dully.

"Yes." He latched onto her words eagerly as though anxious to get past this part of the conversation. "Yes. I think you'll make a spectacular Bella representative and I'm ashamed to have ever doubted you."

"But you still think the worst about me, don't you?" she asked. "You still think I slept with you to influence the decision. You still think I tricked my sister in some way. You still think I planned everything from the beginning."

"None of that matters anymore, Vana. That's what I'm trying to tell you. I'm not angry anymore. I allowed my personal feelings to cloud my professional judgment on this, but that's over with. I see now what Jagger and Stephen and Arthur saw all along—the only thing that matters is your potential, your ability to be the Bella Woman. You really were the only choice, and I can admit now that I was foolish to let my personal feelings blind me to that. And I see no obstruction to a perfectly pleasant association between us for the duration of this project."

"Well, you'd better check again, because your blindness has not been miraculously cured." She tried to keep her words calm but she was boiling inside. "There are things staring you right in the face that you don't even suspect! And I'm sick and tired of people sayin' it doesn't matter anymore whether I did or didn't use you and step on my own sister to get this. I'm fed up with hearing that the only important thing now is how good a job I'm doing."

She drew in a heated breath. "It does matter! It matters to me. And if learning to be a big-city somebody means learning to be like you or Jagger or learning to live alone and care only about myself or learning to put my business before my feelings or learning to shuffle aside the rights and wrongs of things as long as they turn out okay in the long run—then, no thank you. I don't want to live like that."

She stood and gathered her coat and purse.

"Vana. Vana please—"

She started for the door.

"Vana!"

He grabbed her arm and she spun to face him.

"I thought you were perfect," she said. "I thought you had everything, knew the meaning of everything. I thought you lived some beautiful, valuable life that I could only dream of." She laughed and the sound was hollow and false in the silence. "I was so dumb." She shook her head and sighed heavily. The heat was gone. She was just tired.

"I'm glad we've had this little evening together," she said "It's added greatly to my education. And now, well, it's been a very long day for me and I'd like to go home and get some rest."

There was something going on in his eyes, but she didn't bother to try deciphering it. She felt numb. Schuyler Van Dusen could take off to live on the moon and she wouldn't care. The emotional roller coaster she'd been on ever since that first day he'd looked at her was finally at an end. She was so drained that she felt nothing at all but a need to go home to bed.

Chapter Eight

For the hundredth time, Vana scanned the faces crowding into the baggage area. She'd been waiting nearly two hours and the anxiety mounting inside her was beginning to make her feel queasy. She desperately wanted this to go well. She needed to be friends with her sister again. Had Meg had a change of heart and decided not to come?

Finally, Meg's champagne hair appeared in a wave of people. Vana eagerly pushed through the crowd toward her, rising on tiptoe to wave every few seconds until she finally caught her sister's attention.

"There you are!" Meg called as though Vana had been negligent in some way. "I can't believe I flew all the way to New York and you didn't even meet me at the gate." Meg's forehead was creased in a frown and she looked rumpled and miserable beneath her burden of bulging garment bag and overstuffed shoulder tote.

"Here, let me take those!" Vana quickly took the luggage from Meg, attempting to give her a little hug in the process. Meg pulled back and eyed her accusingly.

"It's the security," Vana explained. "I've been here a long time, but they won't let people without tickets into the gate areas. I'm sorry."

Meg ignored the explanation and instead stared at Vana's face as though suddenly noticing it. "My God, you don't look like the same person." She tilted her head to stare at Vana from different angles. "They've done some kind of surgery on your face, haven't they?"

Vana shook her head in surprise. She didn't know whether to be flattered or offended. "I don't go around done up like this all the time, but I had a photo session this morning and I haven't had a chance to wash my face. You'd be surprised what makeup and hair can do," she said, "but then you were a hairdresser. You know all about that, right?"

"Humph," Meg snorted. "I know about making somebody look better, but I never learned to perform miracles." She examined Vana's hair suspiciously. "Some cut," she muttered. "And this color...if you were gonna let them color your hair why didn't you get something really jazzy like mine?"

"Oh, it's not colored. It just looks a lot different because of the cut and—"

Meg laughed sarcastically. "Sure, sure," she said. "I do know about hair, Vana, and I've lived with you your whole life and I'm no dummy."

"Let's not fight, please," Vana pleaded. "Let's try to make this work."

Meg gave her an evil look, then fished in her purse for her baggage claim ticket as the carousel behind them began to spit out suitcases and boxes. She maintained an accusatory silence, watching as Vana arranged for the bags to be taken outside and hurried down the sidewalk to signal the car and driver that they were ready.

"You're kidding!" Meg exclaimed as a sleek burgundy limousine pulled up to the curb in front of them. "We're riding in that?"

"I was planning on a cab, but Sky heard I was coming out to pick you up and he insisted on us using one of the company cars." Vana helped the driver stow Meg's bags in the trunk and apologized to him for the long wait.

Meg's eyes were wide as she settled into the back seat.

"Pretty wild, huh?" Vana said. "I was the same way the first time I rode in one. But very few people drive their own cars around here and a lot of the companies seem to have these things available. It's a whole different world, Meg." Excitement crept into Vana's voice. "I can't wait to show you everything."

"So Sky is lending you a limousine," Meg said acidly. "I guess he's back in the picture then. He must not have stayed mad at you too long."

Vana drew in a deep breath. She had hoped to stay away from any points of conflict for a while, but it was obvious that Meg had stepped off the plane itching for some kind of battle.

"Sky and I have a business relationship," Vana said. "He's very interested in this big promotion for Bella, and I happen to be the key element in that promotion. We are forced to see each other a lot, but it's purely business."

"You told Mama he wasn't even speaking to you," Meg said, sounding pleased with herself for having the information.

"He wasn't...at first," Vana admitted. "Then we were thrown together for a charity ball thing, and, well, we kind of buried the hatchet. Everything's very...nice and polite since then."

That wasn't exactly true of course. Sky had sent her flowers the day after their Chinese dinner with a note saying he was afraid he hadn't made himself absolutely clear at dinner and that he was willing to forget everything she'd done and that he thought it was was in both their best interests to work together on the Bella promotion as friends. She had torn the note into tiny bits and burned the pieces and flushed the ashes down the toilet.

What was she supposed to do now—fall on her knees and give thanks for his good business sense? Was she supposed to be grateful for his generous offer to overlook her previous crimes and put aside his anger and loathing in favor of a rational business arrangement?

How dare he make it sound like he was the only one with things to overlook or put aside! How dare he make it sound like every problem and difficulty sprung directly from her and he was this sane and reasonable person, who was doing her such a favor! And how dare he act as though they'd never lain so warmly together in the night, or wanted each other, or whispered things....

She had stayed furious at him for days. She had wanted to rant and rave at him. She had wanted to lock her hands around his throat and squeeze. But by the time she saw him again her fury had nearly burned itself out, and she was able to return his polite smile and sit across from him in a meeting without losing control.

He was willing...hah. Her wrath had subsided but a tiny kernel of it stayed to fester inside her. How dare he treat her like that!

She sat across from him through dinners and meetings. She accompanied him to a party and a premiere. And she had remained polite and civil, her lapses into sarcasm controlled, her verbal attacks on him toned down enough to sound like sharpened kidding. The people around them always seemed comfortable so she knew that her efforts were convincing, but every once in a while she would catch him studying her from the corner of his eye and she wondered if he knew she was seething inside.

"How handy," Meg said sarcastically. "The boss wrapped around your finger."

"Come on Meg...get off this! This is old territory. Mama said you were willing to meet me halfway on patching things up, but I don't hear any halfway at all. I don't know why you bothered to come."

"I had a break from rodeoing and I was bored. And you sent me a ticket," Meg said petulantly.

"I sent you tickets before," Vana reminded her.

"I know. I cashed them in and used the money."

"There's more money, Meg. There's plenty if you want some. You wouldn't believe what they're paying me."

"I don't want your money!" Meg flared. "I don't want your handouts."

"I thought we shared things. I thought we took care of each other. I thought it didn't matter who actually—"

"Yeah, yeah, yeah. I've heard that before."

"Because you're the one who said it! You're the one who thought it was fine for you to be the success and me to come live with you and help you coordinate your wardrobe. How can you forget that those were your ideas?"

"That was different, Vana. I'm the one who was supposed to do big things. I'm the one who was supposed to take care of *you*."

"Why?" Vana asked softly. "Why were you supposed to take care of me?"

Two silent tears ran down Meg's cheeks. "Because," she said weakly. "Because I had to be good at something. Because it was the only way I could ever show you up and prove to Mama that I was as good as you."

"I don't understand. Why—"

"Oh, don't give me that innocent act! You know exactly what I'm talking about." Meg wiped angrily at her tears. "Mama always thought you were little Miss Perfect. You never needed help with anything. You never made a fuss. You never got into trouble."

"Me?" Vana said in amazement. "Mama barely noticed I was around. The attention was always on you. Not that I'm complaining," Vana added quickly. "You really did make us all proud of you."

"There you go!" Meg shouted. "Still being Miss Perfect and trying to make me feel better. You want to have everything now, don't you? You took all of mine away—you made me look like a fool, and you still want to be all the other stuff, too."

"What are you talking about? We've been over this and over this, Meg. I did not take anything away from you. I did not take the Bella contest from you. I had no idea what was going on, I didn't know who Schuyler Van Dusen was and I didn't influence them one way or the other in their choices. In a fair world the honor would have been yours. I'm sorry it wasn't . . . but I'm tired of feeling guilty over it and I'm tired of being blamed for things I didn't do."

Meg laughed bitterly. "I know you didn't do any of those things. I found out I was never even considered as a possibility so you didn't steal anything from me by winning. And I know you well enough to believe it when you say you didn't know who Van Dusen was." She shrugged. "I only jumped to those conclusions, I guess, because if it had been me I probably would have been guilty of everything."

Vana stared at her in astonishment. "If you know all that, then why are you still mad at me?"

"Because you ended up with it all," Meg accused fiercely. "I'm the one who got the looks and charm, remember? That's always been the way it was. You kept us going through all the rough spots and you were the one Mama always said was her rock, her blessing—while I was her trial. And you were the one who never caused any trouble or worry and you were the one who finally got Papa's approval, but me . . . all I had was a natural talent for fluttering my eyes and attracting men. I could never compete with you. All I could ever do well was enter contests and parade myself around."

Meg sagged back into the plush seat and looked forlorn. "Now what have I got?" she said pathetically. "You're even better at *that* than I am. The contest you walked away with makes every title I've ever won look like chicken feed."

Vana was momentarily speechless. Meg had seen her as perfect? Meg had been jealous of her? Meg had been trying to measure up to her in some way? The ideas were almost incomprehensible. She had always felt so plain and uninteresting beside Meg. She had envied Meg in nearly every way. She had spent so many of her first-star wishes asking to be just like Meg.

"I—I don't know what to say. I had no idea."

"Humph." Meg glared at her, but the look was as vulnerable as it was harsh. "You were too busy being perfect to notice."

"Why didn't you ever say anything? Why didn't you give me some hint of how you felt? I mean, after we were both adults couldn't we have talked about this?"

"Let you know that I knew you were better than me? Let you know how much everything got to me? Let you know I really wasn't so oblivious or constantly happy or convinced that I could set the world on fire? Not on your life. The only things I had to hang onto were the thought that I had what it took to get us out of Zeckendorf, or at least I had you convinced I did, and the belief that you needed me around to kind of balance things out for you—that you couldn't make it on your own."

Vana smiled gently. "I didn't believe I could do anything on my own, either. For most of our lives I probably did need you to help me and watch out for me. I guess at some point I grew beyond it, but that doesn't make you any less valuable to me now. You shouldn't—"

"God, there you go . . . making me sound less awful than I really am, whitewashing my motives and ignoring some of the things I've admitted. And trying to turn it around into something positive. You've always painted me as better than I am and then made me feel so terrible when I couldn't live up to your standards."

Meg reached out to grip her sleeve. "Why don't you just yell at me? Why don't you let loose and scream terrible things at me so I can have a good reason to resent you? That's what would make me feel better!''

"What a mess." Vana leaned back and closed her eyes briefly in an effort to sort out her thoughts. She opened her eyes and looked at her sister helplessly. "I don't have any instant answers. For you or for myself.

"I'll tell you some secrets, though." Vana bowed her head. "I'm not perfect and I never have been. I've been envious of you since the day you were born and I've always thought you were Mama's favorite. I'm not innocent of thoughts like that. And I can't even count the number of times I wished you would die and I could inhabit your body. And I spent my whole life feeling like a big nothing because I couldn't hold a candle to you."

"You're making that up!"

"No." Vana crossed her heart with her finger. "I swear it's true. I saw you as the perfect, golden child and me as the family embarrassment. And I spent a lot of time trying to live up to what I thought you expected of me."

Meg scrunched up her face with the effort of her thoughts. "Jimminy," she said finally. She looked around the posh interior of the limousine as though seeing it for the first time, and laughed. "Just look at us! Two lil' ole gals from Zeckendorf, Kansas sashaying around New York City in a car big enough to haul hogs to market."

Vana joined in her laughter, but she felt she could have just as easily cried. Somehow they had just breached a barrier that had been in place for their whole lives. And she felt closer to her sister and more loving than she'd ever felt before.

She opened the concealed door to the tiny refrigerator and took out two cans of soda. With a flourish she popped the cans open and handed one to Meg, who was rolling her eyes at the decadent absurdity of a refrigerator in the backseat.

"To a new beginning," she said.

"A new beginning," Meg repeated, then grinned evilly. "And lots of New York men!"

Meg's laughter and Meg's enthusiasm and Meg's outrageous pursuit of men filled Vana's days and made her finally feel at home in her new city. They settled into a routine of Vana spending the day working at Stephen's studio while Meg shopped and caroused, and then meeting for dinner and a night of seeing sights and going to the theater and enjoying the special energy of Manhattan after dark.

Nafa joined them for several evenings and Vana found herself bridging a gap between the women. She fell somewhere in between now. She was not and never would be as cosmopolitan or sophisticated as Nafa, but she was no longer the midwestern girl that Meg was, either. She had changed. Everyone told her so. Even Meg insisted that she talked different now. And being with both Nafa and Meg made her feel the truth of it. She was a different person now. Or was she?

Meg's visit stretched from one week to two and beyond. Vana marveled at how quickly Meg learned to get around and how tireless her sister was in her pursuit of fun. She fit into the city life like a missing puzzle piece and in no time she had men calling on the phone and issuing invitations. Occasionally Meg mentioned getting back to the rodeo circuit and not letting her horse lay off too long, but it began to be apparent to Vana that her sister was in no hurry to leave.

"Now Vana," her mama told her on the phone, "don't you be lettin' Meg get into any trouble. Them big-city men might be too much for her."

"Don't worry, Mama," Vana said, laughing. "Meg's doing fine."

"And when's she figurin' on gettin' back to her barrel racing? Has she said?"

"Not really, Mama. This is all pretty exciting for her and I suppose she thinks the rodeo circuit will still be there when she gets back."

"Well..." Mama drew out the word meaningfully. "I won't be t'all surprised if she don't go back to rodeoing. I think she fancies that city life you're leadin' a darn sight more'n she ever fancied the rodeo life. She talked for nigh onto ten minutes long distance about that limousine car you been riding her around in."

The following day Vana reported Mama's call to Meg. "And she thinks you won't ever go back to barrel racing...that you'll just stay on here," Vana added.

"Maybe she's right," Meg tossed off flippantly.

"But your dream of being a famous barrel racer...what about your dream?"

"I don't know. I guess it was never really very important to me. I think I talked about it mostly because it seemed to impress you so much. Fact is I would probably still be the top blow-dryer in Zeckendorf if you hadn't been pushing me all the time to go after what I wanted. I never could bring myself to tell you that I had kind of gotten to the point where cutting hair in Zeck felt pretty darn good."

"I can't believe that! You're changing things around. That's not really how you felt. You were as desperate to get out of that place as I was."

"Nah...I only talked big about it. I never had half the nerve you did. I never told you, but I had money saved all along. You know that hair cutting paid pretty good, and well, I kind of just squirreled it away and didn't mention it 'cause I was kinda' used to the not-bein'-able-to-afford-it stuff as an excuse. And I never wanted you to know that I probably could afford it even if you couldn't, 'cause I was afraid you'd shame me into usin' it to get away on my own."

"So Mama's sacrifice to get the trailer for us didn't mean anything at all to you? Our big chance to escape didn't mean anything at all to you?" Vana was incredulous.

"Oh, I wouldn't say that. The two of us gettin' to take off like that for the rodeo circuit was pretty exciting...pretty romantic and all. That part was fun."

"Jimminy, Meg, sometimes I think I've never known you at all."

Meg shrugged and grinned. "Makes us even. The only difference is you used to think you knew me—I never thought I knew you...never. And ya know, I've decided it wasn't so bad that I tried to live up to what I thought you wanted for so long. Maybe I ended up better for it."

Vana stared at her in silence a moment, wondering. She had lived with Margaret since she was born and yet their lives were a tangled mess of miscommunication and misunderstanding. Were all relationships this complicated and this difficult? Were all people this baffling and unreadable?

A picture of Sky's face filled her mind. She didn't have to wonder how badly he had misunderstood her—the evidence was plain—but could she have misread him as well?

"So how about this shindig tonight?" Meg asked as she applied bright pink polish to her nails. "I get to go, don't I? I mean, I've been askin' you now for a week!"

"Of course, if you want to. I'm afraid it will be boring for you, though." Vana had tried to avoid discussing the party in hopes that Meg would forget about it and make other plans.

"A big party full of hotshots and rich people! How could that be boring?"

"Believe me, Meg, rich people and hotshots are not that much fun. If you say or do one wrong thing they treat you like dirt."

"No problem," Meg announced airily. "Which dress can I borrow?"

The phone rang and Vana picked it up. It was Jagger wanting to know when she'd be by the office for her makeup and hair work.

"About an hour," Vana told him. "And I'm taking Meg to the party so could we fit in a little makeup time for her?"

Meg, listening to Vana's end of the conversation from across the room, jumped up and down with silent excitement.

"You're taking Meg to the party?" Jagger asked doubtfully. "Does Sky know?"

"Not yet. I was just going to call him."

"He might not be able to get her in," Jagger cautioned. "And even if he can . . . do you think it's wise to take her?"

"Do you think you can fit her in for makeup or not?" Vana asked firmly.

"We'll work out something," Jagger retorted as though offended. "If she has to go at least we should try to do *something* with her."

Vana hung up the phone and immediately dialed Sky's number. She explained the situation to his assistant, indicating that she expected Sky to get Meg in somehow.

"It's amazing the way you can get anything you want, Vana." Meg picked up the polish and turned around and around as though dancing with an invisible partner. "I want to get in solid with all these bigwigs and rich people so I can get anything I want, too."

Vana didn't comment. She had begun to worry about Meg lately and about Meg's new attitudes. Was it her imagination or was Meg setting herself up for a big fall? She felt like an inexperienced parent confronted by a problem child. She didn't know how to handle any of it or stop the progress. All she knew was that she loved her sister and wanted her to be happy.

Meg's eagerness was infectious, though, and she soon forgot her worries and was caught up in the excitement of getting ready for the party. Most of it was a breeze now. She had a wealth of clothes to choose from and Nafa had taught her how to match her outfits to the occasion. Tonight was important enough to warrant a designer gown she'd not worn yet.

The sessions at Jagger's had become relatively brief, and painless, too. She had ideas of her own now about how she wanted her hair, and the stylists and makeup artists she worked with were familiar enough with her now to do the job in the dark.

She and Meg were both ready with time to spare and relaxing with Nafa in the lounge over a cup of tea when Sky arrived to pick them up. Meg jumped up eagerly to show him her "get-up." But Vana knew the moment she saw Sky's set expression and curt nod to Meg, that something was wrong.

"I need to have a conference with Vana," he said shortly, and Nafa quickly gathered her cup and started out.

Vana nodded reassuringly to Meg, indicating that she should leave, too, but that everything was all right. Meg shot a curious look at Sky as she left the room.

"What do you think you're doing?" Sky demanded when they were alone. "You can't take Meg to this thing."

He looked so wonderful in his black tuxedo. Every time she saw him it was always a surprise to her—how blue his eyes were and how beautifully silver his hair was. Every time she saw him and the aching softness started to spread inside her, she had to remind herself of all that had happened between them, and refresh her righteous anger and wounded resolve to keep from making a fool of herself.

"Meg is my guest and my sister, and she wants to go tonight."

"Be that as it may, Meg should not be taken to this sort of gathering."

"Why?"

"Vana, this is not just an average party with an eclectic assortment of guests from here and there. You remember what that charity ball we attended was like? That was nothing compared to this. Tonight's gala is one of the blue blood's premiere social events of the year. Meg will not enjoy this."

"No. What you mean is that these people will never like Meg. You're afraid she'll embarrass you, aren't you? Just like you were afraid I'd embarrass you the first time."

He pulled back and his expression became cool and impersonal. "Very well," he said calmly. "It's your decision. Are we ready to leave then?"

Vana settled into the limo between Sky and Meg. Once again she felt like she was bridging some sort of gap between Meg and someone else. Did Meg ever sense it? she wondered, as she tried to ease them both into pleasant conversation.

"Something to drink?" Sky asked politely. "We have champagne, soda, mineral water and Scotch in here tonight, I believe."

"Nope, not for me." Meg giggled. "I don't want to have to pee right away, you know. Rich ladies probably don't pee a lot, right?" She giggled again.

"Nothing for me either, thank you," Vana said.

She glanced over at Meg with a sinking feeling. Her sister was still giggling. Excitement sparkled in her eyes, making her even more pretty than usual, but Vana was suddenly aware of Meg's champagne hair and 3-D earrings and fluorescent-pink nails and the fuchsia lipstick she'd insisted on adding after the makeup people were finished. And was that a sprinkling of pink glitter that Meg had added to her hair?

Meg bounced around happily and when she moved forward Vana saw the drift of pink sparkles that had settled on the pale gray seat. Sky glanced down at it curiously. Maybe she had made a mistake by giving in to Meg's pleas. She didn't give a damn whether these snotty people liked Meg or not, but what if they snubbed her to the point that they hurt her feelings?

Meg giggled and oohed and aahed through the entire process of checking their coats and entering the ballroom of the grand old hotel. "It looks like a fairyland," she whispered to Vana when they were finally inside.

Vana smiled and squeezed Meg's arm. The room did look like a fairyland with fractured prisms of light reflecting from huge crystal chandeliers and buffet tables studded by ice sculptures of mermaids and King Neptune. The air was perfumed with the mingled fragrances of fresh flowers massed in breathtaking displays and woven into garlands to festoon the tables.

Had it been only two months since that first society bash she'd attended with Sky? Vana smiled to herself. It seemed like a lifetime ago. She had been so nervous and insecure then.

"What's that secret smile about?" Meg asked, and Vana laughed.

"Secret smile?" Sky asked.

"Sure...that little mysterious look Vana gets sometimes—like there's something going on but only she can see it."

Sky peered into Vana's face intently as though expecting to see the look Meg was talking about.

"I'd have thought you'd have noticed it by now," Meg told him pointedly, "as much as you stare at her all the time."

Sky's face flushed crimson and Meg laughed.

"You two..." Vana scolded, but she couldn't help studying Sky's flustered face. Did he really stare at her all the time? And why was he so undone by Meg's mention of it?

"I have some people to speak to," Sky announced gruffly, and left them to disappear into the crowd.

"I guess he's mad at me now," Meg said, sounding fairly unconcerned.

"I don't know. Anyway, let's forget it and look around."

It was fun having Meg there to share with. Vana was relaxed in her role now and ready to enjoy her new experiences, but often she was in the company of people who kept her feeling guarded, so she hid her wonder and interest. Now with Meg she was safe in exclaiming over the beautiful room and sharing her delighted amazement.

They wandered past tables and stopped to watch the dancing.

"Have you ever seen so many beautiful dresses?" Meg whispered.

"Sure," Vana teased. "At the Zeckendorf junior-senior prom."

"You didn't get to go to the junior-senior prom," Meg reminded her dryly.

A short, serious-faced man stood several feet from Meg watching the dancers. Meg nudged Vana's ribs and winked. Before Vana could stop her, Meg sidled up to the fellow, cocked her head to the side and said, "Aren't you famous for being some kind of scientist or genius?"

The man stared at her in shock a moment, then recovered enough to blink furiously behind his no-nonsense black-framed glasses and tug nervously at the collar of his tuxedo shirt. "No," he said, "however, I was well-known in my fraternity for my scientific mind. How extraordinary that you should sense something of that sort."

"Oh—" Meg twinkled and fluttered "—I could just tell by that look in your baby-blue eyes that you had one of those genius brains. So is that what you do...inventions and things?"

"No," he admitted reluctantly. "I help my father manage his affairs."

Meg burst out laughing and nudged the man's arm as though sharing a hilarious joke with him. "That's good," she said finally. "You're a funny guy."

His dark brows knit together in perplexed confusion and he tugged on his collar again.

"You come alone?" Meg asked coyly.

"Yes...no...I mean, I came with my sister. Just with my sister," the man stammered. He reached up to frantically comb his fingers through his dark hair as though suddenly convinced it was not neat enough.

"Why, I came with my sister too!" Meg exclaimed. "This is my sister, Vanessa, and I'm Margaret, but you can call me Megi," she said sweetly.

"And we have to be moving along," Vana inserted quickly. "We were just on our way to—"

"Vana! Don't be rude! My friend..." Meg motioned with her hand for him to fill in the blank.

"Barclay," he said, clearing his throat and smiling for a tenth of a second.

"My friend Barkie was just going to ask me to dance." Meg looked at Barclay expectantly.

Vana winced at the reduction of Barclay to Barkie and wondered how in the world she was going to get Meg away before this high society jerk did something to hurt her feelings. To her surprise Barclay gave a courtly little bow and offered his hand to Meg. "I would be charmed if you would give me this dance," he said stiffly, and Vana heard Meg giggle as they moved off together into the crowd of dancers.

Vana stood on the edge of the dance floor, leaning and shifting and standing on tiptoe in an effort to keep Meg and Barclay in sight. She felt as nervous and responsible and helpless as a mother watching her daughter on her first date. She shouldn't have brought Meg here. It was clear to her now. Instead of giving in to Meg's pleading, she should have been mature enough to realize the potential problems and firmly tell her no.

"Don't tell me she's already off in pursuit of trouble?" Sky said, and handed Vana a stemmed glass of white wine. He held another glass of wine that he'd obviously intended for Meg.

"Thank you," Vana said, and took a sip.

"It's a peace offering. I shouldn't have said anything about Meg coming."

"Why not?" Vana asked him. "You were thinking it."

Sky took in a deep breath, puffed his cheeks out with it and then expelled it with a frown. "You can be the most exasperating woman...."

"Ah, it's all right," Vana said with a sigh. "I'm thinking I shouldn't have brought her either. What if these stuffed shirt creeps start being nasty to her? I mean, I've spent my life putting my foot in my mouth and learning to deal with bad reactions from people. But she goes to pieces when she thinks she's being rejected or disliked."

"We'll just have to take care of her then, won't we?" Sky said gently.

"You mean you'll help me?"

He smiled down at her in answer and her heart did a little flip-flop in her chest.

"Where is she now?" he asked.

"Dancing with some guy. It looks okay so far." She stood tall and peered around. "I've lost track of them now, but they seemed to be waiting on the floor for the next dance."

Sky nodded. His eyes met hers, swept down her body and returned to lock onto hers again. A shiver ran through her.

"You are very sexy in that dress," he said appreciatively. "The folks back home would gape."

"Really?" she said, and looked down at herself in mild surprise.

Nafa had fallen in love with this gold satin. It was very fitted with a defined waist, a long narrow, slit skirt and a shirred bodice held up by two delicate rhinestone straps. She knew it fit her like a glove and bared a lot of her back and arms and shoulders, but still, it was a surprise to hear that the effect was sexy. She'd never been referred to as sexy in her life, and she'd never imagined herself as being capable of sexiness.

"Really," he assured her, and smiled. "Since we're waiting, why don't we dance, too?" he asked lightly, but his sea-blue eyes were intense and hopeful.

Vana couldn't trust her voice. She nodded and moved onto the floor without taking the hand he offered. But she had to touch him eventually. She turned toward him and lifted her arms hesitantly. It's just a dance, she kept telling herself. Friends dance. Relatives dance. There's nothing scary about dancing with someone.

She held herself back as far from him as possible and rested her hands properly in the dancing position. But he wasn't satisfied. He pulled her closer, close enough to feel the warm length of his body brushing hers. His hand touching the bare skin of her back sent a thousand tiny currents through her. She closed her eyes, and she could hear the whisper of his breathing.

The music flowed around them, enveloping her in a liquid unreality. Every inch of her skin felt heated and alive. She was aware of her own pulse, and she could sense the beat of his heart and the rushing of blood through his veins. The slightest pressure of his thigh against hers or the brush of her breasts against his chest burned through her entire body. Every point of contact became a focus of heat and electricity until she felt like she could glow in the dark.

"I want you," he whispered. "I've never wanted anyone as much as I want you."

She stopped and pulled back, staring at him in confusion. Couples glided by around them.

"Can't you feel it between us?" he asked softly. "It hasn't gone away. I've been fighting it and you've been fighting it, but it's still there."

She turned and zigzagged her way out of the dancers, back to the edge where it was safe. Her knees were shaking so badly she was afraid she might trip and fall. He caught up to her but did not try to reach out for her.

"You can't run away from it, Vana," he said simply. "Just like I can't. It's something with a life of its own, connecting us whether we encourage it or not."

She put her hands to her cheeks. Her fingers felt icy against her burning face. Every cell in her body ached for him, but she was frightened and uncertain. She felt caught in the grip of some awesome power. She dropped her hands to her sides and stared down at the floor.

With one strong, gentle hand he reached out and tilted her chin up so that their eyes met. "Come home with me tonight, Vana. Please. We need to be together. It's right."

She looked into his eyes and saw warmth and an almost painful yearning. The room spun crazily around her and moments fractured and split, making each pinpoint of time into infinity.

"Excuse me...please excuse me." A male voice penetrated her consciousness like a distant sound breaking into a dreamy sleep. "Excuse me, Mr. Van Dusen. Your driver needs to speak with you. He's waiting by the outer door."

Vana watched Sky move away through the crowd of people until he disappeared from her view. She shook her head against the haze that filled her mind, and suddenly she was aware again of the music and the laughter and the press of humanity surrounding her. Oh, God! Where was Meg? How long had she been unconsciously floating in never-never land?

Frantically she moved along the edge of the dance floor, searching, stretching and bending and craning her neck in an effort to catch a glimpse of Meg's turquoise dress and champagne hair.

"Hello there."

Vana turned to see Danielle Whittenboro zeroing in on her. That was all she needed!

"Hello, Danielle."

"A gruesomely dull affair, isn't it?" Danielle asked dryly. Her shoulders were bony and pale, protruding from a strapless, stiffly ruffled black taffeta dress.

"A little too much excitement for me," Vana countered drolly.

Danielle sniffed in amusement. "Actually, I've been watching for you," she admitted. "I couldn't remember after our last little chat whether you said that exclusive school you went to was in Europe or not."

"Oh you couldn't?" Vana asked as though puzzled.

"No," Danielle responded eagerly.

"Didn't I say?"

"You must not have," Danielle encouraged.

"Perhaps I didn't." Vana smiled. "Then it was my oversight, wasn't it? Terribly sorry. How silly of me."

"Oh no...don't give it a thought," Danielle said quickly with a vaguely puzzled expression.

"How kind of you." Vana smiled again. "I won't then." She turned her head back to look at the passing dancers. "I was just watching the dancing," she said, hoping Danielle would find that boring and go away.

"I don't dare watch the dancers," Danielle announced dramatically. "My reserved, priggish brother is out there making a fool of himself with some...some dime store glitter girl." She rolled her eyes and set her mouth to indicate disdainful amusement. "I'll never hear the end of it from my friends."

Vana tried to ignore her. She continued watching for Meg and hoped that, without encouragement, Danielle would fade away soon.

"Here he comes now," Danielle said. "God!" Her voice dripped with indignant disgust. "What a delightfully charming couple. Look at that pink glitter all over his shoulder, will you! My parents would just die if—"

"I don't know who the nerd in the tuxedo is," Vana said, squaring her shoulders and staring Danielle straight in the eye, "but the young woman you're pointing at happens to be my sister!"

Chapter Nine

Your sister! You can't be—'' But before Danielle had a chance to finish her thought they were descended upon from all sides.

Sky approached from behind them, unsuspecting and unaware, and generously offering a neutral smile and a polite greeting to the woman he had previously referred to as the Whittenboro Witch. And before that exchange could be dealt with, Meg and Barclay plopped into their midst, fresh from a fast dance, laughing and clutching their chests and breathing in big gulps of air.

Everyone tried to talk at once. "Do you know my...?" "Is this your...?" "How did you two...?" "I didn't know you had a..."

"Isn't this a coincidence!" Meg finally exclaimed in a breathless voice that silenced them all.

"Who's going to begin the introductions?" Sky said, still blissfully unaware of the situation.

"This," Danielle finally said in an exaggerated upper-crust tone, "is my brother, Barclay Hughes Whittenboro the Fourth."

"Barkie!" Meg giggled. "I've never met a Fourth before!"

Danielle stared at Meg in horror. "Barkie?" She sniffed as though the word had a foul stench to it.

Through all of this, Barclay appeared more relaxed and happier than Vana would have guessed it was in his nature to be without the aid of generous amounts of alcohol or that gas that dentists sometimes used.

"I'm Schuyler Van Dusen," Sky said, holding out his hand to Whittenboro the Fourth. "I've done business with your father on numerous occasions."

Barclay nodded and stiffened a little as he shook Sky's hand. "Yes, I'm well aware of who you are, Mr. Van Dusen."

"Schuyler...please," Sky told him.

"And I'm Vana Linnier, Meg's sister." Vana held out her hand and smiled warmly. She was more than grateful for his generous treatment of Meg. "But then I guess you've already heard that from Meg."

"The Bella Woman," Danielle put in with a snotty emphasis that made the title sound like an obscenity.

"That is my sister, Danielle," Barclay said to Meg as though Danielle was somewhere off across the room.

"Danielle Anne Whittenboro," Danielle said haughtily. "As in the Mayflower Anne Whittenboro."

"And I—" Meg affected a ridiculous late-movie parody of a cultured Englishwoman's voice, playfully poking fun at Danielle's snobbishness, and clearly kidding rather than being hostile "—am Margaret Colleen Linnier the First. You know, as in the Hole-In-The-Wall-Gang Linniers." She giggled and elbowed Barclay, whispering, "Get it? Get it?" to him and treating him to a silly eyebrow wiggle.

Danielle's face turned a dark red. Barclay covered his mouth with his hand and coughed in an effort to hide the wide grin that sprang to his face. Sky looked startled, then puzzled, then worried in a lightning-fast sequence of expressions. Vana absorbed it all and felt like an observer at a buffalo stampede. There was absolutely no good way to stop this.

"The humor of your remark escapes me...though I'm certain you intended humor," Danielle said to Meg acidly.

"Oh, come on. It was just a joke. This is a party and we're here to have fun, right?" Meg said with all the midwestern charm she could muster.

"This is not a party—it is a *charity gala*," Danielle retorted. "And I've never heard the purpose reduced to something so trivial as 'having fun.'"

"What's wrong with having fun?" Meg's eyes were beginning to cloud and her voice was wavering. The full impact of Danielle's rejection was finally hitting her where it hurt.

"There's nothing wrong with having fun," Vana assured her sister in a soothing tone. She flashed arrows at Danielle. "And I'd say anyone who doesn't know how to have fun is a little perverted."

"The difference between the upper class and the lower masses is an ability to rise above the trivialities of life," Danielle shot back pointedly. She swept Meg with a disdainful up and down look. "And the lower masses appear to be well represented here."

"That's enough, Danielle," Barclay said, causing everyone to stare at him in varying degrees of surprise, his own sister appearing the most surprised.

"How dare you speak to me that way in public, Barclay?" Danielle said in a shocked tone as soon as she'd managed to regain control of herself.

Barclay ducked his head and tugged at his collar. Then he glanced over at Meg's moistening eyes and turned back toward Danielle with squared shoulders and a lifted chin. The straightening seemed to make him a good foot taller in stature and Vana realized that he was almost handsome in a studious, intellectual way.

"I won't have you treating Meg this way," Barclay said to his sister.

Again Danielle registered shock, but this time there was a little fear mixed in with it. "Wait until Father hears about this!" she said.

"Oh, gosh," Vana said, unable to resist the temptation. "I hope your papa won't spank poor Barkie when you tattle. I'll bet—"

"I think that's about enough, Vana," Sky cut in, sounding like the wise elder breaking up a childish squabble. Vana hated him for it. She felt the humiliating comment was directed solely at her.

"Oh yes," Vana attacked him. "We wouldn't want to be nasty to Danielle Whittenboro, would we? We wouldn't want to embarrass or humiliate a Whittenboro—even if she deserved it!"

"Calm down, Vana," Sky said in a voice that was too commanding for her taste.

"Is that an order?" she demanded.

All of her anger at Danielle and the whole snobbish system, all of her fears for Meg and all of her collected baggage of hurt and anger over Sky suddenly ignited into one brilliant beam focused directly on Schuyler Van Dusen. He was betraying her. Just minutes ago he'd held her close and said he wanted her and now he was selling out like a lowly grub worm—groveling before the power and influence of the Whittenboro name.

"Yes, that's an order," he said, softening the word with a smile. "And I also order you to take another relaxing sip of wine and then to dance with me again."

"No, thank you. Why don't you ask your buddy Danielle?" Vana turned abruptly to thread her way to the refuge of the ladies' room.

As soon as she was safely inside she sank against the wall, knees suddenly weak and hands trembling. She wanted to burst into tears and sob against her mother's comforting shoulder. She wanted to be back on the farm and away from all this insanity. She wanted to go back to a time when all that mattered to her in the world was whether she got to ride a horse after school or not.

Meg peeked her head inside the door. "Here's where you are," she said as though they'd been playing hide-and-seek.

Vana drew in a deep breath, straightened and moved to sit in a dainty chair as Meg entered the room. Without a word Meg pulled up another chair and sat down beside her.

"So this is where the rich ladies pee," Meg said, turning her head all directions to study the room. "Where's the toilets?"

"In there." Vana nodded toward another door. "This part is called the lounge."

"This is where you recover from your ladylike faints, huh?" Meg joked.

"Or sneak a ladylike cigarette," Vana added.

"Or hide when you're embarrassed," Meg said meaningfully.

"If you think I'm embarrassed, you're wrong," Vana said defensively. "I have nothing to be embarrassed about."

"Oh, Vana. You're so hard on people."

"What does that mean! Do you think I should have been nicer to that evil witch while she was sharpening her claws on your hide?"

"No." Meg grinned. "The gun you used on that sow was just the right caliber." She chuckled. "You always were lethal, Vana. God, even the big-shot football players were scared of your temper when we were in school. Nobody wanted to get near you unless I was there to protect them." She shook her head. "I might have been the toughest one in some ways, but you were always the scariest."

"People were scared of me?" Vana asked in amazement.

"Everybody but me. You even scared Mama sometimes. And Papa... well, I think that's finally what sold him on you. He must have figured anybody who could scare him deserved his respect.''

Vana stared down at her hands and frowned. Could that possibly be true? That people hadn't disliked or shunned her or been bored by her—they'd just been afraid of her?

"Intimidating, I guess you'd call it,'' Meg mused. "You've always been so damn intimidating. I used to try to copy you, you know, to get a little respect from people. But they'd always just laugh at me like I was some pat-it-on-the-head baby doing a cute trick.''

"So,'' Vana said, feeling calm now and ready to accept guilt or whip up some regret, "you think I made a fool of myself out there?''

"Not really.'' Meg grinned. "I thought you were pretty brave. But you were kinda' hard on Sky, you know?''

"No. I don't know. Just what do you mean by 'hard on Sky'?''

"Just what I said before. You're so hard on people. If somebody weakens of falls down one little bit in your opinion you come down on 'em with a sledgehammer.''

"I'm not like that with you, am I?''

"No.'' Meg's mouth twisted into a little rueful smile. "But sometimes I think the only reason is because you see me as a walking screw-up, your poor sister who's so dumb or scatterbrained or babyish that she can't be responsible for anything she does.'' She chewed on the corner of her lip and blinked as though holding back tears. "I've always tried so hard to impress you, to get you to take me seriously. Sometimes I've tried to push you, done awful stuff just to see how much you'd let me get away with. I guess since I couldn't ever get your respect, sometimes I tried for your hate.''

Meg took a deep breath and smiled. "Anyway I'm glad it never worked. I'm lucky you don't hate me. I realize now that you're a pretty terrific sister—'' she grinned self-consciously "—and I guess I'm crazy to be complaining because you excuse everything I do and protect me all the time. Most people would probably die for a sister like that!''

Vana groaned and pretended to let her head fall help-lessly to the side. "It's all too complicated for me," she said. "Maybe Sky's right. Maybe we should all live by ourselves and not even try to get along with other people except professionally."

"Sky said that?" Meg asked.

"Not exactly, but almost."

"Well, you can if you want—" Meg wiggled her eye-brows with comic suggestiveness "—but not *me*." She grinned slyly. "As a matter of fact I'm on my way to din-ner with Barkie right now."

"You're kidding."

Meg shook her head smugly. "He's crazy about me. You know, he's really smart. I always had a soft spot for brainy guys, the kind with the slide rules and automatic pencils poking out of their pockets, but none of 'em ever asked me out."

Vana laughed. "Well, have a good time. You have your key to get in don't you?"

"Yes, Mother. Right in my purse. Now why don't you go out and have Sky take you somewhere quiet for a drink?"

"No. I don't want to see Sky. I don't want to talk to him."

"But maybe—"

"No," Vana insisted firmly. "I've had it. I'm tired of the way he's convinced I'm tainted, but keeps stooping to of-fers of friendship or...well, I'm fed up with it all. And now, tonight, when I saw the way he sided with Danielle—the way he automatically jumped in to defend his upper crust asso-ciates—"

"Oh, Vana," Meg said helplessly. "There you go mak-ing—" She stopped herself short and sighed. "Maybe the biggest problem is that you and Sky are too much alike."

Vana watched her go and then headed out in a circuitous route for her coat and a cab. She went home and straight to bed and didn't answer the phone when it rang.

Her mind was kept occupied for the next few days by preparations for her first television commercial. The print-ad photos Stephen had been shooting had pleased everyone concerned and though they hadn't appeared yet in any publications, the Bella people were convinced she was putting across the image they wanted, and they were anxious to schedule more. Arthur had managed to sandwich a video-taped spot into the schedule, though, before they began work on another round of magazine shots.

It was all so routine for Vana now. Posing in front of the still camera was nothing. And since there was no speaking role involved, the coming video session didn't seem much different. Modeling and being the Bella Woman didn't feel much different some days than getting up in the morning and going to work at the Zeckendorf bank.

The incident at the charity gala had left her feeling brittle and empty. She refused to think about it or to discuss it with Meg, hoping time would simply ease it into insignificance if she ignored it long enough. There had been too many emotions stirred up that night and the thought of trying to sort them out and deal with them frightened and disturbed her. Could Sky dislike her and want her sexually at the same time?

She avoided Sky, which was relatively easy because he was not exerting any real effort to make contact with her. And she kept her mind on her modeling and her gym workouts and Meg's continuing infatuation with "Barkie."

Meg had come home very late the night of the gala, humming to herself and grinning ear to ear. The next morning there had been an outrageous three-dozen pink roses delivered to her at the apartment. "Oooh!" she had squealed. "He guessed pink was my favorite color!"

The whole thing had struck Vana as funny at first. It served Danielle Whittenboro right that her brother was smitten with someone so lowly in Danielle's eyes. But her amusement had only lasted from the delivery of the flowers to Barclay's arrival promptly at noon to take Megi—as he referred to her now—to the Russian Tea Room for lunch.

When Barclay walked in, stiff and uncomfortable in his obviously expensive but still curiously wrong three-piece suit, bearing yet another bouquet of flowers and looking at Meg like a lovesick puppy, it was still funny. But when Meg rushed out of the bedroom and met his lovesick puppy look with a moonstruck gaze of her own, Vana's amusement turned to dread.

Vana was afraid for Meg as soon as she realized Barclay did indeed mean something to her. She had no doubt that the Whittenboro's upper-crust machinery would not hesitate to crush Meg into an emotional pulp if they felt threatened by her in any way.

Lunch at the Russian Tea Room was followed by dinner that night at Four Seasons, lunch the following day at the Quilted Giraffe, dinner the following night at Lutece and so on until the itinerary sounded like an eating guide to Manhattan's finest. The apartment filled with enough flowers to supply a street corner vendor for a year and when there was no room for any more, bouquets of pink balloons arrived instead.

Vana tried to engage Meg in a heart-to-heart talk that would enable her to work up to some kind of warning. But Meg skipped blithely along, beaming and unsuspecting and starry-eyed—in too much of a lovestruck rush to sit down and talk and listen to Vana's warnings and cautions. Every waking moment of Meg's time now seemed to be taken up by dates with Barclay or getting ready for dates with Barclay.

Vana applied herself to the video work and, when it was wrapped up, took some welcome days off to explore museums and parks. And she worried. Meg couldn't possibly take care of herself against a bunch like the Whittenboros of Connecticut. Somehow Vana had to find a way to protect her.

In two weeks she would be on vacation; she'd insisted on the time off so she and Meg could fly to Kansas and celebrate theirs and their mother's birthdays, just as they'd always celebrated since the girls had become adults. Vana's and Meg's birthdays were one month apart and Kate's fell almost exactly in between, and the combining of all three into one glorious evening together was a tradition Vana didn't want to upset or lose. She felt a strong need for some connecting thread to her old life.

Meg had suggested prying the stubborn Kate out of Kansas and forcing her to fly to New York for the occasion, but, though Vana did want her mother to experience New York, she also had an urge to return to the farm and Zeckendorf and see what the old home felt like now. She wanted to put off the trial of convincing Kate to come east for a Manhattan visit for another time. Meg agreed and cheerfully told Vana to go ahead and make the plans—anything was all right with her.

In the middle of Vana's vacation planning, Nafa called to surprise her with the news that Mr. Van Dusen had offered her a terrific position with Bella and she'd jumped at the chance.

"What about Jagger?" Vana asked. "Is he mad?"

"No. He knew I'd be leaving soon. That's the way he works—he finds somebody green and teaches them the ropes while he works them to death for four or five years. Then they become experienced enough that he doesn't want to pay them what they're worth so they strike out for somewhere else and he starts all over again."

"I'm really excited for you," Vana said.

"Well, then prove it, girl! Get yourself over to this fancy new office of mine and let me take you to lunch and christen my brand-new expense account."

Vana laughed and agreed to a time. She was happy for Nafa and eager to share in her triumph. She felt good all the way over in the cab in spite of the weird chanting of the driver, but when she stepped out onto the sidewalk and realized it was Sky's building she was going into, her spirits deflated. The last thing in the world she wanted to do was run into Sky.

And so of course that's precisely what happened. When she walked into Nafa's plushly carpeted, new-paint smelling office, Sky was standing, big as life, right in the center of the room.

Nafa smiled broadly in greeting and Vana had the sneaking suspicion that maybe Sky's presence at that exact time might not have been an accident.

"Come in, come in," Nafa called.

Vana stood self-consciously in the doorway. "It looks like I'm interrupting something so why don't I just wait—"

"Nonsense." Nafa hurried over to take her arm and pull her into the room. "We're almost finished. I just asked Mr. Van Dusen to come by and look over the outline I've drawn up for my first project here."

Sky recovered from his obvious surprise at seeing her, cleared his throat and set the papers he'd been reading down on the shining new desk. "Yes. I've seen as much as I need to for the time being . . . so you two feel free to—"

"How about that!" Nafa made a show of checking her watch. "It's lunchtime already!" She reached into a cabinet for her purse. "Mr. Van Dusen is joining us, Vana. Isn't that terrific?"

"Oh, no," Sky began quickly, "I couldn't—"

"Oh, no," Vana said at the same time, "I don't want to—"

"This is working out perfectly, isn't it?" Nafa said brightly, ignoring both of their stammering protests. "We're all very much involved in Bella now, and we're all friends, so this lunch kills two birds with one expense account."

Vana set her teeth and glared over at Sky. He met her look with an accusing glare of his own.

They walked to the restaurant Nafa had already chosen. Nafa chattered along the way, while both Sky and Vana contributed little more than nods and grunts—and those only when there was no escaping a response. The day was sunny and bright with that special brilliance late spring can cast in the city, and the warm breeze on Vana's face broke through her funk and made her feel happy to be alive. They rounded a corner and passed a fountain. The water tumbled beside them, the sun catching droplets and transforming them into flashing points of light as they fell.

Vana didn't realize she had stopped until Nafa asked if something was wrong.

"No. I'm sorry. The fountain is just so magnificent today, I guess I was caught up for a minute." She moved forward on the wide sidewalk to join them. People hurried past her on all sides, their eyes straight forward and their faces determined. "Isn't it sad the way no one in this city takes the time to enjoy anything?" she said, more to herself than to anyone else.

Sky turned his head and gave her an indecipherable silent look and Nafa humored her with a mumbled agreement as they stepped inside the restaurant. It was an intimate little country-French place with exposed brick walls and waitresses in starched white aprons. They were shown to a table set for three with damask napkins and sterling flatware, and settled in with handwritten menus.

After they had ordered, Nafa began working at a conversation that included all three of them. She talked about her new job at Bella as product development consultant and when that produced little in the way of responses, she began asking questions about the Bella Woman promotion that she addressed to both of them.

"So exactly what stage is the promotion in?" she asked them.

Vana fiddled with her fork and waited. Sky sipped at his water and waited. Finally Vana broke down and said, "I don't know."

"Well, have any of the print ads been published yet so that we have a sense of how they're being received?"

This time it was Sky who relented with an answer. "No. The first magazine exposure will be two to three weeks from now. For all we know Vana might be a big flop in the public eye when they finally get a chance to see her."

"Hah. I doubt that," Nafa countered. "I heard Stephen talking about entering a few of the shots in some high-level commercial photography contest because he thought they were so good. I can't imagine the public won't respond."

"Stephen's a good photographer," Vana said. It still made her a little uncomfortable to listen to compliments that were even indirectly aimed at her modeling. She wanted to make certain all the credit went to Stephen.

Sky shot her that indecipherable look again and she wanted to scream at him to stop.

"I think the campaign based around Vana is going to give Bella a whole new image, don't you agree?" Nafa directed this question right to Sky so he couldn't avoid answering.

"Yes. Vana is exactly what Bella needed—a natural woman. She comes across on film as a believable, heartland-of-America golden girl...sexy yet wholesome, tough and independent yet vulnerable, smart and sassy, warm and fun." Sky turned and looked at her with a level measuring gaze that made her seethe. "If Vana can't sell Bella, nobody can."

"You make me sound like I'm not even real—just some advertising gimmick created to please the public," Vana accused, meeting his gaze with a heated one of her own.

"Isn't there some truth to that?" he asked coolly.

"What do you mean by that?" she demanded.

"I mean that Vana Linnier barely existed before Bella picked her up and transformed her into a presence."

"Oh no," Nafa cut in. "With all due respect for the boss, Vana had more natural presence than anyone I've ever worked with. Her only problem was she wasn't aware of it and didn't know how to use it."

"Barely existed?" Vana repeated his words with distaste. "Barely existed?" Fury mounted inside her and she wanted to leap on him and wrestle him down to the floor and make him cry uncle, just as she'd done to all the boys in her second grade class after they'd laughed at her during recess.

"I suppose I barely existed that day you couldn't stop staring at me in the Astrodome! I suppose I barely existed when you chased me around in a party and made me talk to you! Or how about when you were so eager to see me you drove all the way out to the rodeo grounds at dawn! Did I barely exist then?"

"Whoa, now, fellow diners," Nafa said, holding up her hands. "Anger is bad for the digestion."

"Why don't you say the rest of it?" Sky baited her. "Why don't you say how *you* were staring at *me* and how *you* asked *me* to—"

"Don't you dare say it," Vana interrupted, leaning across the table toward him with her clenched fists resting between the bread basket and her plate. "Don't you—"

"What?" Sky asked with infuriating mock innocence. "I was just going to remind you of how you asked me to go out for Mexican food with you."

The waitress arrived just then with their baked salmon and Vana settled back into her chair to steam. Schuyler Van Dusen had some nerve. Angry retorts and vicious remarks flashed in her head. She folded her hands in her lap and studied her salmon while the waitress added more food and fussed with the butter and refilled their water glasses. By the time the woman was finished Vana's breathing and her blood pressure had calmed considerably.

Vana picked up her fork and glanced sideways at Nafa. Nafa picked up her fork and glanced sideways at Vana. From the corner of her vision she saw Sky glancing across at her and then picking up his fork.

"I'm so glad we could all get together for lunch like this," Nafa said as if totally serious.

They ate in silence for some time.

Finally Nafa made a brave attempt at conversation again. "What's this I hear about Meg seeing what's-his-name Whittenboro?" she asked casually.

Vana sighed involuntarily. There it was, surfacing again in her mind, a nagging cloud of worries about Meg.

"She calls him Barkie and he calls her Megi," Vana retorted dryly.

"Oh . . . that bad?" Nafa sympathized. "Must get a little nauseating to be around."

Vana put down her fork and rubbed the spot right in the middle of her forehead where she seemed to be getting a constant pain lately. "That's not what bothers me. It's . . . well, you know Meg. Do you really think the Whittenboro clan is going to stand for her being their Barclay's steady date? I'm afraid she's in for a real fall."

Nafa nodded. "I understand what you're saying."

"She's a big girl," Sky said. "Why don't you let her lead her own life and face her own problems for a change?"

Vana felt her mouth drop open and her eyes widen.

"Are you trying to butt into my relationship with my sister?" she asked incredulously. "Does my contract with Bella entitle you to run my personal life, too?"

"Just a little friendly advice," Sky said in a maddening pat-on-the-head tone. "If you hadn't been so quick to attack and defend her that night at the gala, she and Barclay would have had a chance to stand up for themselves against Danielle, and the whole thing might have been resolved then and there."

"Sure, you would have liked it if I'd stayed out of it at the gala, wouldn't you? That way you could have stepped in and smoothed everything over so your precious blue-blood buddies didn't have to be publicly embarrassed or scandalized in any way."

"Is that what you thought I was doing . . . protecting the Whittenboros?" Sky looked at her as though she were a mental patient predicting the end of the world.

"It was pretty obvious whose side Mr. Schuyler Ahrent Van Dusen of the grand old Vandy family of Manhattan was on. Too bad you're not a Third or a Fourth. That really helps with the one-upmanship, doesn't it?"

"You really think that? After knowing me?"

"What's to think? I was there. I saw and heard."

"You're way off base on that one. In the first place, I wouldn't give Danielle Whittenboro the time of day. In the second place, the Van Dusens are just barely above white trash in the eyes of the diehard blue-blood families. Those people aren't interested in anything except family trees that stretch back to the Mayflower and family money that hasn't had to be worked for since recorded time. No one in their right mind would lump me in with that set."

Vana smiled with false sweetness. "How sad for you. You don't get to be one of them. But you're still ready to lick their boots and butter them up whenever you can, I'll bet. It must be good for both business and social reasons, right?"

Sky shook his head. The line of his jaw was set and his eyes were narrowed and dark.

"You," he began in a slow, dangerously measured voice that made Nafa cringe visibly, "are a stubborn, hot-headed, bad-tempered, illogical and exasperating woman. And someone ought to teach you better manners at lunch."

He stood, threw his napkin down beside his plate, nodded a goodbye to Nafa and then stalked out.

"Hmm," Nafa muttered, "there's a brilliant idea that backfired."

"Was this all your idea, Nafa?" Vana demanded. "Or was he in on the surprise lunch, too?"

"I'm afraid I get all the credit for this one," Nafa admitted. "What a disaster, huh?"

"I could have told you that in the first place." Vana glared at her friend, then softened.

She couldn't be too angry at Nafa. She had learned to think of the woman as a close friend, in fact the closest friend she could remember having with the exception of Meg, and she knew that, whatever Nafa's reasoning, the woman had meant well.

Her friendship with Nafa had taught Vana that closeness meant not only caring but mutual trust, and the relationship had nurtured a wonderful secure feeling inside her. She had absolute faith in Nafa. She knew that the woman would never intentionally hurt or humiliate her and that any criticism expressed or mistakes made were in a spirit of concern.

Vana marveled at and cherished this relationship. She felt almost humbled by the responsibilities involved. Not only did it allow her to have absolute faith in another human being, it required her to offer Nafa the same things in return.

"You gonna attack me with a Sherman tank now, too?" Nafa asked lightly, but Vana could tell her friend was worried.

"No. Of course not. But what in the world possessed you to do this?"

Nafa gave a little derisive snort. "Too smart for my own good, I guess."

The woman toyed with her water glass a moment. "See, it's like I'm up on this mountain looking down on a lake and I can see you and Van Dusen both floundering around in the water and about to drown. And I'm not sure I'm seeing things right at first but then Jagger mentions something to me and Meg mentions something to me and Stephen starts babbling therapese to me on the subject, and the picture I'm seeing gets clearer and clearer."

Nafa drew in a deep breath as though about to take a plunge into the mythical lake herself. "And what I realize is that the reason you and Van Dusen won't save yourselves is that there's only one life preserver and you'd have to share it. But you're both so stubborn and hardheaded that you won't come to terms and work things out and take hold of the thing together—you'd both rather drown to prove your points. Or maybe it's that you'd both rather drown than concede. Either way I just got tired of watching you two spit and sputter and thrash around in circles sooo..." She shrugged. "I was just trying to jump in and give you both a little push."

"Cute story," Vana said sarcastically. "Have you ever thought of writing children's books?"

The waitress appeared with their coffee and Nafa's outrageous chocolate meringue confection with whipped heavy cream on the side. They were both grateful for the distraction as they went through the ritual of tasting and moaning and declaring it good enough to eat in a dark closet.

"See why I like this place?" Nafa asked with a grin. She took another slow, appreciative bite. "Sheer decadence. My greatest vice."

Vana laughed. She felt completely relaxed and unthreatened now. "I'm so glad I met you," she said spontaneously.

Nafa looked surprised and then momentarily flustered by emotion. "Damn, girl, are you just trying to sweet-talk me into giving up half of my dessert?"

Vana smiled and shook her head, then grew thoughtful and serious. Why not share her fears and problems with someone who cared about her? She always felt the need to hide her worries from her family, but she had no compulsion to protect Nafa from anything. She had no doubt that Nafa could handle hearing any emotional nonsense without upset or disapproval.

"I can't keep Sky out of my mind," Vana admitted with some difficulty.

Nafa stopped eating and signaled complete interest but didn't say anything to encourage her.

Vana fought down the familiar urge to close herself off and make a joke, and she searched for a place to begin, a way to express her jumbled thoughts.

"When I met Sky, he seemed so unbelievable, so much a man from my fantasies, so absolutely perfect. Then... I don't know...everything started going wrong. He believed all that awful stuff about me using him and trying to steal the contest—just like you did at first—and I was so hurt by it that I didn't even try very hard to convince him of the truth. The very fact that he had believed it without giving me a chance to explain was such a terrible blow for me.''

Vana shook her head and took a sip of coffee while she sorted through her thoughts. In telling Nafa this she was also confronting herself and forcing herself to understand her own motivations and actions for the first time.

''I began to see that he wasn't perfect, that he could make mistakes and be irrational and emotional at times, that he could misunderstand—that he was human instead of a fantasy. And I was disillusioned and angry as well as hurt. I had this growing feeling that he'd let me down, that he'd betrayed me—not only by accusing me wrongly, but also by not living up to my image of him.''

Nafa remained silent.

''Does that make sense?'' Vana asked hesitantly.

''Yes.'' Nafa said. ''But do you understand it yourself?''

''I think I do now. I didn't before, but I do now. That's why I was so upset with him at the gala, too. I didn't know how to cope with all the longing I was feeling for him. The need I felt for him was frightening. I mean, it seemed to be reaching inside me and twisting me up in spite of the fact that I'd decided he wasn't who or what I wanted. In spite of the fact that he could never love me. So when he jumped in to calm me down and defend the Whittenboros I seized on it. You know, more clear proof of his imperfection... another betrayal...more cause for anger and hurt.''

''And?'' Nafa urged.

''And, I guess I was eager to be mad at him, to find reasons to attack him, reasons to prove to myself that he wasn't a man I could love.''

''Why? Why did you want to prove that to yourself?''

''Because... To avoid the pain I guess. To convince myself that I could never accept his humanity and love him. To find reasons to hate him instead of love him because I know that he can never love me.''

"But why do you think he can never love you?'' Nafa pressed.

"I'm not quite sure—even though I know without a doubt that it's true. Maybe it's something to do with me not living up to his expectations. I didn't measure up for him in the beginning . . . and I have to admit that one of the things that convinced me to take the Bella contract was the sneaky little hope that I would be made into someone sophisticated and perfect—someone Sky would be impressed with. I realize now that even in the middle of all the anger and rejection and hurt I was still thinking in terms of Sky.''

Vana smiled bitterly. "But it didn't work, you see. It doesn't matter what kind of veneer you put on me or how much polish. Sky still knows who I was and what I am underneath.''

Nafa shook her head and compressed her lips in a resigned look. "Lordy girl, you've convinced me. I won't be jumping in to help anymore. You're in way over my head. You two aren't in some little ole lake floundering around—you're smack in the middle of the ocean.''

"You think it's hopeless? Do you think I'll ever get over this and stop thinking about him?''

"Those are two distinctly different questions. As to the getting over him, I have no idea. As to the hopeless . . . Is what hopeless? Exactly what are you hoping for? A life with Sky? Or an end to the confusion?''

Vana stared down into her coffee a moment. "I don't know. I honestly don't know.''

Chapter Ten

This is so exciting!'' Meg squealed, bouncing on the seat as if she could make the car go faster.

Vana smiled at her antics, but kept most of her attention on the narrow road before her. The rental car was a big, sturdy sedan but even so it was drifting and jerking on the ridged gravel and sand road.

Early summer was kind to the Kansas farm country. The wheat and corn and hay crops thrived in the endless, flat fields. Berry vines and tiny wild plum bushes and wild grapes sprawled in a tangle in the ditches and along the fence rows, their spindly branches laden with fruit. Roses and lilacs bloomed in the farmyards and the Osage orange trees marking the sections and breaking the wind between fields were brilliant green and supple in the breeze.

After months in the city Vana had to admit to herself that the farm country had a certain appeal.

"Oh, look at the Hirschbergers' lambs!" Meg cried, and Vana looked out across a pasture dotted with late lambs, playing and jumping in the grass while the ewes quietly grazed. The lambs were cuter than she remembered lambs being.

Her heart picked up a little when she turned into the driveway to the farm. The white clapboard house was as pristine and spotless as always, but it looked so much smaller! She pulled the car up to the graveled circle in front of the barn to turn it around, and stopped in back of a shiny new silver Mercedes. She wondered if her mother had ever driven the car as Vana had intended, or whether it had become just another yard decoration like the plastic windmill with its whirling blades. The fancy Mercedes looked comical parked as it was on a dirt driveway and surrounded by scratching hens. A scruffy cat lazed in the sunshine on the car's hood.

"Is that the car you won?" Meg asked reverently.

Vana's yes was drowned out by the screeching and banging of the old porch door as Kate burst from the house to greet them.

"Well, I'll be," Kate muttered several times as she stood and watched Vana get out of the sedan.

Vana pulled her into a hug, then Meg descended and they all hugged together.

Vana unloaded their luggage from the trunk and Meg grabbed a handful and rushed into the house. Everything looked so different, Vana thought, sweeping the fields and pens and outbuildings with a searching gaze.

"Don't just stand there," Kate chided. She smoothed her print apron and stiffened her spine and turned toward the door. "Come on in now."

Kate had never likeed the out-of-doors. She had never understood the girls' obsession with riding horses out in the weather, and she probably wouldn't understand Vana's interest in the barns and pastures now.

Vana slammed the trunk, gathered the remaining suitcases and followed her mother and sister into the house. Baskets of new potatoes and onions and unshelled peas lined the enclosed porch. She stepped into the kitchen, fragrant with the aroma of roasting meat, and she had to grin. Everything was just as it had been! Mama had not changed anything in her kitchen by so much as a fraction of an inch.

"What's so funny?" Kate asked suspiciously. "Not good enough for ya anymore?"

"No. No, Mama," Vana assured her. "Just the opposite. It feels so good. You haven't changed anything."

"Why should I?" Kate huffed. "Haven't had a notion to change nothin' around this place for forty years. Why would I start now?"

"Since we're gone now, Mama," Meg teased, "and you have all this extra room, Vana thought you'd probably made some changes...you know...pool table in the living room, component stereo and big screen television in our old bedroom, sauna and whirlpool in the attic."

Kate blinked her eyes in confusion, then reached over to swat Meg with a dishtowel. "If I was gonna do all that, the first thing I'd get me was one a them alarm detectors. Only, 'stead of fire, I'd get it to detect when you girls was pullin' my leg."

Vana sat down at the kitchen table. She still remembered when her mother had so proudly ordered the chrome and Formica replacement for the scarred old wooden hulk of a table that Heinrich had repaired and repaired through the years. Kate had declared reverently at the time that the table was the largest catalog order she'd ever placed in her life.

No sooner had Vana seated herself than Kate plunked a huge glass of iced tea down in front of her.

"How 'bout a cookie or some chips maybe?" Kate asked.

"Now Mama, I won't have you waiting on me while I'm here," Vana insisted.

Kate frowned and tugged at her apron.

"You can wait on me," Meg quipped as she raided the snack cupboard.

After several minutes of persuasion Kate was finally convinced to sit down at the table and join them instead of hovering like a maid on duty. She sat down stiffly, pulling up a chair and folding her gnarled hands primly on the worn mint-green Formica.

"Wait till you see this, Mama." Meg's eyes shone with excitement as she bent over to fish in her carry-on bag. She produced a glossy fashion magazine and flipped through it hurriedly.

"Oh, Meg," Vana said self-consciously. "Can't it wait?"

"Nope." Meg had the magazine open but was holding it so her mother couldn't see the page. "Close your eyes, Mama," she ordered.

Kate sighed and obediently closed her eyes. Meg laid the open magazine on the table in front of her.

"These just came out, Mama! The first ones..."

Kate opened her eyes and gasped. She clutched one hand to her bosom and reached out hesitantly to touch the glossy page before her.

The first ads had come out nicely, Vana thought. And it wasn't that she was ashamed of them in any way. But seeing herself there—and especially seeing someone else seeing her there—all made up and posed in living color just like she was somebody glamorous, made her very uncomfortable.

"Holy Mother..." Kate muttered as though suffering shock.

"Pretty exciting, huh, Mama?" Meg asked.

Kate shook her head. "A beauty. A movie star," she said in a voice heavy with sadness.

"What's wrong, Mama? Don't you like the picture?" Vana asked in alarm. "Is the dress too low cut? Do I look too conceited?"

Kate looked across at her with moistened eyes. "The picture is beautiful, Daughter...and you're beautiful sitting here in my kitchen. And so...so grand. I barely knew ya when ya drove in. You're a butterfly come out of the cocoon, that's what you are, and I feel as stupid and blind as a post for not seein' that butterfly was in there all along."

"Anybody'd be beautiful if they had all the work done on 'em that Vana's had," Meg said with a sniff. The twinge of jealousy in her voice was unmistakable.

"Shush now, Margaret. That's uncalled for," Kate scolded.

"Well, it's true." Meg pouted. "They just started from scratch and spent a zillion dollars and redid everything. Right, Vana?"

"Margaret, I'm tellin' you..." Kate warned.

Meg's face screwed up and she jumped from her chair and slammed out of the room.

"Well, sorta' appears things are back to normal already," Kate remarked dryly.

"She's afraid you'll love me better now," Vana said softly.

Kate sighed and shook her head. "Gracious me, what a trial that child's always been."

"I don't think I'd mention that," Vana cautioned. "About her always having been a trial. She's a little touchy on that subject, too."

Kate eyed Vana suspiciously. "Whatda' you two been comparin' troubles and talkin' bout what a bad mama I been to ya?"

"No, not at all, Mama. Just the opposite, in fact. We always talk about what a good mama you were... even when things were rough."

"Yeah, it was hard sometimes bein' a good mama to you girls and pleasin' Heinrich at the same time."

"If our real father had lived—" Vana began.

"No..." Kate blew air through her nose as though almost amused at the idea. "Your real papa was cut from the same cloth. A different load of troubles on his mind, but not much difference in the way he treated me or you two babies. Men's men, ya know."

Vana was startled by the revelation. "Well, I—I mean you never talked about our real papa, but I've just always assumed..."

"Nah, he weren't no better. No worse, but no better...just different. I was sorry to see Seamus Dennehy pass on so young, a course, but mostly I was sorry cause it was pert near impossible for a woman alone to survive with two babies back then."

Vana was amazed at the way her mother was suddenly opening up and discussing the past without evasion. "You never told me any of this, Mama."

"You're a grown-up now, it's plain. No reason to be sugarin' up the facts anymore, is there?"

"I didn't realize you ever had," Vana said.

"Humph, just wait'll you have kids," she said knowingly.

"Tell me the unsugared version of why you married Papa, then, if you're ready to."

"Not much to tell. I had two babies and was livin' on my brother's good graces and takin' in ironing to earn what I could. Heinrich came to town on some sort of farm business. It was the first time he'd been more'n fifty miles from his home in his life. He came by my brother's place to look at some dairy stock and he stayed to dinner. He wrote to me regular for about six months, then he came and got me and we married."

"But why?" Vana pressed. "That doesn't tell my why."

"Like I said, I couldn't make it on my own and my brother's patience was wearin' thin. I never came across much for eligible men, living out on my brother's farm like that, and when Heinrich's eyes kept sliding down the dinner table toward me I saw my chance right off. His family didn't consider me much of a catch, but they'd adopted him to help work the farm after his brothers had all got big enough to leave home, and so he wasn't really blood kin—not really one of them, ya see. That's pretty much the reason he hadn't hooked up with a local girl before then, most folks probably were afraid that he wouldn't inherit none of his family's ground or be given a start if he married, so they kept their daughters away from him. Anyway, the Linniers finally came around.''

She frowned in thought a moment. ''They weren't too generous about settin' us up with any ground of our own, though. Just kind of loaned Heinrich patches. I got my own house out of the bargain, though—in my time a woman couldn't ask for much more.''

Vana shook her head. ''I'm sorry you had it so rough, Mama. And I'm sure glad that times are different now.''

''Humph,'' Kate snorted. ''Not so different as you might figure. I kinda' keep track a my neighbors hereabouts and their kids who are marryin' and settlin' down. Men are still men, that's for sure. A woman still doesn't have no say over her life once she marries unless she has money of her own—unless she's built something for herself before she ties that knot. Only way a wife can talk back to her husband is if she has the money to walk away anytime she pleases.''

''Things change slowly in some places, I guess. But I don't think every place in Kansas is like Zeck...and I know some real nice city men.''

''Don't you bet on it. They may act different but then maybe they're just cagier while they're courting.''

''I've been thinking a lot about being in love and what it all means,'' Vana offered hesitantly.

''Just don't go getting any ideas you want to get married,'' Kate cautioned.

''But why? I should be safe. I've earned enough money and success to be able to walk out anytime I please.''

''That's just it . . . you've gone too far. No man worth his salt is gonna be interested in you. He'd never be able to hold his head up knowin' how famous and successful you were. It would belittle him, cause folks to doubt his manhood.''

''You're probably right, Mama.'' Vana smiled.

''Maybe somethin'll happen and you'll lose your job modeling,'' Kate said as though the thought might be consoling.

The thought occurred to Vana that she was indeed a grown-up. The proof had just transpired. She had suddenly seen that her mama's advice wasn't always worth a hoot, and she felt that their roles were curiously reversed for the moment. She was listening to her mother like an indulgent parent would listen to an adored child.

"So I can't make heads or tails, Mama, about whether you think being married is good or bad in the long run."

"No good or bad to it. Just somethin' nature does to a woman when she's young. Makes her want a home and another live person to share it, and makes her start thinking babies."

"Something nature does to a woman but not to a man?" Vana asked.

"Ummm, I suppose to a man, too. But the wantin' wears off the men real soon and they start bein' grouchy and resentful. I think they get to feelin' nature cheated 'em somehow by tricking 'em into marryin' and saddling 'em with troubles."

This new mother-daughter honesty inspired Vana to open up a little herself. "I've got a man on my mind, Mama. And I can't get him out. But I can't seem to get along with him at all. How do you explain that?"

"It's that nature workin'," Kate said. "She's a tricky old gal. Trick folks into all sorts of mischief."

"Maybe so." Vana laughed.

"I've got a man on my mind too, Mama." Meg stood in the doorway sheepishly. "Fact is, I think I'm really in love. His name's Barkie Whittenboro and he's the smartest man I've ever met."

Vana winced but kept silent.

"He's so wonderful."

"Well, I hope you're watchin' yourself in that city, daughter," Kate said, then added, "I hope Vana is keepin' you out of trouble."

"I don't need Vana to keep me out of trouble," Meg retorted.

"She's a big girl," Vana put in quickly.

"Bein' big don't mean nothin'," Kate declared. "Now what happened with all those barrel-racin' have-to's of yours and the hair fixin' you spent so much time learnin'? You been flittin' around from one thing to the next and now there you are livin' off your sister."

"Mama!" Vana cried.

But instead of dissolving, Meg's face went into a determined scowl. "Well maybe I won't need Vana for much longer. Maybe I'll just get married!"

Kate shook her head in resignation. "You just won't never learn, will ya, Margaret?"

Meg ignored the comment. She obviously had something else she was wanting to say.

"Aren't you gonna ask me about my boyfriend?" she prompted.

"Ask you what?" Kate said.

"Ask me what he's like and how he looks, you know."

"All right. Tell me about him."

"You're gonna meet him! It's a surprise. He's flying in for a couple of days to meet you and see the farm."

"Oh. Real nice." Kate looked suddenly nervous. "You don't reckon he'll be put off by farm life do ya? I mean, bein' a city boy and all he might think this was all pretty shabby and poor out here."

"Oh, no, Mama. He's not like that at all. You're gonna love him."

Vana groaned inwardly and a little seed of dread began to form in the pit of her stomach.

The visit settled quickly into a quiet, restful routine. They cooked, they gardened and they visited about unimportant things. Kate's new blunt honesty was put back on the shelf and she became her old evasive self. Vana kept away from discussing personal problems just as she always had. And Meg entertained and irritated and inspired them.

The party was scheduled for the third day of the visit, on Kate's birthday. That morning they drove the four miles into the town of Zeckendorf for groceries and a few last-minute gifts for one another.

Vana strolled down the sidewalk of Zeck's four-block downtown area with a sense of something akin to disbelief. Had she really invested so much emotional energy in worrying whether the people in this town liked her or not? Had she really been crushed when no one asked her to the annual street dance or the prom? Had she really let the disapproval of this severe and suffocating little place make her miserable?

"Let's go to the soda fountain for a cherry limeade," she suggested and Meg eagerly agreed.

They lined up at the fountain on the high swivel bar stools and watched as the counter girl squeezed limes and mixed cherry syrup with carbonated water from the spigot.

"This is something I haven't found in New York," Meg announced as she sipped at her drink.

"Well it sure ain't no reason to move back," Kate countered gruffly.

"When are you coming to New York for a visit?" Vana asked. "I'm anxious to show you the things they do have."

"I don't know about me flyin' all the way to New York," Kate said doubtfully.

"Mama, come on! Flying is nothing. It's like sitting in your own living room with a bunch of company over and some waitresses bringing you snacks," Meg said.

"It ain't the flyin'...though I ain't too keen on that neither. I just figure I'm here where I belong and I oughta stay here."

"Mama! You hate it here in Zeck. You told me once you still felt like you were visiting after twenty years of living here," Vana reminded her. "I was thinking you might even want to move one of these days," she added tentatively.

"I never said I liked it here," Kate bristled. "I said I belong here. It's the spot where I fit. The town where I was raised is all changed, and my brother and his wife have moved off their farm to some fancy retirement getup. Where else would I go? I never had much for an education and I can't talk fancy or write or spell good—city folks would think I was a fool. So where would I go?''

Before Vana could answer a small group of teenaged girls came giggling in to order milkshakes. They all stared at the three Linnier women and then one screamed, "It *is* you! You're the lady in the magazine!" She had a copy of the new fashion issue under her arm.

All the girls erupted into squeals as she thumbed open her book and insisted on Vana autographing it.

"Oh, God, you're so beautiful," one of the girls gushed.

"What are you doing *here*?" another one asked.

"I used to live here," Vana answered.

"You're kidding!" they exclaimed in unison.

"She used to go to the same school you go to and come to this same soda fountain and after she graduated she used to work right over there at the bank. She was nothin' but a teller in the Zeck bank for years," Meg announced smugly.

The girls all stared out the window at the beige brick bank and then back at Vana in disbelief. Vana nodded as though to confirm the truth of it.

Vana started to say something to the girls about how she had gotten lucky, but that being out in the world had made her see how the only thing that had ever kept her in Zeckendorf was herself, and that they could do things with their lives, too, and that just because they were born in Zeck didn't mean they had to feel the rest of the world was closed to them.... But before she could put it all into words Meg cut in.

"So, see," Meg said. "She's just like you. Only difference is she got lucky and won this big contest. It could have happened to any of us. If you girls were old enough, it could have happened to you and all those beauty experts would have taken you to New York and made you into somebody gorgeous. They can do it to anybody, ya know."

The girls gave one another pointed looks as if to ask if Meg was for real.

"Bet you've seen some of my awards in the lobby trophy case there at the high school," Meg said as though she was shy about the idea but being forced to discuss it. "I won more titles than any girl in the county ever had. That record's still unbroken today."

The girls looked blank. "We don't ever look at that trophy case," one of them finally said.

"Well I used to cut hair here, too... right up to less than a year ago. I was the first hairdresser to do blow-drys in Zeck. Before me you had to drive over to Halsey to get a blow-dry," Meg announced proudly.

"Oh yeah," one of the girls said with dawning recognition. "I think you used to cut my mother's hair."

The milkshakes were finished and lined up on the counter in to-go cups. The girls scooped them up and left in a giggling rush.

"What can you expect?" Meg said as they left. "What a bunch of airheads."

"Remind me of you when you was that age, Margaret," Kate said matter-of-factly.

Vana suppressed a laugh and rubbed her folded paper napkin across her mouth to camouflage the grin that was trying to surface.

"Oh, Mama, you can't be serious," Meg wailed.

"Don't let this place get to you, Meg," Vana said. "We're both past this town now. You don't have to prove anything in this place anymore, and neither do I."

"That's easy for you to say, Miss Famous. But what have I got to hold up when I'm thumbing my nose?"

"So stop driftin' around like a dust mote and settle yerself into somethin'," Kate ordered unsympathetically.

"Mama, why are you bein' so mean to me all of a sudden?" Meg pouted.

"Cause it finally hit me that I always babied you along because I feared you was too fragile to make it on your own, but, could be the reason you stayed so fragile was that I babied you along the whole way. You bein' gone and then comin' back kinda' showed me the other side a the cow. Started me thinkin' if you was tough enough to behave so damn ornery and jealous-hearted and selfish, then you was prob'ly tough enough to take bein' treated like regular folks. Might do you some good . . . though I kinda' doubt it at this point.''

Kate grinned and picked up her glass. "Or could be I'm just gettin' old and I'm takin' advantage of not havin' no man around expectin' a shut mouth from me. Speakin' my mind to folks is beginning to feel pretty darn good.''

Kate took a long drink as if the speech had made her thirsty. Meg stared at her mother as if suffering major shock.

"What say we move along?'' Vana suggested to smooth things over. "There are things I want to get for the party and Zeckendorf Dry Goods is calling to me.''

Covering the four blocks of Zeckendorf made Vana feel stronger than she had ever felt. She was truly beyond all this, and the prejudices and strictures of this tiny old world community couldn't touch her at all anymore. It was no longer threatening or a source of irritation or disgust or anger or misery. It simply didn't matter.

She could see the town for what it was now. It was inherently neither good nor bad. Neither idyllic nor terrible. It was simply a place where there was one set of rules, one pattern of accepted behavior, and any person who wasn't happy living by those rules or conforming to that behavior would not be nurtured or warmed.

Now that the place no longer evoked an emotional response, she suddenly realized that the town was like an organism fighting for its life. Zeckendorf had been founded as a small German farming community, and it had thrived for generations with the collective values and rules the early settlers brought. The town was besieged on all sides now with the ideas and problems of a changing world, and it was trying to cling to the old ways and ignore the encroaching steamroller of progress in a desperate bid for survival. Zeckendorf had become obsolete and irrelevant—not only to Vana, but to the modern world.

She looked around and was engulfed in a wave of sympathy. Zeckendorf was dying. Its brightest young people were leaving. Its businesses were drying up. The grain elevators and railroad loading platforms—once the very heart of the town—stood like abandoned skeletons. What had been for generations a bustling center of life, now consisted of a small bank, a dry goods store, a beauty and barber shop, a gas station with a Coke machine, a small grocery, a café, a hardware and drug store combination, a domino parlor and a four-page weekly newspaper.

There were surrounding small towns, towns within a radius of fifty miles, that were healthy and well. But they were places where change had been allowed and welcomed; places where the young were encouraged to dream and the outside world was acknowledged; places where prejudice and fear and narrow-mindedness hadn't been allowed to cripple the community. As they got back in the car to go home Vana noticed that the newspaper office was boarded up.

"What happened to the *Zeckendorf Record*?" she asked with a feeling close to dismay.

"It folded," Kate said. "So many folks got to readin' the *Halsey Independent* that they just folded."

When they returned to the old farmhouse it felt different again to Vana. It felt like a haven now. Someplace warm and good, safe from the despair of the doomed town. As the girls fussed over dinner, forcing Kate to sit in a chair and watch for a change, and then went through the ritual of candles and singing and multilayered German chocolate cake from scratch, Vana felt a new certainty growing inside her.

The reason this felt like a haven had nothing to do with the familiar clapboard house or the tattered furniture. It had to do with the people and the giving and taking. She suddenly knew that she wanted more than those vague ephemeral dreams she'd treasured. She wanted something real to hang onto. She wanted a family; she needed warmth and love and caring to flow through her life. Her airy dreams were wonderful, but she needed solid ground beneath her to survive.

She lay awake that night, warmed by thoughts of their party and spinning through all the new feelings and ideas she was having. She felt a sense of wonder at her human capacity to change and grow, and through the dark hours she groped through her past with her eyes wide open, trying to fully shape a new understanding. She didn't fall asleep until dawn.

She woke to the sound of voices. A lively conversation was apparently taking place out in the kitchen. She couldn't make out words or specifics but she could hear both male and female voices. She rubbed her eyes and looked at the clock. Noon! Her sleepless night had caused her to doze half the day away.

She splashed her face with cold water, brushed her teeth and ran a brush hastily through her hair. Men in the kitchen, she grumbled to herself as she pulled on jeans and an old T-shirt. Probably the mailman or the road grader or a neighbor had stopped by and was jawing at the kitchen table so now she had to get dressed instead of being able to slouch out in her robe for coffee.

She felt cross and grouchy as she always did when her sleeping patterns were off. But she needed coffee and if the mailman or whoever it was didn't like her scowling face, that was too bad. She picked up her shoes, changed her mind and threw them back down and marched through the living room and into the kitchen.

She stopped dead inside the kitchen door and stared at the cluster of people seated at the table.

"Surprise!" Meg called gaily.

"Surprise!" Barclay echoed from beside Meg.

"Good morning," said Schuyler Van Dusen quietly.

"Coffee?" Kate asked, but she bustled over to the stove for the pot without waiting for an answer.

"Isn't this exciting!" Meg wiggled in her chair. "Barkie missed me so much he came a day early."

Barclay grinned and blinked a few times behind his glasses. He had on a brand-new, starched chambray shirt that looked as if it had been hand tailored for him on Madison Avenue.

"Close your mouth and sit, Vana," Kate ordered, plunking a cup of hot coffee down on the table.

Vana slid into a chair mechanically. She turned to stare at Sky who was in her mother's kitchen, sitting in her mother's chair and resting his elbows on her mother's Formica table just as if he belonged there.

"What the hell are you doing here?" she demanded.

"Now, Vana," Kate chided, "drink your coffee before it chills and don't cuss in my house."

Vana obeyed by instinct, sipping at the steaming liquid but keeping her glare trained on him over the top of the cup.

"That was...kind of an extra surprise," Meg said. "Since Barkie was coming we thought it would be fun if Sky got to see the farm and meet Mama and..." Meg's voice trailed off and she smiled weakly.

He was wearing an old denim shirt, soft and faded from hundreds of washings. His eyes looked tired but intensely blue, and there was a faint stubble on his face. He looked very sexy in an earthy way and that added to her anger. She knew she looked terrible.

"We would have cleaned up," he said, "but the bathroom was so close to where you were sleeping...we didn't want to wake you."

"How thoughtful," Vana said sarcastically.

His eyes were on her. She knew he was taking in her swollen eyes and her barely combed hair.

"How dare you come here!" Her anger and outrage exploded. "This is *my* home. Just get out and go right back to New York where you belong!"

"No daughter o' mine is rude to company in my kitchen!" Kate declared fiercely. "If you wanna yell and cuss go out to the barn."

"All right!" Vana jumped from her chair so fast she banged her shin on the table leg. She hopped on one foot, massaging the hurt and clamping her lips together to keep from swearing again.

Sky stood and crossed the room to open the door and hold it for her as she hobbled out. The action sent her right to the boiling point.

Once outside, he reached for her arm as if to render assistance. She jerked free and struck out across the lot in a determined, forceful stride to prove she didn't need it. Her shin throbbed insistently. She swung her arms and drew in deep aggressive breaths through her nose and blew them out forcefully through her mouth. By the time she reached the barn the throbbing had diminished but the anger had not.

He followed her into the cool, hay-filled structure and she spun to face him.

"So you couldn't leave it be! You had to come all the way to Kansas to prove what a joke I was, to laugh at my home and my mother and—"

"No!" Sky protested. "That's not why I came."

"Why, then?" she shouted.

The words echoed in the huge old barn, disturbing the swallows high up in the rafters; they fluttered, leaving their perches to dip and soar through the still air.

Sky was startled by the birds. He jumped back, then tilted his head to follow their flight with an expression of alarm.

"They're just barn swallows," Vana said contemptuously.

Sky looked at her helplessly a moment, then rubbed a hand across his face. He looked exhausted.

"I wanted to," he said simply.

"And everything Schuyler Van Dusen wants, he gets. Is that it?"

He turned to a bale of wheat straw and sat down. "Will you stop it, Vana?" he said in a worn voice. "I know you. I know about your temper and about how you attack whenever you feel threatened. And I know you have this wealth of emotion stirring around inside you...emotion that I think confuses and frightens you."

Vana sank down on a bale several feet from his and stared at him mutely. She wanted to yell at him again but she couldn't think of any specific words. There was a strange burning behind her eyes and her throat felt tight and blocked.

"In many ways we're alike, Vana," he said softly. His lips curved briefly into the barest of smiles. "It took me time to realize that, but it's true. Maybe that's why you seemed so familiar to me the moment I met you. It was like meeting myself ten or fifteen years ago."

The silence of the barn settled around them. The swallows had flown out into the sunshine and the few hens that had been scratching on the straw-covered earthen floor had moved outside, too. The shafts of sunlight piercing through the cracks and chinks in the old wood of the roof were filled with golden, floating specks and Vana was overcome by fleeting images from childhood. She had always hidden in this barn, in the secret places where the stacked bales didn't come together and pockets and caves were accidentally formed.

She had spent hours reading here or watching the floating dust dance and settle in the sunlight or staring up at the nesting swallows. The barn had been her hiding place, her refuge, her escape whenever something hurt too bad or someone came too close to breaking in on her private self.

Now here she was feeling like she wanted to run and hide from Sky's words and his probing eyes and his gentle voice, but he was sitting here in *her* barn and she had no place else to go.

"What do you want?" she asked, and she hated the weakness in her own voice.

"I want to be friends." He studied his hands a moment and then looked back up at her. "I can't afford to lose you as a friend."

"Can't afford to?" His choice of words seemed strange.

"Yes. I'm a very important person. I have scores of business associates with whom I have professional relationships, and I have social acquaintances with whom I maintain a polite civility, but I have almost no real friends. I am protective of my mother and stepsister and indulgent toward my father but I am not able to be friendly or sharing with my family, either."

He paused for a moment and she had the urge to reach out for his hand.

"I'm not an easy person to be close to or understand...like you...and it's cost me. It cost me a wife. It's cost me extraordinary loneliness. When I was younger—" that bare suggestion of a smile touched his mouth again "—being alone didn't matter. I saw it as independence and was proud of myself for it.

"But I've had a lot of solitary years and it doesn't feel good anymore. I feel...disconnected somehow, like an outcast or a lost soul rather than a free spirit. I want people in my life. I want—" he shook his head and held his hands up "—I don't know...communication, I guess. Real communication.

"I think that's possible between the two of us. I think we're, I don't know, kindred spirits or karma sharers or reincarnated identical twins...." He chuckled self-consciously.

"We seem to have totally blitzed the romance angle, but can't we try to start again as friends? I'm damn well in need of a friend and it wouldn't hurt you to have one, either."

Vana swallowed hard against the threat in her throat and blinked to clear her eyes.

"All right," she said gruffly. "I suppose it wouldn't hurt to have a friend. But that involves more give-and-take than just professional courtesy, you know."

"I know." He stood and moved to stand directly in front of her. Hesitantly she rose to face him. He held out his hand. Slowly she extended hers. The handshake felt as solemn and binding as a vow.

He drew in a deep breath, tilted his head back to look up and then around. "Sooo..." he said, with almost comical nervousness, "this thing sure holds a lot of hay, doesn't it?"

"Yes," she agreed, yielding reluctantly to the smile that tugged at the set line of her mouth. "Not quite as much as the Astrodome though."

Chapter Eleven

The three days that Sky and Barclay stayed on the farm went quickly. With Meg as ringleader, they explored the fields and pastures and the town of Zeckendorf. Barclay and Sky learned how to gather eggs and feed chickens and milk cows and work the vegetable garden, and Meg engineered field trips to the neighbors so the men could see the lambs and tour the shearing barns.

Vana enjoyed the fun but remained watchful. Slowly, her bad feelings toward Sky were dissolving. His fall in the creek and his battle with a mad hen over an egg and his skin-of-the-teeth escape up a tree when an angry sow saw him as a threat to her litter, all made her roar with laughter. He took the lumps and the laughter good-naturedly, he joined in to laugh at himself and, one by one, the walls between them melted away.

He was making himself completely vulnerable, exposing himself to ridicule, showing the human being beneath the untouchable Schuyler Van Dusen facade and Vana couldn't help but respond. By the third night when Meg had an elaborate going-away dinner scheduled for the men, Vana found herself joining in the festivities with wholehearted enthusiasm and being genuinely disappointed at the thought of Sky's leaving early the next morning.

"Dah-daah!" Barclay trumpeted as he and Sky placed the dessert on the table. They had agreed to the idea of Meg and Vana cooking dinner only with the condition that the men would furnish a surprise dessert.

"Crème brulée for the lovely ladies," Sky said with a courtly bow.

"Looks like some kind of custard to me," Kate said.

"You're right," Sky agreed good-naturedly. "It's nothing but a fancy name for custard."

They all tasted and complimented and kidded one another about various events during the past three days.

"It went too fast," Barclay said wistfully. "When I was little I used to dream of living on a farm like this."

Vana, Meg and Kate all groaned at the same time and everyone burst into laughter.

"There's times even now when I wish I could just move right on into town," Kate said. "When those big clumsy Linnier boys swarm all over here to plant or bale . . . what a darned ruckus!"

"Linnier boys?" Sky asked.

"Guess they'd be my nephews if anybody cared to figure that out," Kate said.

"Papa's family never gave him title to this farm," Vana explained. "Being adopted, he wasn't a full-fledged family member in their eyes so they didn't ever let him actually own or inherit any of the family ground like they did his brothers. The Linniers have a lot of land in these parts and they've always gone to great lengths to keep it 'in the family,' so to speak."

"And now after all these years, this farm doesn't belong to Mama at all," Meg put in bitterly. "They let her live in the house, but it belongs to all of them. And I don't think it had anything to do with Papa being adopted. I think it was because he adopted us and then never had any children of his own. They hated us! They were afraid we'd end up with it.''

"It's most likely due to the fact that Heinrich never had sons mor'n anything else," Kate corrected. "They never have let a girl inherit, 'cause soon as she marries she ain't a Linnier anymore. They prob'ly figured since Heinrich had no sons to pass it on to he shouldn't get hold of it in the first place.''

"Anyway, they cheated Mama out of having anything once Papa died. They claimed everything of value belonged to them and they'd just been loaning it to Papa,'' Meg said.

"What's the difference?" Kate asked. "I'm not wantin' for anything. Specially now, with Vana tryin' to give me things right and left.''

"It's the principle, Mama," Meg said, but her huffy attitude seemed more a result of Kate's mentioning Vana's generosity.

"Well if it's principle you're talkin', then look at it this way. This has been Linnier ground for four generations. Don't mean nothin' to you girls and me, but it means a lot to them folk. Once Heinrich was dead we prob'ly woulda' sold the whole caboodle if we coulda', just like they feared we'd do. So they was smart to do what they did. And they say I can live in this house till I die. And I got the trust to fall back on...so stop all this complainin', 'cause I'm doin' just dandy.''

"The trust is what galls me." Vana couldn't keep from saying it even though she knew Kate wanted the subject dropped.

"Yeah," Meg chimed in. "Papa putting all his assets into a trust so after he was dead you still couldn't have any say over anything—it's like he can still boss you around even after he's dead!''

"She has to ask permission to use money from the trust or sell anything of Papa's that hasn't already been sold," Vana explained to Sky and Barclay. "And the trustee is one of the Linnier brothers, a hard-nosed old coot who thinks buying anything but the bare essentials is a sin."

"Gads!" Barclay exclaimed loudly. "This all sounds as bad as my family! And here I thought farm life was so simple and idyllic."

"Would you mind if I had one of my lawyers look into the trust?" Sky asked. "I know nothing about that sort of thing but maybe there's a way to change trustees or—"

"I can help Mama with her business," Vana said firmly, dismissing his offer. The thought of Sky having such a definite connection to her mother was unsettling. "You can just tell that old goat to go to hell," she instructed her mother. "'Cause I've got money enough for us all now anyway."

"Vanessa! Watch your language," Kate ordered. Then she started to chuckle. "You shoulda seen his face when he drove by and saw that fancy silver car they delivered sittin' in the drive. He blew in here like a tornado thinkin' I'd somehow got hold of everything and gone wild over a car." She chuckled again at the memory. "Seein' him all red and puffed up like that was even better when I told him just to load Sassy up and take her as he went."

"Sassy?" Meg asked.

"Yeah, the Linniers give me one a their prize-winnin' milk goats just before that fancy car came. Old Sassy took a real shine to that car right off and wanted to sleep on it nights and play mountain goat on it days. Her climbin' on that car was the excuse I needed to pack her right back to her happy home."

Vana and Meg looked at one another and burst into laughter.

"Mama hates goats!" They laughed in unison. "And the Linniers keep trying to give 'em to her."

"Remember that one you shot with the rock salt so many times she was bald?" Meg said.

"And no matter how many times you shot her she still ate all your roses," Vana added.

"And the bark off the trees and the siding off the well house and the little flag you put out for Memorial Day," Meg finished.

"Yup." Kate frowned. "Had a heck of a time findin' an excuse to give that one back. Them Linniers don't set much stock by roses or yard trees or flags."

"I always thought goats were so cute," Sky said. The three women groaned and Vana reached out to box his arm lightly.

The phone rang and Vana answered. It was Arthur raving about a special project and insisting that he needed to talk to Sky immediately.

"Something big has come up," Sky said apologetically after he'd hung up and turned back to the group. He didn't sit back down at the table and Vana felt a twinge of disappointment. She knew that he was leaving before he said a word.

"I need to be in New York first thing in the morning for an important meeting, so Arthur had arranged for a private jet to fly me back tonight."

The three women voiced varying expressions of regret and Kate insisted that he visit again soon, with or without Vana and Meg.

"You're welcome to ride along, Barclay," Sky offered.

Barclay tugged at his collar and blinked and looked over at Meg.

"Oh no," Meg cried. "He's staying until that flight at noon tomorrow, like he planned."

Kate stood, announcing that she was going to pack Sky a snack box to take with him on the flight and then she muttered something about the way young people seemed to jump around and change their minds and travel at the drop of a hat.

"Oh no," Sky told her playfully. "We think about going places for days usually. Take Vana there...." He grinned and Vana knew by the look in his eyes that something was up. "She's got five whole days to get ready for her trip to Rome."

"Rome!" Meg screamed.

"Rome?" Vana whispered.

"Rome?" Kate mouthed.

"In Italy?" Vana asked reverently.

"Where the Pope's at?" Kate asked, but it wasn't really a question so much as an expression of disbelief.

"That's what the call was about," Sky explained. "I didn't want to mention it until it was a certainty, but now we're all set and the meeting tomorrow morning is just a formality. We're taking a crew to Rome to shoot on location, and we're launching a whole series tracing Bella's roots in Rome and the struggles in bringing it to America."

"Rome," Kate breathed. "One of my girls is going to see the Pope."

"What if he's not home, Mama?" Meg teased.

Long after Sky had tucked the king-size snack box under his arm and hurried away, Meg and Barclay had disappeared out into the warm night and Kate and she had both turned in, the name echoed with wonder through Vana's mind.

Rome. Such a short time ago she'd thought driving a hundred miles from Zeckendorf was fulfillment. Then she'd gotten a taste of travel on the rodeo circuit, and Houston, Texas had seemed like a dream come true. Then there was New York, the unattainable city of her fantasies, to savor. Now Rome? She had surely fallen into the pages of a storybook.

And Sky had said "we": "we're taking a crew...we're all set...we're launching." Did that mean Sky would be there to see Rome with her?

Two days later, when they'd extracted a promise of a visit from Kate and assured her that they'd be back to see her often, too, Vana and Meg drove away from the farm, headed toward the airport and their return flight to New York. Vana felt a twinge of sadness as they pulled away.

"You know, I never thought I'd see the day when I felt bad about leaving this place," she told Meg.

Meg continued her primping in the rental's visor makeup mirror and didn't bother to comment. In fact Meg was strangely quiet the whole way to the airport and throughout the boarding process.

Once seated Meg didn't accept the magazine the flight attendant offered, and she continued her unusual silence, staring vacantly as if she were troubled by something.

"What's wrong?" Vana finally asked. "I've never seen you so quiet."

Meg turned to look at her as though suddenly waking up to her surroundings. "I'm worried about a lotta' stuff," she admitted.

"Did Barclay say or do something upsetting to you?" Vana asked, immediately jumping to conclusions.

"No. Why, should he have?" Meg unfastened her seat belt and turned her body toward Vana. The middle seat in their row of three was unoccupied, and she pushed up the armrests to open the space between them. "It's ... Well, I can't figure out what to do with myself. I mean, if I don't care about being a famous barrel racer anymore, what do I want to be? An actress maybe, or a singer?"

"What brought this on so suddenly?"

"It's not that sudden. It's been kinda' nagging at me ever since I realized I didn't want to go back to the rodeo circuit. I always wanted to be a barrel racer—it's even in the school yearbook that my dream was to be a barrel racer— but I know now that it's not really the life for me. So what's my dream now? What great thing do I want to be?"

Vana considered how to reply. She'd been the one who'd always encouraged Meg to have a grand dream. She had expected it of Meg, she supposed. Because she so treasured the dreams that had always danced secretly in her own head, she had just naturally assumed Meg thrived on dreams, too.

But lately she'd begun to realize how different she and Meg were, and how much she'd misread her sister through the years. Maybe her assumption that Meg was fueled by motivations identical to her own was one of the expectations she'd had of Meg that she shouldn't have. Maybe she had unknowingly pushed Meg into creating and striving for goals that were not that important to her own happiness or self-satisfaction.

"Do you have to want to be or do some great thing?" Vana asked tentatively.

Meg looked almost disoriented by her answer. "I don't know," she said in a perplexed voice. "Haven't you and Mama always said I should—"

"Forget all that old stuff. Seems to me you and I have both been living up to other people's standards ... or standards we thought other people had. I think it's time for both of us to listen to our own hearts for a change, don't you?"

Meg smiled in a puzzled way as though working at comprehending the full meaning of Vana's words. "Yeah," she said tentatively, "maybe you're right. Maybe I don't want anything grand at all."

She sat quietly in thought a moment and then turned to Vana with her brows knit in question. "What you said about both of us, does that mean you're sorry you've made this big success of yourself?"

"No." Vana breathed deeply. "But I'm beginning to think that focusing on success and goals exclusively can be a miserable, dead-end life, too, even when that success or whatever was truly important to you."

"What do you mean? Aren't you happy with everything?"

"Yes. I'm surprisingly happy with my life, considering how unmodel-like I was in the beginning." She smiled. "Who'd have ever guessed I'd get to do and see everything I dreamed of this way? Only—I feel terrible admitting this, but it's not enough."

"Not enough! God, what do you want to be, Vana—queen of the world or something?"

"No! It's nothing like that. I just think I've maybe listened to Mama a little too much all these years. I'm beginning to feel there's more to needing a man than financial security and babies, that's all."

Meg stared at her in surprise. "You're thinking that way, too! I thought I was the only one."

Vana laughed ruefully. "So, where does that leave us? I wonder."

"I don't know where it leaves you, but it leaves me asking why in the heck wouldn't it be okay to just ignore all Mama's preaching and fall in love with somebody and get married." Meg grinned. "When I'm with Barkie..." The line trailed off in a moony sigh.

"Oh, brother!" Vana rolled her eyes and made a face designed to tease Meg unmercifully.

"Oh sure, make fun of me!" Meg defended herself. "I've seen the way you look at Van Dusen sometimes and the way he looks at you. Only difference is you guys are both fighting it like it's a disease or something. Pretty dumb, if you ask me. I'd rather be icky and happy than dumb and miserable."

Vana let her head fall back against the headrest and stared straight ahead at nothing. "Maybe you're right," she admitted wearily. "But me and Sky—" she shook her head "—it's too messed up."

Meg raised her eyebrows in question.

"He makes me too mad," Vana declared with a sudden infusion of energy. "He hurts my feelings too much. He...he upsets me and scares me and destroys my concentration and ruins my sleep at night. It's better to just leave it as a friendship."

"Better or safer?" Meg asked. "Do you think you can be in love and not be hurt or mad or disturbed sometimes? What are you looking for—a nice unemotional, boring love affair?"

The validity of Meg's point made Vana irritated and defensive. She was looking for sympathy from her sister, not criticism or advice.

"He's never apologized for accusing me of all that ugly nonsense during the contest. For all I know he still thinks it! And he made a fool of me in front of Danielle Whittenboro...and he has all these little sneaky secrets about his past—like did you know he was married before? And he told me I barely existed before I was made over into the Bella Woman!"

Vana was becoming angrier and angrier as she talked. "How could I ever forgive or forget all that? How could I ever—"

"Oh, simmer down," Meg ordered in an exasperated tone. "Jeeze." Her forehead creased in a frown of disapproval. "Have you got any secrets from him? Have you made any mistakes and upset or misjudged him? Have you ever apologized to *him* for anything?"

Vana glared at her silently. How dare her own sister say things like that?

"My opinion," Meg said dryly, "is that you two ought to be locked up together for about a week. At the end you'd both be madly in love or you'd be dead and the whole thing would be solved."

"Cute," Vana said sarcastically. She pulled the flight magazine from the seat pocket in front of her and plopped it in Meg's lap. "Here, why don't you read awhile?"

"You started it," Meg reminded her self-righteously as she picked up the magazine and flipped it open.

Vana squeezed her eyes shut and pretended sleep, but her thoughts went round and round in a dizzying emotional spiral. By the time she finally closed her blinds to the lights of Manhattan and climbed into bed that night, she was exhausted from more than the trip. She had done enough thinking to last for years.

Nafa woke her bright and early the next morning with a stack of Rome guidebooks and a list of packing suggestions and a printed shooting schedule.

"So you'll know what to take and what to see when you get there and how much free time you'll have," Nafa explained.

"Thanks. Are you coming too?" Vana asked her hopefully.

"No. No Rome for me this time. But I'll get there one of these days." Nafa smiled. "Now, I'm heading to the office and I'd suggest you get in gear. Two and a half days isn't that long to get ready for a trip like this."

Vana bounced out of bed eagerly and Nafa started out. "Oh," she said, turning back toward Vana, "you might want to give the boss a call. I think he'd like to hear that you're back and getting ready and everything."

"Why? Did he say that?"

"Not exactly. Not directly anyway."

"Well, he can always call here," Vana said. "Nothing's stopping him."

"Sounds like he had a great time at your mom's," Nafa said casually. "He's told a couple of funny stories."

"Yeah, we had fun. We decided there was no reason we couldn't be friends."

"Wise," Nafa said solemnly. "Very wise."

"You wouldn't know who else might be going on this Rome shoot, would you?" Vana asked innocently.

"The usual crew." Nafa paused and scratched her head as though thinking. "Seems I recall something about Mr. Van Dusen going too." She gave Vana a wide-eyed look. "You could call him and ask...if you're curious or anything." She wiggled her fingers in a wave. "Bye now. See you later."

Vana plunged herself into sorting through her clothes and cosmetics and running to the cleaners and the store. The list of Nafa's suggestions seemed endless: A blow-dryer, a travel iron, a curling wand and a hand-held clothes steamer capable of adjusting to the different electrical setup. Travel sizes of every possible necessity including shoe polish, stomach soothers and cold water detergent for hand washing. The list included items she'd never owned or even used before in her life, but she felt obligated to follow Nafa's suggestions.

The frantic activity kept her mind occupied, kept the tingle of anticipation she was feeling about the trip from becoming a full-fledged nervous condition and kept her from succumbing to the lure of the phone and the sound of Sky's voice. She barely saw Meg. Their comings and goings seemed to be overlapping to the point of allowing only waves or quick greetings in passing. One of them was always hurrying somewhere.

The morning of the big trip Vana awakened to find a note from Meg. "Wake me up and let's go to breakfast. I have some big news!"

With a feeling of dread, Vana walked beside Meg to the little natural foods restaurant in their block. Big news? Meg didn't really think she could possibly have any future with Barclay Whittenboro the Fourth, did she? Vana was worried sick and afraid to hear the announcement, but she kept quiet and waited. Meg obviously wanted to make a big deal out of this newsflash, waiting until after they were settled at their table before beginning.

They ordered fresh fruit and giant bran muffins and coffee, and the food was delivered immediately.

"Are you ready?" Meg leaned forward across the table and beamed with excitement.

"Ready as I'll ever be," Vana said apprehensively. She knew it was Barclay and she knew Meg was heading for a disastrous fall. She dreaded hearing the details.

"I have a job!" Meg stopped, held up her hands and corrected herself. "No. I have a career!"

"You're kidding!" Surprise and relief flooded through Vana. "Tell me . . . tell me!"

"Nafa and Jagger helped me. I'm going to start working with this superstar big-name hair stylist...you know, learning from him and kind of learning the ropes at the same time. Then eventually I'll get my own spot in his shop and I'll work with Jagger on consulting and I might get some movie work and—"

"How...how did this happen?" Vana asked.

"After our conversation on the plane I just got to thinking...and I went in and talked to Nafa about what she thought about my chances of getting on with a good shop here in Manhattan. I mean, when it comes right down to it, Vana, I like doing that as well as I like anything, and if I could get into the big league here—you know, the really exciting stuff...

"So anyway Nafa called Jagger and he got me an immediate tryout or audition or whatever you call it with this *famous* guy who's a friend of his." She paused and grinned with infectious pride and delight. "And he liked me! He said he—" she paused to clear her throat and imitate the man's exact words "'—liked my irreverent attitude' and thought 'it could be translated into my hairstyling technique.'"

"I am so happy for you, Meg." Vana rose and leaned across the small table to hug her sister's neck.

"It's not anything as amazing or grand as what you're doing," Meg said self-consciously. "But I think it's good for me."

"I think it sounds plenty amazing and grand," Vana said warmly. "And I think you were incredibly smart and resourceful to put it all together."

"Really?"

"Really."

As soon as she returned to the apartment, Vana put the finishing touches on her packing and waited for her ride to the airport. Meg's news and the thrill of the trip had combined to put her in a wonderfully buoyant and joyful mood. All was right with the world and Italy was waiting for her.

"Your car's here, Ms. Linnier," the doorman announced over the intercom promptly at one o'clock.

"Thanks. Tell the driver I'm on my way," she answered.

Eagerly she shouldered her garment and tote bags, took hold of the leashes of her two big rolling suitcases and headed out for the elevator. She pushed the button and waited. After several minutes of clicking and whirring the polished brass door slid slowly open. And there stood Sky.

He had on a finely tailored charcoal-gray suit over a blue-and-white striped shirt with a subtly figured silk tie in a silvery blue shade. The color combination made his silvery hair look even more impressive and turned the blue of his eyes to something extraordinary.

He smiled and Vana's knees nearly buckled.

"I thought you might as well ride out to the airport with me," he said casually, "instead of each of us having a separate car. Is that all right with you?"

"Sure," she said quickly, and busied herself with hefting her luggage into the open elevator.

He reached out immediately to help and they fumbled around, each grabbing for the same straps and handles. Every time his hand touched hers, her pulse picked up another beat. And by the time they were settled into the elevator together with the luggage there was a roaring in her ears and a crop of butterflies in her stomach. She stared up at the lighted numbers as they descended and refused to meet his eyes.

She remained nervous on the ride out to Kennedy Airport and throughout the lengthy boarding process. She was going to fly over the ocean today! She was going to go to Europe! And she was going to do all this sitting right next to Schuyler Van Dusen.

She was worn out from nervous excitement before they'd spent three hours in the air. She'd already broken out the stomach soothers from Nafa's list and read and reread portions of the guidebook. Sky's presence in the seat next to her made her jumpy and constantly on edge. Three weeks in

Rome. Three weeks of constantly being thrown together. Could they stay friends or were they destined for a blow-up?

"Vana...Vana. We're here."

Vana sat bolt upright in a disoriented start. She'd been dreaming about Sky.

"You were sound asleep, but I thought you might want to see Rome from the air as we land." Sky smiled and a shiver went through her.

"Are you cold?"

"No...no." She leaned over toward the window.

"It's about eight a.m., Rome time," he remarked as he leaned over to share the view with her.

The aircraft was descending through a cover of clouds. She blinked away the sleep from her eyes. And suddenly they broke free of the clouds and Italy was spread before them.

"Ohhh," she breathed.

The countryside was a rich quilt of greens and tans bathed in a golden glow of sunlight.

"I had no idea there'd be so much farm country," she said in amazement. "I thought..." Her words faded upon first glimpse of Rome.

"There it is," Sky said softly. His voice was touched with wonder.

In the distance the fabled city shimmered in hazy relief as if it were a mirage.

Excitement surged through Vana as she helped Sky gather their things and then lined up for the deplaning. When next she stood on firm ground she would be on Italian soil!

She hurried down the snaking jetway beside Sky. Someone ahead of her was discussing customs. Customs. Just like in the movies. She exchanged grins with Sky and his eyes were as full of delight as she imagined her own were.

First she heard the language. The musical cadence of a language she couldn't understand floated all around her. Even the little children knew how to speak Italian here! She turned to share that silly thought with Sky, but as she did she caught her first glimpse of an Italian policeman, or what she supposed was a policeman. He was dressed in something akin to military fatigues and was casually cradling what looked like some kind of machine gun. Right there in the airport—a real machine gun! She gaped and pointed to show Sky.

"I know," he said. "And look, there are more."

She turned her head and saw the same sort of figures strolling about through the unconcerned airport crowd. And that was when the reality of it all hit home to her—she was truly and absolutely in a foreign country, or rather *she* had suddenly become a foreigner. Her expectations and her notions of what was standard or normal were meaningless here.

The ride into the city from Fiumicino airport was full of surprises. Vana couldn't get over the number of pastures, orchards and fields existing so close to the famous city. She'd imagined it would be more like New York, a sprawling urban environment with tentacles spreading for miles. But as their rented van sped down the highway from the airport, then negotiated the city streets, Vana saw that nothing here was even vaguely reminiscent of the large U.S. cities she'd seen. The plastic-and-chrome veneer so common in the cities she'd seen barely existed here. And the taller-is-better or newer-is-better mentality was not in evidence here at all.

This was a world lifted straight from the pages of a history book. Looking out the window she realized that if all the funny little cars zipping along the streets could be taken away and the people in modern dress were removed from the picture, the buildings and squares and fountains would look almost the same as they had back in some distant time.

The crew settled into their hotel, the Raphael, then split up and headed out for food and a brief exploration of the adjacent public square. Stephen insisted that they begin shooting at first light the following morning so they were ordered to use this day primarily for rest and jet-lag recovery.

Vana walked into the center of the long, open square that her guidebook called Piazza Navona. She stood very still, absorbing everything, then slowly turned to face yet another direction and another dazzling scenario. The sound of water tumbling and falling in the fountains filled her ears, and she stared in wonder at the intriguing palazzos and ochre-washed houses and drowsy sidewalk cafés ringing the piazza and winding away down the narrow streets in an unbroken line.

"Unbelievable, isn't it?" Sky said. He, too, was taking it in, trying to capture every minute detail of the scene. "Even the sunlight seems different . . . clearer somehow, purer."

They took turns reading aloud from the guidebook. The fountains on either end were the fountain of Neptune and the fountain of the Moor. Seen separately they would have been breathtaking, but arranged as they were, the lovely fountains were eclipsed by the piazza's central offering—a stunning introduction to Rome's marvels—the fountain of the Four Rivers.

Vana circled the Four Rivers in awe, studying the rugged rock base and tilting her head back to look up at the obelisk. Against the rocks were four large human figures representing great rivers of the world. The fountain was a fascinating blend of massive roughness and fine detailing and Vana felt the power and essence of humanity through the ages generating from the age-old work of art. She tried to imagine the care and patience and inspiration that had gone into the creation of the mysterious figures, the windtossed palm and the fiery horse.

"Shall we eat?" Sky suggested, and he headed toward a cluster of outdoor tables at the far end of the piazza.

Vana lagged behind, unable to tear her eyes from things or concentrate on her direction. He paused to wait for her, smiling his understanding, and as she hurried toward him he held out his hand. Without thinking she reached out and took it, and the connection between them felt perfectly right.

Chapter Twelve

Long hours of shooting were interwoven with enchanting moments of discovery in the days that followed. Vana had little free time at first as the crew was anxious to put work before pleasure, but even the twenty-minute walking breaks she and Sky fit in periodically to relax yielded the most amazing finds.

Around every bend in the narrow streets there was always a surprise. Sometimes it was another piazza, a breathtaking fountain or piece of statuary—other times it might be a charming old street-corner icon, a fragment of some ancient pillar or a quaintly and humorously crafted antique drinking spigot mounted on the side of a building.

"I don't understand why you've never traveled to Europe like this before," Vana said as Sky chuckled in obvious pleasure over a comical rendering of a pudgy child pouring water—the surviving portion of an old animal watering trough.

"I've always wanted to," he said, "but not alone. When Cynthia and I married..." He shook his head. "Sorry, you don't want to hear that."

"Of course I do," Vana insisted. "I want to hear everything you have to say... everything you want to say."

"I don't like to talk about her usually," he explained self-consciously. "I was very young and so was she, and we hurt each other a lot." He tried to smile. "I didn't understand anything about love or friendship then."

"And you do now?"

"Yes. Finally. I was a slow learner, though."

"So was I," she admitted. "It's a hard thing to learn I guess. I'm still not sure I have it right."

He looked at her a moment as though about to say something, then he changed his mind, his expression lightened and he smiled in a mildly sarcastic way. "Anyway, I soon found out that Cynthia would only go to places where there were beaches and luxury condos and swinging nightspots. We took all of our trips to Acapulco or some island or another. Not that those places weren't beautiful—but sunning all day and dancing all night can get old after a while."

"I'm glad we're here together," Vana said, feeling a surge of warmth toward him. "I don't know anyone else I could have shared all this so easily with." She chuckled softly. "Meg would have wanted to spend all our time following cute Italian men and Nafa says museums give her hives—and Mama! God, can't you just see Mama in Rome? She hates walking, she dislikes being outside too much and riding in cars too long makes her nauseated. How could she ever see anything!"

Vana took his arm as they started back toward the shooting location, and they laughed all the way about the absurdity of Kate traveling to a foreign country. She felt so close to him now, as though they had known each other forever. Now that he was familiar with the farm and Kate and the town of Zeckendorf, and even the old brick high school that had been the setting for so much teen angst, she was able to make references and jokes that linked them together like longtime friends.

With his hesitant mention of Cynthia she knew that he too felt the intimate link between them. In some ways the bond they were slowly forging was made even stronger by their earlier difficulties.

But still, whenever she reminded herself of the contest ugliness—of his refusal to acknowledge her innocence and his stubborn inability to apologize for his accusations and anger—a steely coldness arose in her. And whenever she found herself trusting him too much or enjoying him too much—or wanting him too much—she called up the memory, conjuring the coldness to protect herself.

They finished the shooting ahead of schedule with a free week and a half left to spend on nothing but fun. Arthur and Stephen joined them for the first five days and together the four of them steeped themselves in the magic of the coliseum and the forum and the Pantheon and the Villa Borghese and the Vatican. They browsed and indulged themselves in the exclusive Via Condotti shops and they ate meal after memorable meal, sampling wild boar and pigeon and vegetables they'd never heard of.

By the time the two men left, Vana was perfectly comfortable at the thought of spending the remainder of the time alone with Sky. In fact she looked forward to the opportunity to simplify all the arrangements. It was much easier to plan an itinerary around the enthusiasms of two people instead of four.

They spent their first morning together enjoying the Doria Pamphili Gallery. Vana was eager to go inside the old palace but somewhat anxious about seeing the tapestries and sculptures and paintings housed therein. She knew nothing at all about art. Would her lack of knowledge be obvious? She worried about what Sky would think if he realized that she knew absolutely nothing about the pieces on display.

But as soon as she saw the magnificent Caravaggios and Carraccis and Brueghels she forgot all of her uncertainties.

It didn't require knowledge to be appreciative of their beauty. She stood transfixed, completely captured by the timeless spells they cast.

"I know so little about art," Sky said regretfully as they studied a particularly spectacular work entitled the *Flight Into Egypt*.

She smiled and reached out for his hand. "You poor soul," she teased. "Now if you'd been raised in one of the culture capitals of the world like I was..."

He gave her a playful poke in the ribs and she retaliated by trying to pinch him as they joined the guided tour to the private apartments.

They ate lunch in a rooftop restaurant with a view of the Spanish Steps. An unlikely assortment of young people, obviously college students from different countries, was clustered together on the steps singing out of tune rock 'n' roll oldies in heavily accented English, and the strains drifted up to their table on the warm breeze. The spontaneous gathering of apparent strangers was oddly touching, but their singing was dreadful. Vana and Sky dissolved into laughter as the group broke into each new number, often more out of key than the last.

After lunch they headed along the river walkway to the Temple of Apollo and the Arch of the Moneychangers, then on to the lovely old church of Santa Maria in Cosmedin with its twelfth-century bell tower. In the porch leading to the church they stopped to wonder over the Bocca della Verita.

The guidebook explained that the name meant mouth of truth and that the big stone disk with its slightly ominous carved face and gaping hole for a mouth had been used to test the truth of someone's words. The suspect put his or her hand into the mouth and then answered questions. Legend had it that the mouth would snap shut on the hand of anyone telling a lie.

Playfully Sky inserted his hand in the hole. "Okay, ask me anything," he announced.

"Umm." She tapped her finger against her lips. "Who is the most charming and fun companion you've ever had in Rome?" she asked.

"Vanessa Linnier!" he answered forcefully and then made a fearful show of checking to see that his hand was still there.

"And who do you want to have dinner with tonight?"

"Again, Vanessa Linnier!" He grinned proudly. "Boy, I'm good at these guessing games, aren't I?"

She made a face at him. "All right..." she said, a note of real challenge creeping into her voice. Suddenly the need for truth was real and not a game. "Do you still think I was trying to trick you or engineer some kind of a fix in the Bella competition?"

His face sobered instantly, but he didn't remove his hand. "No."

"Why haven't you ever told me that, then, or apologized?"

"I just wanted to forget about it. I was ashamed of myself for having behaved that way in the first place. Then, after I finally realized why I'd seized on the accusation so wholeheartedly—and why I persisted in maintaining it long after I knew better—I was even more ashamed...more embarrassed."

"And why was that?"

"At first I was made crazy by it because...well because I'd developed such a dismal history of being used during my time with Cynthia, and I guess it left me too careful, too on the lookout for a recurrence. And then, instead of cooling off and seeing how wrong I'd been, I held onto the feelings for exactly the reasons you accused me of in the catering truck that day. I was afraid. I was fighting it, and I was clinging to the anger as an excuse."

"Why were you afraid?" she asked, but she already knew the answers.

His expression spoke of almost too many reasons to recount. "It happened so fast! I mean, there you were and you were reaching right down inside of me and twisting me up in a way I'd never come across before. When I thought you'd be staying in the midwest it was fine. I planned on writing to you and calling and feeling my way along. But suddenly you were coming to New York and involved with my company, and I felt trapped.

"I was afraid of being hurt. I was afraid of being used. I was afraid of being made a fool of. I was afraid that you weren't what I imagined you were."

"And," she said softly with remembered hurt tearing at the edges of her voice, "you said that I barely existed, that I was nothing until Bella made me over."

"I was..." He drew in a deep breath. "It was a stupid, childish attack. I didn't mean it. I was just lashing out at you, going for a soft spot. The moment I saw you, I knew you were someone valuable." He shook his head in wonder. "The miracle to me is that Bella didn't change you, not on the inside where it's important."

She stood silently, studying his face and searching his eyes. She wanted so much from him, but only if he gave it voluntarily. The last thing in the world she wanted to do was trap him into anything.

"Come here," he said.

She walked up to him and he reached out to hold her with one arm, keeping the other firmly inside the stone mouth.

"I'm so sorry, Vana. What an ignorant fool I've been."

She buried her face in his shoulder and cried softly.

"I'm sorry, too," she whispered. "I've said things to you..."

"Uh-uh," he chided gently. "How do I know you speak the truth?"

She smiled through her tears and reached out to put her hand in the mouth with his.

"That's better," he said. He looked into her eyes. "I love you, Vana. I want to marry you."

She couldn't have been more stunned if the ancient stone mouth had suddenly chomped down on her wrist and eaten her hand.

"My God, Sky! I don't ... I mean, I can't ... I ..."

"You don't have to answer this minute," he said quickly.

"I do love you," she said, recovering from her loss of senses.

Vana spent the rest of the day in a dreamlike state, drifting from the wonder of an ancient ruin or a lovely fountain to the wonder of his arm so tightly about her waist or his eyes so full of warmth and love. They found a charming little place called Cappanina for their celebration dinner. The food was wonderful and the host was a jovial man who introduced himself as Nunzio and managed to hold an animated conversation with them and wish them well without understanding or speaking more than five words of English.

The magic built through dinner and carried them through the warm Italian night to their hotel. No words were needed. They went straight to Sky's room.

She felt no hesitancy or uncertainty this time, and she saw a new confidence and trust in his eyes as well. There was no more need for pretense or self-conscious small talk. As soon as the door closed they were in each other's arms.

"Sky, Sky," she whispered, clinging to him with a fierce hunger fueled by the press of his body against hers.

She drew back, wanting to savor the moment and capture it with her eyes before she became totally lost in it all. He tried to pull her close again, but she resisted, holding him at arm's length.

"I want to look at you," she explained softly. "I want to memorize everything."

He smiled, a smile so chest-clutchingly full of love that it brought a lump to her throat. She reached out to touch the planes of his face and the curve of his neck and the width of his shoulders, tracing his features as intently as a blind person might. She unbuttoned his shirt, marveling at how wonderfully solid his chest felt.

"I love the differences between us," she said.

He smiled again, playfully this time, and began unfastening her blouse. "Two can play at this game," he said.

She gasped as the warmth of his hands met the heat of her breasts. She tried to circle his neck with her arms and embrace him, but he swatted her hands away.

"No, no," he grinned. "My turn."

He kissed her forehead. He covered her closed eyes with feathery kisses and skimmed the tip of her nose. His lips traveled down the length of her neck and into the hollow spaces at her throat and shoulders. She leaned her head back, swimming in the liquid sensations he aroused. Then, suddenly, his mouth was at her breasts, kissing and tasting her through the sheer lace of her bra.

A soft moan escaped her lips and the sound of it brought a renewed urgency to his lovemaking. He shrugged out of his shirt and gathered her into his arms in one fluid motion. He carried her quickly to the bed. She clung to him tightly, and they fell together, bodies molded and lips eagerly seeking in long searching kisses.

He pushed her trailing blouse from her arms and unhooked her bra. Her freed breasts felt swollen and pulsing with need. He caressed the softness with his palms and brushed her hardened nipples lightly with his thumbs.

"You are so beautiful," he breathed in a voice filled with reverence and awe.

And she felt beautiful. Truly beautiful. His love created a glow of beauty that warmed and enveloped her.

"Sky," she murmured. "Sky—" Her words were cut short by the explosion of pleasure as his mouth sought her bared breasts. The sweet pull at her nipples coursed through her until she was consumed by a burning, throbbing need.

"I want you inside me," she whispered, and he tore off the remainder of their clothing in a heated rush.

He pulled her close, kissing her deeply. The room spun around her. She pressed herself tighter against his solid muscled length. The sensations were exquisite and intoxicating—her tender breasts against his firm chest, her yielding belly against his searing hardness. And every moment, every touch, every slight pressure fueled the growing white heat at the center of her womanhood.

He pulled back, hovering over her, devouring her with his eyes. Then he lowered himself, connecting and fitting with her as though they were one. She rose, accepting him, meeting him, hungrily pulling him into a total joining, and the world reeled and dissolved beneath the power of their fulfillment.

Later they lay in the tangle of sheets and listened to the faint sounds of the water splashing outside their window in the fountains of the Piazza Navona.

"Marry me, Vana," Sky pleaded. "Please. I love you. I need you in my life. I need to feel . . . connected to you, so badly."

Vana pulled back from him a fraction. Fear raced through her at the thought of what the word yes would mean. But it wasn't just the lifetime of preaching from her mother about men's treatment of their wives, or the million other vague uncertainties nagging at the borders of her mind. It was Meg, too. Didn't Meg still need her? Didn't she have an obligation to see Meg on her feet and settled before she could enter into some other binding emotional commitment?

"Just think," he said lightly. "We could have an apartment in town and a great place out in country big enough for animals and kids. Hey! Maybe a house for Kate there, too. We could even buy her a goat!" His voice trailed off as he saw her expression.

"Do you have doubts about me, about us?" Sky asked.

"No. It's just so sudden. So—"

"Waiting is for people who don't know themselves or each other well enough to make a commitment or for people who aren't mature enough to accept the responsibility of a commitment." He reached out to stroke her cheek with his fingertips. "You and I have made enough mistakes and had enough life experience to be past all that. If I hadn't been fighting against everything so hard I think I'd have realized almost from the start that you were the person I wanted to share my life with."

"Oh Sky, I love you so much. I am certain of that. I can't even imagine a life without you now . . . but . . . what about Meg?"

"What about Meg? She likes me doesn't she? I don't think she'll object to me as a brother-in-law."

"It's not that. She's trying to make a life in a new city, and she's trying to find herself and start a career, and I'm certain she's about to have her heart broken by Barclay. We just patched things up between us such a short time ago, and I think she still feels a little jealous and inadequate over my winning the Bella contest and—"

"What are you trying to say, Vana?"

She had to look away from him to be able to say it and still her voice was weak. "She needs me, too."

She kept her head bowed and peeked up at him in fear. Would he understand? He stared silently but his eyes darkened.

"Don't you see? To marry and leave her now, or even to announce that I was planning on marrying . . . it could ruin everything. I couldn't do that to her."

"Meg's a grown woman, Vana. Didn't you just recently learn your lesson on that? You have to let go. You have to stop babying and protecting her, especially when doing so is at such great expense to yourself."

"But don't you see? If I marry you now, in addition to everything else wonderful that's happened to me, I really will have it all. I don't know if she can handle that."

"That's nonsensical! You're running away just like I did. You're conjuring up excuses so you won't have to confront your feelings on this. I thought we were past all that!"

"No." she shook her head urgently. "It's not an excuse. Meg and Mama mean so much to me. I hated myself before for causing Meg so much grief when I won this contest. I couldn't do that to her again."

He sat up and pulled her up to face him.

"You marrying me has nothing to do with your sister!" he insisted. "You're not ready, Vana. Can't you admit that to me? There's something very wrong if you're still working at fooling both me and yourself."

"Please, don't be hurt," she begged. "Please. If you could just be patient...just until she's a little stronger. I do love you."

Sky looked suddenly sad and the change frightened her more than his anger had.

"You aren't giving up, are you?"

The look he gave her brought an unswallowable lump to her throat.

"I can't," he said. His voice was filled with pain and worry. "I won't push you on this Vana. It's all up to you. But please be careful. Don't destroy this. Please."

And he was true to his word. He didn't push her. They spent the remainder of their time in each other's company constantly and Vana checked out of her room and moved into his, but he did not speak of marriage again.

Vana held his hand tightly on the flight home. She was happier than she'd ever been in her life. But she was also very, very afraid.

He dropped her at her apartment and they said goodbye reluctantly. He had untended business waiting for him. As soon as he was gone Vana felt an emptiness begin inside her. The thought of even a day away from him made her ache.

The phone rang and she was treated to the cheery sound of Nafa's voice. "Sky just buzzed into the office," Nafa reported suggestively. "And I do mean buzzed. What have you been doing to the boss man over there in that foreign place?"

"Nafa!" Vana giggled. "Say, you don't know what Meg's up to, do you?"

"Oh, yeah. She's busy as a beaver at that new hair styling job, and I didn't get any of the particulars, but I got the impression she's in the middle of a real dilemma with old Barkie or whatever his name is. Which reminds me, that Whittenboro witch has been wanting to talk to you. She called here yesterday wanting to know when you'd be back and how she could get in touch with you. Said it was *confidential*."

Vana chuckled at Nafa's description of Danielle and also at her sarcastic stressing of the word *confidential*.

"What could she possibly want with me?"

"Don't know, but I'll read you the number. She said it was urgent."

Vana called the number as soon as she hung up and was greeted almost in a whisper by Danielle. "I'm at the family home," she said, "and I don't want anyone to know who I'm talking to."

"Oh, heaven forbid," Vana agreed.

"You must meet me. I have to talk to you about Barclay and your sister."

Vana's heart sank. "All right. Tell me where and when."

She knew that this was it. This was the blowup she'd been waiting for. And this must be part of the dilemma Meg had hinted at to Nafa.

She headed for the meeting with Danielle imagining all sorts of terrible scenes. The Whittenboros wanted to buy Meg off or the Whittenboros were going to threaten to break Meg's legs or shave her hair or put her in "cement overshoes," like in all the old gangster movies. The Whittenboros wanted to get rid of the lower-class little nobody and they were willing to go to any lengths to accomplish it.

As she walked into the little espresso parlor she wished she'd brought a tape recorder so she'd have evidence in case she wanted to go to the police for help.

"Over here," Danielle called to her from a corner table. Her eyes looked as though she'd been crying.

Vana sat down and ordered a cappucino for propriety's sake. The waiter returned with it in an instant.

"So, what is it?" she asked Danielle. She had come ready to do battle.

"Your sister..." Danielle began and Vana drew herself up in preparation. A single tear trickled down Danielle's cheek. "Your sister is making my entire family very unhappy."

The tear and the method of delivery disarmed Vana a bit. "How so?" she asked suspiciously.

"My poor baby brother—" she sniffed into a shredding tissue "—is so crazy about her, he can't eat or sleep. He's told Father he won't work with him anymore and he doesn't care about the family's financial dealings. He refused to come to the annual Whittenboro reunion this last weekend. All he does is sit in his room and stare at her picture."

"I don't understand. I haven't had a chance to speak with Meg since I returned, but when I left everything was fine between them." Vana was puzzled now and beginning to be uncertain about what was going on.

Danielle drew herself up in a show of indignation. "Poor Barclay asked your sister to wear his college fraternity pin...to...go steady. It's the first time he's been serious about a girl since grammar school! And she refused!"

Danielle twisted her tissue and sniffled loudly before continuing. "She told him she just wanted to keep dating him, that she didn't know if she was ready to make any promises or settle down yet, that she had a new career and a new life and...and she told him she couldn't possibly be officially linked to him because he had—" the words appeared to stick for a moment "—such a rude sister."

"Hmm. I see," Vana said. It was hard to be serious when she felt so much like laughing. Little Meg! Little Meg had brought the whole Whittenboro bunch to their knees. "I like Barclay and I'm very sorry to hear he's been so upset by this," she said sincerely.

"My whole family is simply destroyed!" Danielle wailed. "He came to my parents with the news of his intentions and they were aghast. Barclay Hughes Whittenboro the Fourth involved with a girl like that.... It was dreadfully terrible for them."

She shook her head sorrowfully. "But Barclay is so important to them, and since he met her he's been happier than anyone has ever seen him...and they decided they couldn't break his heart by saying no even when it was the only suitable thing to do. So they swallowed their pride and dignity and slapped generations of Whittenboros in the face—they told Barclay that if it made him happy, they would learn to accept her."

Danielle's eyes blazed. "They warned all their friends so no one would be shocked and they planned a big party as a welcome for her. Do you know what her refusal did to them? They are humiliated!"

"I'm sorry to hear all this, Danielle. But I don't know what I can do about it."

"You can talk to her," Danielle insisted. "Influence her. She doesn't understand anything. You know how the world works and what's important. Tell her how old our name is. Tell her how wealthy and powerful the Whittenboro family is. Make her see how lucky she is to have an opportunity like this."

"I can't possibly speak for Meg," Vana said evenly. "I have no idea what her intentions are or even whether she really said everything you've told me. All I can promise is that I'll tell her how upset Barclay is. Knowing how fond she is—or was—of him, I'm certain she'll want to speak to him. And that's the only way any of this can be settled—between the two of them."

Danielle stood stiffly as Vana said goodbye. "Thank you for coming," she said formally. "And you can assure your sister that in the future I will behave toward her with the utmost cordiality."

"I'll tell her," Vana said. She managed to hold in her laughter until she was all the way back out on the sidewalk and hailing a cab.

She shook her head and chuckled, muttering, "Little Meg!" as the cab wound its way through the busy city traffic. The cabbie peered at her suspiciously in the rearview mirror. When had Meg become so self-reliant? So able to fight her own battles? When had Meg gotten so strong and smart? When had Meg stopped needing her so completely?

The thought that her sister truly didn't need her anymore was difficult to absorb at first. It tugged at her painfully, as though she had just lost something irretrievable. But then she realized that all she had lost was the past. Meg's new strength and independence meant the beginning of a better and freer relationship between them. And it meant...

Oh, God! It meant there was no reason in the world she shouldn't or couldn't marry Sky.

She drew in a ragged breath and covered her face with her hands. She was trembling, she realized. She was frightened. One part of her was reduced to that little scared rabbit inside, while the other part of her was watching like some curiously detached observer.

She shook herself and straightened, fighting to keep the rabbit under control. The cabbie was gawking like a child now, and she had the urge to stick out her tongue at him.

She was absolutely positive that she loved and needed Sky Van Dusen, so why had this terror descended upon her? She looked out the window at the visible pieces of jagged Manhattan skyline. It still sent a thrill through her, a residue of excitement left from childhood dreams. And suddenly it was all very clear to her.

Sky had been right. She was subconsciously afraid of marriage. She had been grasping at excuses. Just as remnants of the old childhood dreams still lingered within her, Kate's teachings and example also retained a strong hold on her. Vana shook her head, marveling at the durability of some emotions. She had gently put aside so much of childhood, yet the fear her unhappy mother had instilled in her could even now seize her in its irrational grip.

She couldn't deny the fear—it had been nurtured inside her too long. But she would not let it control or ruin her life. She would fight it. And she knew Sky loved her enough to help her fight it.

She leaned forward. "I've changed my mind," she said firmly. "Take me to the Vandy building."

Full of joyous determination and purpose she rode the elevator up to the executive floor. She wouldn't listen to the secretary who insisted Mr. Van Dusen was too busy. She breezed past the flustered woman and burst into Sky's spacious office unannounced.

"Vana!" he exclaimed. Waving off the angry secretary behind her, he instructed the woman to hold all calls.

"What are you doing here?" he asked in pleased puzzlement. "I thought you and Meg would have so much catching up to do...."

Vana shrugged and grinned. She could barely contain her excitement. "You're a pretty smart guy, you know," she said cryptically.

He smiled and held out his hands in mock humility, but his eyes were full of questions.

"I can be hard to get along with," she said.

A tiny glimmer of hope appeared in his expression, but she could tell he was afraid to voice it.

"So can I," he said lightly.

"Do you still remember how to say anything in Italian?" she asked innocently.

"My *bella stella*," he said affectionately as he moved around the desk to hug her. Beautiful star was his favorite of the Italian phrases he'd learned.

"That will come in handy," she remarked thoughtfully, ignoring the hug.

"Oh?"

"Sure. I mean . . . we loved Rome so much we'll want to go back, and when in Rome, we should speak some Italian . . . and endearments are expected on a honeymoon, so—"

"A honeymoon? You mean . . . you want . . . you don't want to wait anymore?"

"No." A tear slid silently down Vana's cheek. "I've been waiting for you my whole life already."

* * * * *

*. . . and now an exciting short story
from Silhouette Books.*

*

HEATHER GRAHAM POZZESSERE
Shadows on the Nile

CHAPTER ONE

Alex could tell that the woman was very nervous. Her fingers were wound tightly about the arm rests, and she had been staring straight ahead since the flight began. Who was she? Why was she flying alone? Why to Egypt? She was a small woman, fine-boned, with classical features and porcelain skin. Her hair was golden blond, and she had blue-gray eyes that were slightly tilted at the corners, giving her a sensual and exotic appeal.

And she smelled divine. He had been sitting there, glancing through the flight magazine, and her scent had reached him, filling him like something rushing through his bloodstream, and before he had looked at her he had known that she would be beautiful.

John was frowning at him. His gaze clearly said that this was not the time for Alex to become interested in a woman. Alex lowered his head, grinning. Nuts to John. He was the one who had made the reservations so late that there was already another passenger between them in their row. Alex couldn't have remained silent anyway; he was certain that he could ease the flight for her. Besides, he had to know her name, had to see if her eyes would turn silver when she smiled. Even though he should, he couldn't ignore her.

"Alex," John said warningly.

Maybe John was wrong, Alex thought. Maybe this was precisely the right time for him to get involved. A woman would be the perfect shield, in case anyone was interested in his business in Cairo.

The two men should have been sitting next to each other, Jillian decided. She didn't know why she had wound up sandwiched between the two of them, but she couldn't do a thing about it. Frankly, she was far too nervous to do much of anything.

"It's really not so bad," a voice said sympathetically. It came from her right. It was the younger of the two men, the one next to the window. "How about a drink? That might help."

Jillian took a deep, steadying breath, then managed to answer. "Yes . . . please. Thank you."

His fingers curled over hers. Long, very strong fingers, nicely tanned. She had noticed him when she had taken her seat—he was difficult not to notice. There was an arresting quality about him. He had a certain look: high-powered, confident, self-reliant. He was medium tall and medium built, with shoulders that nicely filled out his suit jacket, dark brown eyes, and sandy hair that seemed to defy any effort at combing it. And he had a wonderful voice, deep and compelling. It broke through her fear and actually soothed her. Or perhaps it was the warmth of his hand over hers that did it.

"Your first trip to Egypt?" he asked. She managed a brief nod, but was saved from having to comment when the stewardess came by. Her companion ordered her a white wine, then began to converse with her quite normally, as if unaware that her fear of flying had nearly rendered her speechless. He asked her what she did for a living, and she heard herself tell him that she was a music teacher at a junior college. He responded easily to everything she said, his voice warm and concerned each time he asked another question. She didn't think; she simply answered him, because flying had become easier the moment he touched her.

She even told him that she was a widow, that her husband had been killed in a car accident four years ago, and that she was here now to fulfill a long-held dream, because she had always longed to see the pyramids, the Nile and all the ancient wonders Egypt held.

She had loved her husband, Alex thought, watching as pain briefly darkened her eyes. Her voice held a thread of sadness when she mentioned her husband's name. Out of nowhere, he wondered how it would feel to be loved by such a woman.

Alex noticed that even John was listening, commenting on things now and then. How interesting, Alex thought, looking across at his friend and associate.

The stewardess came with the wine. Alex took it for her, chatting casually with the woman as he paid. Charmer, Jillian thought ruefully. She flushed, realizing that it was his charm that had led her to tell him so much about her life.

Her fingers trembled when she took the wineglass. "I'm sorry," she murmured. "I don't really like to fly."

Alex—he had introduced himself as Alex, but without telling her his last name—laughed and said that was the understatement of the year. He pointed out the window to the clear blue sky—an omen of good things to come, he said—then assured her that the airline had an excellent safety record. His friend, the older man with the haggard, world-weary face, eventually introduced himself as John. He joked and tried to reassure her, too, and eventually their efforts paid off. Once she felt a little calmer, she offered to move, so they could converse without her in the way.

Alex tightened his fingers around hers, and she felt the startling warmth in his eyes. His gaze was appreciative and sensual, without being insulting. She felt a rush of sweet heat swirl within her, and she realized with surprise that it was excitement, that she was enjoying his company the way a woman enjoyed the company of a man who attracted her. She had thought she would never feel that way again.

"I wouldn't move for all the gold in ancient Egypt," he said with a grin, "and I doubt that John would, either." He touched her cheek. "I might lose track of you, and I don't even know your name."

"Jillian," she said, meeting his eyes. "Jillian Jacoby."

He repeated her name softly, as if to commit it to memory, then went on to talk about Cairo, the pyramids at Giza, the Valley of the Kings, and the beauty of the nights when the sun set over the desert in a riot of blazing red.

And then the plane was landing. To her amazement, the flight had ended. Once she was on solid ground again, Jillian realized that Alex knew all sorts of things about her, while she didn't know a thing about him or John—not even their full names.

They went through customs together. Jillian was immediately fascinated, in love with the colorful atmosphere of Cairo, and not at all dismayed by the waiting and the bureaucracy. When they finally reached the street she fell head over heels in love with the exotic land. The heat shimmered in the air, and taxi drivers in long burnooses lined up for fares. She could hear the soft singsong of their language, and she was thrilled to realize that the dream she had harbored for so long was finally coming true.

She didn't realize that two men had followed them from the airport to the street. Alex, however, did. He saw the men behind him, and his jaw tightened as he nodded to John to stay put and hurried after Jillian.

"Where are you staying?" he asked her.

"The Hilton," she told him, pleased at his interest. Maybe her dream was going to turn out to have some unexpected aspects.

He whistled for a taxi. Then, as the driver opened the door, Jillian looked up to find Alex staring at her. She felt...something. A fleeting magic raced along her spine, as if she knew what he was about to do. Knew, and should have protested, but couldn't.

Alex slipped his arm around her. One hand fell to her waist, the other cupped her nape, and he kissed her. His mouth was hot, his touch firm, persuasive. She was filled with heat; she trembled . . . and then she broke away at last, staring at him, the look in her eyes more eloquent than any words. Confused, she turned away and stepped into the taxi. As soon as she was seated she turned to stare after him, but he was already gone, a part of the crowd.

She touched her lips as the taxi sped toward the heart of the city. She shouldn't have allowed the kiss; she barely knew him. But she couldn't forget him.

She was still thinking about him when she reached the Hilton. She checked in quickly, but she was too late to acquire a guide for the day. The manager suggested that she stop by the Kahil bazaar, not far from the hotel. She dropped her bags in her room, then took another taxi to the bazaar. Once again she was enchanted. She loved everything: the noise, the people, the donkey carts that blocked the narrow streets, the shops with their beaded entryways and beautiful wares in silver and stone, copper and brass. Old men smoking water pipes sat on mats drinking tea, while younger men shouted out their wares from stalls and doorways. Jillian began walking slowly, trying to take it all in. She was occasionally jostled, but she kept her hand on her purse and sidestepped quickly. She was just congratulating herself on her competence when she was suddenly dragged into an alley by two Arabs swaddled in burnooses.

"What—" she gasped, but then her voice suddenly fled. The alley was empty and shadowed, and night was coming. One man had a scar on his cheek, and held a long, curved knife; the other carried a switchblade.

"Where is it?" the first demanded.

"Where is what?" she asked frantically.

The one with the scar compressed his lips grimly. He set his knife against her cheek, then stroked the flat side down to her throat. She could feel the deadly coolness of the steel blade.

"Where is it? Tell me now!"

Her knees were trembling, and she tried to find the breath to speak. Suddenly she noticed a shadow emerging from the darkness behind her attackers. She gasped, stunned, as the man drew nearer. It was Alex.

Alex... silent, stealthy, his features taut and grim. Her heart seemed to stop. Had he come to her rescue? Or was he allied with her attackers, there to threaten, even destroy, her?

*   *   *   *   *

Watch for Chapter Two of SHADOWS ON THE NILE coming next month—only in Silhouette Intimate Moments.

Take 4 Silhouette Romance novels & a surprise gift
FREE

Then preview 6 brand-new Silhouette Romance novels—delivered to your door as soon as they come off the presses! If you decide to keep them, pay just $1.95* each, *with no shipping, handling or other charges of any kind!*

Each month, you'll meet lively young heroines and share in their thrilling escapes, trials and triumphs . . . virile men you'll find as attractive and irresistible as the heroines do . . . and colorful supporting characters you'll feel you've always known.

Start with 4 Silhouette Romance novels and a surprise gift absolutely FREE. They're yours to keep without obligation. You can always return a shipment and cancel at any time.

Simply fill out and return the coupon today!

*$1.70 each plus 69¢ postage and handling per shipment in Canada.

Clip and mail to: Silhouette Books

In U.S.:
901 Fuhrmann Blvd.
P.O. Box 9013
Buffalo, NY 14240-9013

In Canada:
P.O. Box 609
Fort Erie, Ontario
L2A 5X3

YES!   Please rush me 4 FREE Silhouette Romance novels and my free surprise gift. Then send me 6 new Silhouette Romance novels to preview each month as soon as they come off the presses. Bill me at the low price of $1.95* each with no shipping, handling or other hidden costs. There is no minimum number of books I must purchase. I can always return a shipment and cancel at any time. Even if I never buy another book from Silhouette Romance, the 4 free novels and the surprise gift are mine to keep forever.

*$1.70 each plus 69¢ postage and handling per shipment in Canada.

215 BPL BP7F

Name _____ (please print) _____

Address _____ Apt. _____

City _____ State/Prov. _____ Zip/Postal Code _____

This offer is limited to one order per household and not valid to present subscribers. Price is subject to change.

SilR-SUB-1D

ATTRACTIVE, SPACE SAVING BOOK RACK

Display your most prized novels on this handsome and sturdy book rack. The hand-rubbed walnut finish will blend into your library decor with quiet elegance, providing a practical organizer for your favorite hard-or soft-covered books.

Only
$9.95

**Approximately
16" x 8"
when assembled**

Assembles in seconds!

To order, rush your name, address and zip code, along with a check or money order for $10.70* ($9.95 plus 75¢ postage and handling) payable to *Silhouette Books.*

Silhouette Books
Book Rack Offer
901 Fuhrmann Blvd.
P.O. Box 1396
Buffalo, NY 14269-1396

Offer not available in Canada.

*New York and Iowa residents add appropriate sales tax.

BKR-2A

Silhouette Special Edition

COMING NEXT MONTH

AVAILABLE THIS MONTH

In response
to last year's outstanding success,
Silhouette Brings You:

Silhouette Christmas Stories 1987

Specially chosen for you in a delightful volume celebrating the holiday season, four original romantic stories written by four of your favorite Silhouette authors.

Dixie Browning—*Henry the Ninth*
Ginna Gray—*Season of Miracles*
Linda Howard—*Bluebird Winter*
Diana Palmer—*The Humbug Man*

Each of these bestselling authors will enchant you with their unforgettable stories, exuding the magic of Christmas and the wonder of falling in love.

A heartwarming Christmas gift during the holiday season... indulge yourself and give this book to a special friend!

Available November 1987

XM87-1